pounding *the* pavement

pounding *the* pavement

a novel

Jennifer van der Kwast

Broadway Books

New York

POUNDING THE PAVEMENT. Copyright © 2005 by Jennifer van der Kwast. All rights reserved. No part of this book may be reproduced or transmitted in any form or by any means, electronic or mechanical, including photocopying, recording, or by any information storage and retrieval system, without written permission from the publisher. For information, address Broadway Books, a division of Random House, Inc.

PRINTED IN THE UNITED STATES OF AMERICA

BROADWAY BOOKS and its logo, a letter B bisected on the diagonal, are trademarks of Random House, Inc.

Visit our Web site at www.broadwaybooks.com

First edition published 2005

Book design by Donna Sinisgalli

Library of Congress Cataloging-in-Publication Data
Van der Kwast, Jennifer.
Pounding the pavement : a novel / Jennifer van der Kwast.— 1st ed.
p. cm.
ISBN 0-7679-1953-X
1. Young women—Fiction. 2. Job hunting—Fiction. 3. New York (N.Y.)—Fiction. 4. Unemployed women workers—Fiction. I. Title.

PS3622.A5854P68 2005
813'.6—dc22
2004051474

1 3 5 7 9 10 8 6 4 2

For Doc,

with all my love

acknowledgments

Oftentimes I wonder what audacity possessed me to think I could ever dare write a novel. I have since decided that the blame falls squarely on my family, whose unconditional love and support made me feel as though I could accomplish anything. So thank you to my mother, Patty, my father, Henry, and my grandmother, Mimi, for always being so proud of me, even before I've given you any good reason to be.

I would also like to thank Jenny Raucher for being a champion from the very beginning; Pilar Queen, whose kind, encouraging e-mails have now been saved in a special folder just for her; and Erin Hennicke, whose invaluable advice, insight, and friendship made the whole process seem a little less terrifying.

Special thanks also go to my agent, Joe Veltre, for his endless patience and guidance; my editor, Stacy Creamer, in whose expert hands I've never felt safer; and her assistant, Tracy Zupancis, for quelling my unnecessary panic attacks.

And finally, I'd like to thank Keith Goldberg, my harshest critic *and* my biggest fan, and the only person in the world who could possibly make "your dialogue needs work" sound like "I love you."

Sarah Pelletier

121 West 68th Street, Apt. 4B
New York, NY 10023
h: (212) 555-1476 c: (917) 555-9317
E-mail s.pelletier@hotmail.com

WORK EXPERIENCE

2000–2002   *451Films.com*   *New York, NY*
Content Development Assistant
- Worked with filmmakers and writers to produce online material
- Scouted films, directors, and creative properties
- Participated in the development of short film showcases
- Critiqued and analyzed submissions

1999–2000   *NYC Film Fest*   *New York, NY*
Assistant Programmer
- Solicited, viewed, and participated in the selection of films
- Edited programmer notes and film descriptions for festival catalog
- Coordinated post-screening discussions and specialty panels

Summer 1999   *NYC Film Fest*   *New York, NY*
Festival Intern
- Responsible for the distribution of publicity materials
- Acted as liaison between filmmakers and festival sponsors

Summer 1998   *The Late Night Show*   *New York, NY*
Office Intern
- Managed all aspects of daily office operations
- Assisted show producers with production needs
- Maintained and updated department databases

EXTRACURRICULAR ACTIVITIES

1997–1999   *The Brown Daily Herald*   *Providence, RI*
Arts Writer
- Contributed film reviews
- Covered all campus-wide arts and cultural events

EDUCATION

1996–2000   *Brown University*   *Providence, RI*
BA in English, Minor in Modern Culture and Media
- Graduated Phi Beta Kappa

chapter one

A certain nostalgia comes with having to revisit a résumé. I long for the days when I was straight out of college, when padding a résumé was the sort of challenge that fostered a liberating sense of artistic expression. In a field I once dubbed "Related Experience" (as opposed to my now dreaded "Work Experience") I could haughtily appoint myself such glamorous distinctions as the *director* of student films, an *editor* of the school newspaper, a *writer* for the campus literary magazine.

My résumé, as it stands now, is nothing but a testament to dashed dreams and aspirations. And sadly, to make room for one disappointing failure after another, I've had to remove the silly tributes to my former glories as a director, an editor, and a writer.

The latest version of this curriculum vitae of mine currently lies faceup on the gray Formica desk in front of me, yet I cannot bring myself to meet its eye. It embarrasses me how my name leaps off the page, so cocky and bold. Yet despite my résumé's seemingly desperate pleas for attention, Mark Shapiro, the stocky, bald-headed man who sits across the desk from me, pays no heed to it at all. Instead he fixes me with a steady, penetrating stare and an eager smile I find rather unnerving.

Mark Shapiro is my last hope. He's a headhunter.

Now, I don't really put much faith in recruiters, staffing agents, or any other slick hustler looking to pimp me out as a two-bit work whore, when really I'd much prefer to think of myself as a classy, full-service, employment escort. But my steady stream of interviews has recently dwindled to a minor trickle, and the tedium of having spent the last six months of my life as a recluse has begun to overwhelm me. So I've scheduled my appointment with Mark Shapiro. If anything, it's just another excuse to get out of the house.

Mark Shapiro is exactly what I expected. Wearing a shirt halfway unbuttoned to display his copious chest hair, he is more desperate amateur comedian than polished professional. He beseeches me like he would an unreceptive audience, hoping I'll find him somewhat likeable and warm up to him eventually. Fat chance.

"So! Sarah Pell-tee-ay!" he says, clapping his fleshy hands together. I cringe. Like most people, he has mispronounced my name. I am too ashamed to correct him, to tell him the name—pronounced "Pell-eh-teer"—is an apathetic nod to my long-abandoned French heritage.

"What are you looking for?" he asks.

"Umm, well, most of my experience has been in the film industry."

He raises an eyebrow. "Uh-oh."

"But I don't *have* to work in film. I was thinking about moving into publishing. Preferably magazine publishing."

"Uh-huh." He nods. "And?"

"And maybe books? Or even television? I'd like to find something media-related."

"Sure you do. So does everyone else in this town. Anything else?"

"And," I am rapidly running out of options, "PR? Advertising?"

"Oooh, that sounds good!" Beaming, Mark finally picks up my résumé. He winks at me. "Let's see what we got." He takes one glance at my résumé and his clown-like grin vanishes. I'm not surprised.

It is torturous to watch his labored reading, his obvious distaste for the document in his hands. His bushy brow is knotted, and his thick lips move as he scans the page. To prove his displeasure even further, when he is done he flips over the page to study the back of it. When has anyone ever included valuable information on the *back* of a résumé?

"Content development assistant, huh?" he asks.

"That's right."

"Did you answer phones?"

"Of course."

"Did you file, catalog, and enter data?"

"All the time."

"You handled faxes and all written correspondence?"

"Yup."

"Then you're an administrative assistant." He tosses me back my résumé as if it were tainted, made tacky with flowery language and an overinflated sense of ego. "Change it. Nobody is looking for a content development assistant."

I blink at the résumé in front of me because I can't imagine how I'd go about changing it again. By now the words no longer make sense to me. I've copied, pasted, edited down, searched for synonyms. The page is only a list of phrases and expressions I think I might have overheard from a distant conversation. They mean nothing to me anymore.

"Okay, look at me," Mark Shapiro commands. I look. He chews on a fingernail. "You see this? Don't do this."

I realize he's mimicking me. I'm the one chewing on a fingernail. But it's not chewing, exactly. It's my pensive, meditative pose.

It's a variation on the pose Rodin used for his *Thinker*. It's the gesture I assume when I pretend I am seriously considering the nonsense little shits like Mark Shapiro spew at me.

I remove my finger from my mouth.

"Good. Now, when you go on interviews, I want your hands in your lap, like a little lady . . ."

I shoot Mark Shapiro a deadly look and he reads it perfectly. Chagrined, he clamps his mouth shut and rubs a nervous hand over the two o'clock shadow on his chin. "You know what you could do?" he muses. "Maybe you could include your computer skills on your résumé. You good with computers?"

I sigh. It's degrading to think someone like me, someone who has, in fact, been a valuable contributor to the workplace at one point or another, would have to list something as obvious as computer skills.

"Oh, I'm excellent with computers," I assure him.

"Really? You know Word? Excel? Powerpoint?"

"Sure," I lie. Powerpoint? Never heard of it.

"Terrific!" He claps his beefy hands together again. "Then we're going to run a couple of tests."

Tests?

He sets up the exams for me in a dark, neglected computer room at the end of the hall. The machine he has selected for me, like the others, is a stained relic of a computer with a grainy screen and indecipherable graphics. It's a computer better suited for a contemporary art gallery than a contemporary workplace.

Pleading a long list of "urgent" phone calls, Mark hands me a crumpled sheet of instructions and leaves me alone in the room with a dusty timer.

"I'll be back in forty-five minutes," he says with a wink and heads out the door.

As soon as he leaves, I crouch down low in my cubicle and hit the timer. There is no point in waiting. I'm as ready as I'll ever be. I begin the typing test, my fingers dancing nimbly on the keyboard.

There is something about the buzz of the fluorescent overhead lights, the shrill of unanswered phones down the hall, the blue glow flickering off my aged computer screen. This anonymous office feels very familiar to me. I am comfortable here.

I sail through the test, one page after another. I hit my stride during the Word exam and my momentum carries me well into the Excel and even the Powerpoint sections. I don't mind tests. In fact, I rather enjoy them. Taking tests reminds me of college, and I was good at college.

The timer rings while I am checking my answers. As if on cue, Mark Shapiro flings himself into the room and lingers in the doorway for a moment, one fat, cocky eyebrow raised.

"So? How do you think it went?"

"Fine," I shrug.

A pained cry erupts from somewhere in the room and I nearly leap out of my chair. I realize the brittle, graying printer is slowly spitting out my test results.

Mark Shapiro yanks out the page and glances at it.

"Not bad," he says, handing it to me. I skim over it quickly.

Typing: 50 wpm
Word: 93%
Excel: 90%

Powerpoint?

96%

I find it hard to stifle a laugh.

When I arrived at the headhunter's agency two hours earlier, it had been raining. Thick, violent sheets of rain. But now the deluge has subsided, and the sun has poked a hopeful head between clouds, peering to see if the worst is over.

Summer has never been my favorite season in New York. Summer is a nasty, bitter, old windbag, armed with blasts of hot air for insult and steel drops of rain for injury. But I do like New York after a rainfall, when the streets glisten with invitation, a gracious perfumed hostess in pearls.

I step out of the office building on Park Avenue and am so pleased by the change in climate I decide to walk home. I do have twelve dollars left on my MetroCard, but I am reluctant to use it. Those are the last twelve dollars I have to my name. As soon as my card runs out, I will be officially broke.

While I stand on the street corner waiting for the light to change, I close my eyes and allow myself a moment to bask in the shielded sun's warmth. Still, I refuse to let the sweet coolness lull me into any sense of false optimism. I know what this summer brings. I know it brings sweat stains on the knees of my pantyhose, damp patches under the arms of my silk button-down shirts, and matted, sticky hair clinging to the back of my neck.

I also know what this summer does not bring. As Mark Shapiro has dutifully informed me, the summer months are notoriously slow for the job market, catering primarily to recent college grads who snap up the poorly paid entry level jobs and feasting on summer interns who toil for nothing more than college credit.

The light changes and I step off the curb. A taxi screeches as it careens around the corner. It doesn't occur to me to step out of the way until it is too late. The cab flies full speed into the pungent puddle in front of me and I remain paralyzed in its wake as the infested wave, a mossy gray stew of urban rot, crashes over me.

chapter two

People *lose* jobs. People *look* for jobs, they *go* job-hunting. But it is also important to remember that people *are* unemployed. Unemployment is, by its very nature, inactive. It is a condition, a state of being, much in the same way that a person can *be* an artist, or can *be* stupid.

There are many rules that apply to job-hunting. But there are just as many, if not more, that apply to being unemployed. You enjoy the time off. You try out new hobbies. You force yourself to be social and meet new people—people who could, potentially, provide access to more job leads. You interview for jobs you have no intention of accepting, if only for the practice. And first and foremost, above all, you develop a routine.

This is mine:

The panic attacks usually start some time around 2 a.m., when the world is dark and quiet and I am slipping into a terrifying dream that either has me missing the deadline for a college term paper or stepping onto the wrong express train, heading twenty blocks in the opposite direction on my way to an interview. I toss and turn for a couple of hours, pounding and fluffing my terror like a lumpy pillow.

Most mornings I wake up before 9 a.m. and that really pisses me off. The 9 a.m. to 11 a.m. slot is the hardest part of the day to kill. Because if I let temptation get the best of me and turn on my computer any time before 11 a.m., I'll discover I've received *no new e-mails* and that *no new job listings* have been posted on the online bulletins. For the rest of the day, I'll have to live with the bitter disappointment. Ideally, I'd prefer to sleep in past noon, leaving only seven (all right, five) hours before I can start drinking when it's still considered socially acceptable.

When I finally do manage to pull myself out of bed it is for one reason and one reason only: there is a Snickers bar in the refrigerator.

My next major event of the day is getting dressed. This might seem like a rather mundane activity to note in the schedule, but its significance cannot be overlooked. It would be all too easy to fall into a bathrobe-and-fuzzy-slipper funk, whittling away the daylight hours with the shades drawn. Miss Havisham at least had her wedding dress. Emily Dickinson was writing poetry. What's my excuse?

That said, I no longer force myself to wear fly-collared blouses and tailored skirts *just in case*. If I do choose to get dressed my daily wardrobe is standard: jog bra, wrinkled gym shorts, anything that might pass for matching socks, sneakers, and a faded college T-shirt marking the year and the event that rewarded student participants with free attire. Today, I boast my contribution to Yale's 1997 A Cappella Fest. It's a lie. I didn't go to Yale. And I am quite positive I didn't visit the campus to take part in the finger-snapping, foot-stomping charade of mediocre vocalists. How the shirt has insinuated itself into my standard daily wardrobe is a total mystery to me.

You're probably thinking my next stop is the gym. You're wrong.

At 10:30 I decide it's okay to start smoking.

At 11—drum roll, please—I make for my final destination: the

Aeron office chair. Fabric web upholstering, backward recline, forward tilt, adjustable aluminum arms, the works! (There's a story about this chair, but I'll get to that in a bit.) I then turn on my computer and log on to my Hotmail account. Today I've received one new e-mail and my heart soars. It is from Marjorie Newman, head of a boutique literary agency.

> Dear Sarah,
>
> Thank you for sending your résumé, but you are far too overqualified for this job. Good luck!
>
> Best,
> Marjorie Newman

Is it thrilling to think someone actually considers me overqualified for anything? Of course not. I know I'm not overqualified. I'm just qualified in a way no one knows how to deal with. Still, I find the letter oddly flattering. So I save it.

At 1 p.m. I decide to take my first break and head to the gym. (Happy now?) I do not go to the gym because I am health conscious. And despite what several magazine articles say about exercise being an excellent stress-reliever, that too is none of my concern. I go to the gym because there are TV sets, all of which receive cable, and no one is going to be there to argue with me when I flip to HGTV to watch homeowners remodel their log cabins. This is the only hour of entertainment I will indulge in. I am not permitted to watch daytime television at any other time. (This is a stringent rule. Without it, I could easily spend the entire afternoon watching marathon reruns of *Newlyweds*.)

At 2 p.m. I come back to my apartment and watch *Newlyweds*.

After the conclusion of one episode, and one episode *only* (yes, I have rules for breaking rules), I head back to my bedroom and ready my lasso. For the rest of the afternoon I will straddle the Aeron, my well-worn saddle, tip an imaginary Stetson on my head, and cock the barrel of my mouse to make sure it's loaded.

And this is how it generally works. Me, a regular Gary Cooper, cruising the online plains—head tilted, eyes squinted, sniffing for trouble.

So. About the chair.

Consider the Aeron a passenger seat on a particularly turbulent flight, and the plane my former company, 451Films.com. I was strapped tightly to that chair for takeoff. And it was all I managed to salvage from the fatal crash.

At 451Films.com we used to pride ourselves on being visionaries with magic wands who tapped the best of New York's undiscovered filmmaking talent. But a week before Christmas, due to failure to remit, our wands were repossessed. So were our watercoolers. And the copy machine we'd been leasing.

Holiday cheer at the time was, at best, waning. A memo had been issued from the cockpit that there was a storm to be weathered, a few bumps ahead, but not to worry—the destination, of course, would be well worth the ride. Unfortunately, by that time everyone in the cabin was too airsick to care. We'd just as soon strap on a parachute and flash a thumbs-up before we leapt out the emergency exit.

Sure, there was still work to be done. But it was menial work, mindless work, work nobody wanted to do anymore. Aspiring filmmakers who didn't know any better sent us their film reels and written proposals, hoping to be featured on our website. We watched, we read, knowing full well that "acquisition" was no longer a word that fit in our company lexicon.

At one point there was a calm, which there always is. And then a ripple of excitement. The office was abuzz with the sort of breathless anticipation we hadn't felt in months. And the word on everyone's fevered lips was "layoffs."

I arrived at the office that Monday morning some time around 11 a.m., much earlier than I usually managed to drag myself in. And still I had to wait another hour before my boss, Gracie—or Princess Grace, as we took to calling her behind her back—came prancing in, two large Henri Bendel shopping bags strapped to her shoulders. An early-morning trip to a tanning salon had left her cheeks glowing a fierce red. She didn't say hi when she walked by (she never did), she merely breezed right into her office. This time, I followed her.

"Oh, good, Sarah, you're here," she said, massaging her neck. "Could you call a messenger to take these bags back to my apartment? My back is killing me."

Princess's blatant disregard of the cut in company expenditures was hardly surprising. As far as she was concerned, the rules never directly applied to *her*.

"Actually, Gracie, we need to talk," I said, taking my familiar seat on her office sofa. She gaped at me with an expression I couldn't quite read. Annoyance? Indignation? Fear? With an exaggerated sigh, she crossed her legs and aimed her pointy-toed shoe at me like a dagger drawn from its sheath.

"I'm listening."

I took a deep breath. "I heard a rumor that all the rest of the assistants are being let go today. Is it true?"

If there was anything Gracie hated most, it was a direct question. So she avoided my eye and toyed with the collar of her candy pink cashmere turtleneck. "You know, I wasn't supposed to tell you until this afternoon—"

"Tell me what? That I'm fired?"

She glared at me. Like it was my fault for putting her on the spot. "In a way . . . yes."

"When?"

"Umm . . ." She fumbled on her desk for a hairpin. "End of the day?"

"You mean, today?"

"Well, actually, no." She stuck the hairpin between her teeth. I watched with no small amount of irritation as she spent the next couple of moments wrapping her Nordic blonde hair into a tight little bun on top of her head. She finally sealed it with the hairpin and sighed again. "Officially, your last day was Friday."

Damn. I must have cut out early and missed the farewell party.

"Do I get any severance?" I asked.

She laughed. "I'm sorry. You're serious? With what money?"

Excellent point. I had almost forgotten we'd had to make do without coffee and toilet paper for the past couple of weeks.

"Well, then, can I take my office chair?" I asked.

Princess shrugged. "Why not? I don't suppose it makes much difference." She turned on her laptop, signaling the end of the conversation.

"I'm also taking the halogen lamp next to my bullpen."

"Fine."

I excused myself from the room.

"Oh, Sarah," she called, as I was stepping out the door. "Don't forget to call the messenger."

I turned back to glare at her.

"Never mind," she said sheepishly. "If you shoot me an e-mail with the phone number I can take care of it."

I smiled politely and continued on.

Despite the exodus of former employees fleeing the building that morning, I did manage to shove the office chair and halogen lamp onto a crowded elevator and head downstairs. I needed a second run, however, to retrieve a metal filing cabinet and a small bookcase. And a third and fourth run to pick up the three empty copy-paper boxes I had stuffed with paper clips, staples, Sharpies, and other supplies. A helpful cabdriver found a way to cram it all into his backseat and insisted I join him up front. The entire ride uptown he ranted and raved about the terrible state of our country's economy, the vicious trick America had played on her citizens.

The cabbie helped me unload my pilfered goods into my apartment lobby. I offered him a gracious tip for his trouble, but he refused to take a dime. He settled instead for a heavy duty three-hole paper punch.

My apartment bedroom is now but a glorified version of my office cubicle. And if you were to see me dwarfed among all my office luxuries, you'd probably think I'd been vindicated. So did I. But in retrospect, I didn't even come close to getting what I deserved. Two weeks after my termination, when the doors to 451Films.com would close for good, one plasma TV would be reported missing and twenty-six laptops would be left unaccounted for. I guess I could very well have walked out with my computer too.

But at least I got the Aeron. And I do love that fucking chair.

At 8 p.m. I decide it's *really* okay to watch television. At 8:30 I decide it's okay to start drinking.

I grab a bottle of Merlot—and a wineglass, for propriety's sake—from the kitchen and bring them both back into the living room. After a few moments of channel surfing, I am delighted to see that *Tootsie* will be on AMC in twenty minutes. I pour myself another generous glass of the wine and get comfortable. This is shaping up to be a perfectly pleasant evening.

And it is all ruined as soon as I hear the rattle of a key chain at my front door.

Bitch. I never hate my roommate more than the moment she's about to walk in.

The jangling at the door scales up for an incredibly long, drawn-out moment until it finally reaches its shrill crescendo. The door flings open and in spills a white blur of blonde curls and long legs.

Amanda straightens, and with one graceful sweep of her long, swanlike arm, she brushes back her curls, smoothes out her white blouse, and delicately plucks down the hem of her skirt. Casually slipping her keys back into her purse, she is the picture of poised perfection. But there is a pink flush to her naturally pale white, porcelain cheeks. I can tell she's been drinking.

Amanda smiles brightly. "You find a job today?"

"No. You find a boyfriend?"

Her smile dips. Opting to ignore me, she breezes into the kitchen.

I can hear her rattling. The refrigerator door squeaks, cabinets slam shut, silverware clatters. Annoyed, I turn up the volume on the TV.

"Hey!" Amanda pokes her rosy red face into the living room. "Any idea what happened to the wine? I know there was at least half a bottle left over from last night."

It is too late for me to feign innocence. My wineglass is poised an inch away from my lips. The empty bottle is on the coffee table, not a foot away in front of me.

Amanda frowns and crosses her arms over her chest. In the background, I can hear Dustin Hoffman pleading with producers who want to cast someone taller—"Oh, I can be taller!" Normally, I'd already be giggling were I not being seared by Amanda's poisoned, humorless eyes.

She cocks her head at the TV screen. "Whaddya watching?"

"Tootsie?"

"Yeah, I don't think so." She grabs the remote control and switches off the television. And the simple, quiet evening I had so been looking forward to goes dark with it.

"I think we should go out," she says.

"No."

"Why? It's not like you have to be up early tomorrow morning."

"But you do," I point out hopefully.

She rolls her eyes. "I'll manage."

I'm fighting a losing battle and I know it. "Where do you want to go?"

"A friend of mine is having an office party in Tribeca."

"Tribeca?" I grimace. "Do I have to get changed?"

"Of course you have to change! You're wearing a bathrobe!"

"Can I wear jeans?"

"Fine!" She throws up her tiny, manicured hands in exasperation. "Wear jeans!"

The bar in Tribeca is not as obnoxious as I had initially feared. The last time Amanda dragged me out to this neighborhood, she took me to a place Citysearch had voted the "Best Singles Scene." It didn't have a name or a sign, just a funny silver symbol above the door. And to make matters worse, the inside looked as though it had been chiseled out of ice. Like the clientele it served, it was cold, sleek, and utterly transparent. I spent the entire evening on tiptoe, trying not to touch anything with sharp edges, in constant fear of breaking martini glasses or knocking over rail-thin models on six-inch stilettos, and grazing past men in slippery, silk shirts. Yet inevitably, as I forged my way to the back room, I smacked straight into some poor, unsuspecting woman. I started to apologize profusely until I realized the woman I had bumped into was my own reflection in a mirror. The back room was but a mirage.

The bar we are at tonight, however, is a welcome surprise. It's a seedy throwback to an era when bars were bars—a saloon for a weary gunslinger, a dive for a thirsty sailor—and not high-gloss hotel lobbies for Bellini drinkers and ditzy cocktail waitresses.

Amanda, as always, lingers by the door. Even at a dingy hole-in-the-wall like this, she still feels the need to make her entrance as if she were a nubile young debutante presenting herself to high society. Her cover girl smile, however, is lost on this crowd. The patrons of this particular bar look as badly shaken as their martinis, their faces soured from having sucked on one too many olives.

Furthermore, as soon as we've walked in, the walls resound with the echo of a shattered glass, followed by an appropriate "Shit!" All heads swivel, not toward Amanda, but to the bar itself where an assembly of stockbrokers—or are they investment bankers?—with discarded jackets and shirttails untucked, cheer wildly. The pound their pints against the wood countertop and chant, "Joe! Joe! Joe!"

A man at the very center, soaked in lager, smiles good-naturedly and fixes his comb-over.

"Well, now that I have everyone's attention . . ." He motions for his friends to quiet down. The middle-aged, gray ponytail-sporting bartender hands him another beer.

"Cheers." He raises his new glass and addresses the room. "Friends, loved ones . . ." He points his glass at an overweight man at the rickety table in front of him, "and Charlie." A few of his colleagues snicker. Charlie holds up his own glass to accept the toast. Joe continues.

"I just want to take this moment to thank you all for the loyalty, the memories, and even the tears. And although I'd like to say the booze is on the house—it isn't. But don't let that stop you. Here's to buying your own drinks, and may there be many more in your future!"

He pauses, waiting for the rallying call.

"And fuck Seaman Partners!"

The members of the bar lift their glasses and respond with a furious, "Hoorah!" Another glass slips and breaks, warranting even more raucous cheers. A thought dawns on me and I turn to Amanda stricken.

"Please don't tell me you brought me to a *pink slip* party."

"Oh, come on." She grins and wraps her arm around mine. "Isn't it wild?"

I am too stunned to resist as she leads me to Charlie's table, smack dab in the midst of all the hoopla, and pulls up a chair.

"Everyone! Everyone!" she calls out. All heads turn. Amanda has that wonderful, mysterious power afforded to strikingly beautiful blondes everywhere. When she commands attention, people give it to her.

"Everyone, this is my roommate, Sarah. Sarah, this is everyone."

Unlike Amanda, I don't really command much attention. The group acknowledges me with a collective nod and a few grunts. But just as soon as they are about to return to their drinks, Amanda makes another announcement.

"Sarah has been unemployed for six months!"

And just like that, I am the life of the party.

I realize now this whole evening has been a setup. After Amanda has paraded me around like Westminster's prize terrier, she introduces me to Monica. Monica is a college friend of hers from U Penn. Because I've never even heard of Monica before tonight, I think I can safely assume her relationship with Amanda consists mainly of a few unreturned e-mails, the occasional trading of voice mails, and canceled brunch plans here and there. Perhaps Amanda just felt a little bit guilty when Monica called this afternoon to tell her she had lost her job. And, ever the humanitarian, she probably offered me up as consolation.

While Amanda leaves to entertain a group of men vying for her attention, I get stuck with Monica at the bar. I'm nearly done with my beer. Monica is staring morosely into her full bottle, as if she can almost see her aborted career floating inside.

"I'm thinking of seeing a therapist," she tells her beer. "My mother thinks it's a good idea. And a friend of mine knows someone who works on a sliding scale. But, I don't know." She looks up at me with big, dopey brown eyes. "What do you think about therapy?"

What do I really think about therapy? I really think it's the East Coast alternative to the Church of Scientology. But I can tell Monica isn't in the mood to hear any of my cynical, albeit astute, observations.

"*Pfft*," I wave off her question dismissively. "I am so beyond therapy. I am actually thinking of seeing a philosopher."

Monica's dopey eyes blink twice. "A philosopher?"

"Uh, yeah . . . See, only a philosopher could answer the questions I have."

"Oh, no, you don't understand!" She becomes inexplicably animated all of a sudden. "Therapy is supposed to teach you the answers are inside yourself."

See? That's exactly the kind of shit I don't need.

I polish off the rest of my beer and figure, to hell with it. I am going to lay it all out on the line. I'm going to tell Monica her mother is absolutely right. She *should* see a therapist. Because pretty soon all her friends are going to get really sick of her fucking whining. And when she can't complain about not having a job, she'll find herself at a loss, completely unable to contribute to a conversation in any other way. She hasn't seen the hot new FedEx deliveryman. She isn't flirting with any cute new interns. Desperate to participate, she'll laughingly bring up Kelly Ripa's latest faux pas. When she is met with only a sea of blank expressions, that's when she'll realize. No one has time to watch morning television. Nobody knows who Kelly Ripa is.

In the end, I don't get to say any of this. Because as soon as I slam down my beer, as soon as I'm about to launch into my tirade, a finger taps me on the shoulder.

I pivot around to find a boy standing behind me. He's a short boy with hair thinning out to carve a permanent yarmulke on the top of his head.

"Hi," he says shyly. "You the girl that's been unemployed for six months?"

He smiles. It's a nice smile, and he's got friendly eyes, so I grin and hold up my empty beer bottle.

"Yeah. Wanna buy me a drink?"

It's a mistake I make only far too often. I am happy to accept free drinks from eager young men simply because I cannot afford my own. But a beer is never just a beer, is it? A beer is a conversation, and usually a dull one at that. The boy plunks down a twenty-dollar bill and immediately the bartender scurries over to take his order. The drinks arrive swiftly and the boy settles down on a barstool beside me.

"I'm Artie." He extends a hand.

"Sarah," I say, shaking it. And already I feel as though I've disclosed too much.

Oh, but it gets worse. Within another few minutes, I learn that Artie's favorite movie is *Braveheart*. And his favorite author is Hemingway. I can feel my eyes rolling around inside my head like a rack of billiard balls knocked cold by the cue ball.

"And what about you?" he asks.

"Me? Well, I kinda like *Who's Afraid of Virginia Woolf?*"

"Isn't that a play?"

"It's also a movie. Liz Taylor? Richard Burton?"

"Oh, sure, I've heard of them." He takes a hearty sip of his beer. "And what about your favorite writer?"

"Haruki Murakami," I say decisively, even though that's not necessarily true. Why risk the fact he might recognize a name like John Irving or Tom Robbins?

Artie gulps hard. I use the lull in our conversation to cast a none-too-discreet glance at my watch.

"Oh, Jesus, I gotta go." It never sounds quite genuine when I say that. Nevertheless, I grab my purse. Artie stands abruptly.

"Which way you headed? Maybe we could share a cab?"

"I'm going to New Jersey," I lie.

"Where in—?"

"I'm just gonna walk over to the PATH." I thrust out my hand before he can even consider moving in for a kiss. "Nice meeting you. And thanks for the beer."

"Sure. Anytime."

I dart for the door without even so much as a good-bye as I slip past Amanda. We wouldn't have been sharing a cab anyway. Earlier, a stockbroker offered to give her a tour of his penthouse loft, so she tossed me ten dollars in guilt cash, making me promise not to travel solo on the subway. She's still where I left her, kneeling under a table trying to locate her cell phone.

To eliminate any chance of Artie coming out after me, I sprint five blocks toward Canal Street. When the bar is safely behind me, I slow down to a trot, and finally come to a breathless, sweaty halt. A hopeful cabdriver creeps toward me, but I wave him away. I still have Amanda's ten dollars in my purse, but I'll be damned if I spend it on anything as frivolous as a car ride.

I crouch down and hang my head between my legs. My whole body aches and my breathing isn't getting any easier. I wonder if it isn't just the running that makes my heart race. Maybe six months of anxiety have finally caught up to me. Maybe I am in the throes of a full-scale panic attack. Just that thought alone spurs another spasm in my back. I lean back against a brick wall, momentarily paralyzed with dizziness.

Someone should cue the bolt of lightning and turn on the rainmakers. And then I could crumble under a torrential downpour, letting it pelt my head and soak my clothes. Because self-pity doesn't really work without a good dose of heavy-handed melodrama.

I blame Amanda. I blame her for convincing me that going to a party would be the answer to all my problems. I had almost forgotten how tedious and exhausting the whole process could be. What is so grand about forcing tight-lipped smiles, shaking limp hands, and nodding in agreement to a comment I haven't even heard? If I really wanted to get all dressed up—put on a pretty skirt, douse myself in orange-scented body spray—if I really felt the need to act all gracious and attentive, I'd be better off just scheduling another interview.

And I blame Amanda for loving it so much. The way she laughs at a terrible pun, the way she can make her total lack of interest in politics sound charming, the way she can talk so passionately about Ben Affleck's love life. And when her favorite song comes up on the jukebox, Amanda is the only one I know who can convince someone to dance with her. Together they'll be the only ones to wiggle their hips under the "No Dancing" sign while everyone else at the bar stares in blatant amusement. Most people would cringe at an act so audacious. But somehow, Amanda makes it seem endearing. That carefree love of life—okay, that joie de vivre. I miss having that.

I step away from the wall, feeling a bit steadier on my feet, and cast a look around to get my bearings. My eyes alight on the glimmering sign across the street. The Screening Room. I check my watch. It's 11:45. *Breakfast at Tiffany's* starts in only fifteen minutes. And suddenly, I feel giddy as I think of Audrey Hepburn floating around her apartment with a cigarette holder. One man holds out a match for her and another man blows it out so he can light her cigarette instead. Now there's a party I would love to attend.

Filled with new purpose, I march toward the theater. And I can't imagine a better way to spend my last ten dollars.

chapter three

It isn't quite fair. All over Manhattan phones are ringing, and in the most inappropriate places. A man will take a woman to a romantic restaurant, lovingly stroke her palm with one hand, flip open his cell with the other. Doors to a bus will slide open, but the line of passengers will halt because someone up front is fumbling in her bag to answer an important call. A Hitchcock revival will be playing at a theater downtown, and audiences will grimace and squirm in their seats, because someone's pocket is trilling Henry Mancini's "Elephant Walk." (Henry Mancini is a brilliant composer, don't get me wrong. But Hitchcock belongs to Bernard Herrmann.)

And here I sit, flossing my teeth in the living room, pleading with my silent, stoic phone. Of all places, this is where you *should* be ringing. *Come on*, I beg. *Ring, ring, ring!*

And then it happens. It rings. At first I think I've only imagined it. But it rings again and it is as if my wildest dreams have come true. In my haste to answer, I only succeed in yanking half the strip of floss out of my mouth.

"Erro?"

"Sweetie-pie, is that you?"

It's my mother. It figures.

"What's the matter, sweetie-pie? You sound strange."

"Umfroshing."

"What? Uh-oh. I can't hear you. Sarah? Sarah!"

She shrieks as if the demons of static were carting me off to their netherworld. Meanwhile, I take the time, patiently, to un-thread the piece of floss wrapped around my molar.

"I was flossing."

"Oh," she says, relieved. "Good. Now, listen, sweetie-pie, I just called to tell you that your father thinks he might have found you a job."

Oh no.

"He was just talking to Carl about your . . . er . . . *situation*. And, well, it turns out Carl has a cousin who is the CEO of a company in New York."

"What kind of company?"

"I don't know. It's called . . . let me see here . . . Pharmateque Capital Corporation?"

That doesn't sound too promising. But I force myself to bite my forked tongue. "What position is he looking to fill?"

"I think Dad said he needs a secretary."

"Mom, people don't *have* secretaries anymore. They're called assistants."

"No, I'm pretty sure he said secretary. Hold on, let me put him on."

"No, Mom, that's okay, really—" Too late. The phone squawks in resistance between changing hands.

"Sarah?"

"Hi, Dad."

"I gave Carl's cousin your phone number. His secretary will be calling you to set up an interview."

"I thought he didn't have a secretary."

"He does. She's leaving."

"Why is she leaving?"

"How the hell should I know! Maybe you should ask her yourself when she calls."

I could snap back, but I consider myself far too old to be sparring with my father. Instead I say nothing, enjoying the tense silence. I close my eyes and imagine my father back home in Denver, squirming in his chair, trying to get a better angle on the television set in the next room.

"So," he says finally. "How are things?"

"Things are fine."

"Really? Mom says you still don't have health insurance."

"Well, no, I don't, but I've been looking into it." Dad sighs. A loud, yawning sigh he's been perfecting ever since I was nine years old.

"You know that's really selfish of you."

"Right, I know."

"What if you were in an accident? Who would pay for your hospital bill?"

"I suppose you would—"

"That's right. Me! You would wipe us out."

"I know, I know. But, Dad, even COBRA still charges over three hundred dollars a month for their continuation policy, and I just can't afford that right now. So, I mean, if *you* don't want to pay hospital bills and would prefer to just write out a three-hundred-dollar check every month—"

"Oh, Jesus." My father lowers his phone, but his voice is no less booming.

"Maggie! Maggie, she's asking for money again!"

"What? No, I never said—" I am interrupted by another squawk of the telephone.

"I thought you said you were solvent," says Mom.

"I am. Just, with health insurance, things are going to get tight."

"You have to have insurance! Don't you worry about your health at all?"

"Of course, I do. Why do you think I was flossing?"

"You're being really selfish, you know."

"Yes, Dad already told me so."

"Don't get snippy."

"I'm not snippy. Mom, I have to go."

"Why?"

"Because I want to call the health insurance offices before they close."

I hang up. Almost immediately, my phone rings again. No longer is it music to my ears. It's probably my mother calling back to demand an apology. Unfortunately, I am in no position to be screening calls so I answer it begrudgingly.

"Hello?"

"Sarah? Mark Shapiro here."

"Oh, hi, Mark."

"Listen, I just found you the perfect job."

"You did?"

"You wanted a media company, didn't you? Well, you got it!"

"What kind of media? Publishing? Film?"

"Commercials!"

Oh. Not quite the media I'd been hoping for.

"You're in luck," Mark continues. "It's a great place. They do lots of steady work. But they just lost one of their employees and they need someone to replace him ASAP."

"What's the job?"

"Hmmm? Umm, hang on . . . let me find it for you." I hear him riffle through pages. "Oh, okay. It's for an office manager. Sounds good, right?"

No. Does not sound good. Sounds, at best, tolerable.

"Yeah, okay. I'll give it a shot."

"Super! They want you to start tomorrow at nine a.m."

"What? I don't need to go in for an interview first?"

"Ummm, not exactly. They really just need a temporary replacement for the time being."

Temping? I groan. "Mark, I told you. I can't temp. If I work for even one day, I'll lose all my unemployment benefits for the week." Yes, I agree: It's one hell of a lousy rule. But, hey, I didn't make it.

"I know. But there's a very good chance it could turn into a full-time gig. If they like you, they might decide to keep you on. Don't you think you should at least look into it?"

"Umm, well . . ." Shit. I've been had. Because, unfortunately, as a rule, I don't turn down potential full-time job leads. "Okay."

"Great. The company is called Stellar Productions. They are located at 581 Broadway. Ask for Gregory."

When I hang up this time, I do indeed yank out the phone cord. Because if any more sticky situations come up, I know for a fact I won't be able to talk my way out of them.

Sharing a workspace is a lot like sharing a toothbrush. This I realize the moment I find myself chewing on the end of a pen that doesn't belong to me. I remove the cap from my mouth and discreetly look to see if anyone else in the office has caught me in so vile an act.

Stellar Productions isn't much of an office. A cunning real estate agent would probably call it "raw space," making it sound exotic and appetizing, like a tray of sushi. Of course, all "raw space" really means is there is no clearly defined reception area, no navigable layout, only a lump of carelessly constructed cubicles. Frankly, I prefer my offices more well-done. Cooked to a crisp, thank you very much.

By as early as 10 a.m., the excitement of embarking on a somewhat promising new job has all but vanished. So has the anticipation. And so has the curiosity. Instead I am filled with a frothy, bubbling rage. I've already decided I hate everyone who works here. I hate the haughty executives who wouldn't deign to introduce themselves to me, who flee to the sancity of their windowed offices in the back, emerging only every now and then to toss their outgoing mail on my desk, without even the courtesy of a "please" or "thank you." I hate the boy who has been hogging the company stereo system, proudly inserting his mixed CDs and taking enormous pleasure in telling us what song is playing, who is singing it, and what year it was recorded (and should anyone ask, he can also supply the name of the LP and the track number). I hate the girl seated beside me because she doesn't need to talk on the phone quite so loudly. And I hate the smug interns, because they know their free labor is a gift they could just as easily bestow elsewhere.

But most of all, I hate being me. Because I am smarter, more professional, and more eager to please than anyone else in this damn office and there's no way for me to prove it. Nobody noticed how quickly I filed my paperwork, nobody thought to mention how polite I sound when I answer the phone. And when I dutifully watched the Stellar Productions reel of sample work and coughed up a few giggles where I thought they might be appropriate, nobody even looked pleased that I made such an effort to pretend to be enjoying myself.

With each passing hour, and with fewer assignments coming my way, I can feel myself peeling back layer after layer of the Professional Sarah, letting a little bit of the Unemployed Sarah shine through. Come to think of it, there's only a fine line between the two (a line made even finer after taxes). I can't help but wonder if my time wouldn't be better spent at home, where I don't have to hastily click out of the Hotjobs website every time someone walks by my desk. Hell, my time would be better spent if I were waiting to get picked for jury duty.

It isn't that I'm not happy to be working. I'm just not happy to be temping. If the company interns are the larvae and the employees the fluttering butterflies, then being a temp makes me the pupa, nestled in the gooey cocoon of my own slime. No one is going to take the time to nurture me and no one is going to give me wings to make me fly. I'm just a waste of space on a twig.

Oh, you know who else I hate? I hate the former dweller of this cubicle, whatever mangy mutt has already pissed on this here fire hydrant. He, with the stacks and stacks of videocassettes—some even mutated to be twice or half the size of regular VHS tapes. And then there's the bookshelf, chock full of binders with budget reports and production notes, and books with such sterile titles as *The Simon Archer Plan: How to Break International Markets*, or *Research Analysis: Volumes I–IV*. What a sad, sad existence this person must lead.

And yet by mid-afternoon, I find myself poring over these tomes voraciously, starved for entertainment of any kind—yes, even the dry, insipid, boring kind. I am delighted to find a talent binder devoted to headshots for aspiring commercial actresses, crushed when the young Alice Zucker's paltry résumé marks the last entry.

I return the binder to the shelf and move on to the next item, surprised to find my index finger take a sudden dip. For the next book down the line is a paperback with a spine so worn and frayed I can't make out the title. I withdraw it curiously and gasp when I see the front cover.

Still Life with Woodpecker? Get out! Since when does Tom Robbins rub shoulders with child star Alice Zucker and Simon Archer, International Market-Man of Mystery?

"Excuse me?"

I look up and find a frown. It's on the rather unpleasant face of a middle-aged man eyeing me carefully. I shove the book back on the shelf and smile prettily.

"Can I help you?" I ask.

"Where's Jake?"

Damn it. Don't people know I'm the temp? Why must they insist on asking me questions I can't possibly answer? Part of me wants to crawl under the desk and mutter, "That's strange. I know he was just here a minute ago . . ."

Instead I shrug and opt for the infinitely more mature, "Dunno."

"Who are you?"

"I'm Sarah. I'm temping for him."

"Great." He holds out one of those minicassettes. "Can you transfer DV to D-Beta?"

Again the shrug. Again the pretty smile. Again the sophisticated reply. "Ummm . . . nope."

"Oh." He looks utterly bewildered. "Jake usually does all the transfers for us."

"I'm sorry."

"Well, do you know anyone who could do it for me, then?"

"I don't know," I glance inconspicuously at the taped-up list of phone extensions under my elbow. The first name reads Abbott, James.

"Have you asked James Abbott?"

The guy blinks at me.

"I *am* Jim Abbott."

"Oh, well, then I'm sorry. I guess I can't really help out."

The phone rings, cutting him off before he can respond. I gladly reach for the receiver on my desk, only to find the lights aren't flashing. The ringing is coming from my bag under the desk.

For a split second I consider acting a true professional and ignoring my personal cell phone calls. But what if it's another job interview? I decide to take my chances.

"Pardon me," I say, holding out an obnoxious finger to silence him. With my other hand I reach under my desk to grab my phone. Jim Abbott skulks off reluctantly to try his luck with the next assistant down the line.

"Hello?" I say into the cell.

"Hi, it's Laurie. I just got fired. Wanna do dinner?"

Laurie can be flippant about getting fired because she is *always* getting fired, even before it was fashionable. Her particular situation, however, is quite rare. She hasn't lost a string of jobs, or even two jobs for that matter. She just keeps getting fired from the same job, over and over again. For three years now she has worked for a megalomaniacal film producer whose violent temper tantrums have achieved an almost legendary status. During his fits, he is likely to flip over his desk and hurl large objects at his television set. And after his outbursts have subsided, if Laurie can't get the office back up and running within fifteen minutes, she gets fired. She got fired last week because her boss dealt the fax machine a crushing blow, and by mid-afternoon she still couldn't get the damn thing to print incoming memos properly. She was kicked out of the office sometime around 4 p.m. By 9 a.m. the following morning, another assistant called to tell her it was safe to come back. So she did. She always does.

"Yeah, dinner's fine," I say. "Dancing Burrito?"

"Sure. Six p.m. happy hour?"

"Perfect. See ya then."

I hang up the phone. Two seconds later, a sudden, sharp trill on my desk makes the hairs on the back of my neck bristle. A loud, deep voice then crawls through the mesh of the phone deck.

"Sarah?"

I freeze. I've never mastered the art of speakerphone parlance. It is one thing to deal with a disembodied voice coming from a tangible phone receiver. Quite another when the voice is an eerie, invisible hiss coming from nowhere in particular.

"Uh, yeah?" I pitch forward and yell.

"This is Gregory."

"Oh!" I yell back. "Oh, nice to meet you!" A positively stupid thing to say to your phone deck.

"Thanks again for coming in today," says the full-throated voice. "You've been doing an excellent job."

"Oh?" I pause. He left large folder of deal memos on my desk this morning. I filed them all within twenty minutes. "Thank you!"

"Been quite a hectic day, hasn't it?"

Rather shamelessly, I find myself agreeing. "Yeah, but I've been managing all right."

"The good news is you'll be getting a little bit of extra help this afternoon. Jake might be dropping by later."

"Umm . . ." I stare at my phone curiously. "Jake?"

"The person you've been replacing?"

"I see," I say, when in fact I don't see at all. Did I just get fired halfway into my workday? "He's coming back?"

"Well," The voice sounds more distant this time. Like Gregory has already given up on the conversation and has literally begun to wander away. "I don't know if he's coming *back*, per se. I think for today he's just going to show you around, explain how the office runs. That sort of thing. He hasn't been very reliable lately. He's been . . ." His voice drops to a whisper. Which isn't very effective on speakerphone. "Well, he's been dealing with personal problems."

"Oh?" For the first time during our entire conversation I perk up with keen interest.

"He's just taking some time off. You understand, right?"

"Sure." Of course I understand. Sounds like heartbreak to me.

"Oh, also," Gregory continues. "I'm having my assistant Marcia bring over more deal memos that need to be filed. Marcia!" I hear him bark, from both my phone and from directly behind me. "Can you bring these over to Jake's temp?" I turn to gaze over my shoulder. A girl seated across from me stands and disappears into the adjacent office. I can make out only a vague silhouette of a man hovering over his desk. "Talk to you later, Sarah."

"Bye!" I say to a phone that has already gone dead.

Not a minute later, Marcia trots over with the stack of deal memos. I'll take my time with this load.

I take a bathroom break and when I return, there is a tall, thin woman hovering about my cubicle. If I were to hazard a guess, I'd assume she's Susanna Carlyle, the executive vice president of Stellar Productions. She scurried past me this morning without so much as a word and fled into one of the back offices. Her door remained closed throughout the day. Call me irrational, but I've never much cared for people who close their office doors. The quest for privacy in the workplace can only mean one thing: someone is going to get fired.

"You're the temp?" she asks me, staring down the long, thin ridge of her nose.

"Yes. Can I help you?"

"The coffeepot in the back is empty."

"It is?" I ask, playing dumb.

"Do you mind making another pot?"

What I would give to be twelve years old again. To be able to snidely reply, "Why me? *I* didn't finish it." But even at twelve, I wouldn't want to risk losing my weekly allowance.

"Sure, no problem," I say brightly as I skip my way into the pantry.

Now, see, I have a theory about being asked to brew coffee. It's a theory I have about being asked to perform any degrading office task. I figure if I absolutely *have* to do it, I'll do it once. I'll do it wrong. And I'll never have to do it again.

My secret to making bad coffee is quite simple. I decided long ago, harking way back to my intern years, never to learn how to make coffee at all. Oh, I suppose if push came to shove I *could* measure out an appropriate amount of coffee grounds. (Or beans? No, grounds. Right?) And I guess I *could* figure out just how much water to add. But I don't much care to fuss with such details. The less effort, the better. Reuse yesterday's soggy grounds, keep the same gaping filter, fill to the brim with tap water, presto!

When the coffee has brewed to my satisfaction, I carefully pour out two full cups. One for Ms. Carlyle, and one for her bitchy assistant for good measure.

Susanna Carlyle's door is, of course, closed. I tap a cute little ditty on her name plate and she answers with a clipped, "Come in." I open the door.

"So sorry to interrupt," I tell her assistant, seated in the guest chair. "Here you go."

"Thank you," says Ms. Carlyle. Her assistant takes her mug wordlessly and glares at me over the rim. To piss her off, I beam her an unnatural, oafish grin.

"You're welcome."

As I prance out of the office and nudge the door closed behind me, I hear Ms. Carlyle speak to her assistant in a purposefully loud whisper.

"Jake's coffee is much better," she says.

Ah, yes. *Him* again. Maybe it's just absence that makes the heart grow fonder. But there was no mistaking Jim Abbott's look of despair when Jake couldn't be found. No ignoring the catch in Gregory's voice when he said his name out loud. And that look of scorn Ms. Carlyle's assistant shot me when it was I who walked through that door? That was a decidedly feminine look, and a hostile one at that—a look generally reserved for the woman holding the last pair of jeans you specifically came to the store to buy. Believe me, that look would have been far softer and more docile if it had been intended for someone else.

These are the only clues I have to go by, but with them I have myself convinced Jake is someone I really, really want to impress. And so when I commence my filing, I pay special attention to my posture. I furrow my brow and look studious. I read the legal memos laboriously, and sometimes I even look off into space and pretend to be absorbing incredibly useful information.

Eventually looking off into space turns into looking wistfully at the door, imagining his dramatic entrance. First I picture him carrying his motorcycle helmet in one hand, a single red rose in the other, which he will gallantly place on my desk to thank me for coming in today. Then I remember the Tom Robbins book, and think maybe he wears glasses, but he also has outrageously wild, red hair. And the interns will leap up when they see him, and he'll goofily slap their outstretched hands with a high-five and tell them the *funniest thing* just happened to him on the subway . . .

At 4 p.m. I figure he must be balding. At 4:30, I decide he is also grossly overweight. And by 5, he is also short. Not just a little short. Like shorter than me short, five feet two at the most.

In the end he turns out to be none of these things. He turns out, in fact, to be just like every other guy.

He doesn't show up at all.

Happy hour at the Dancing Burrito is always packed, but Laurie is easy to spot in even the most crowded bar. She waves to me when I walk in, the pillowy sleeve of her shirt drooping to expose a glimpse of her black lace bra underneath. Laurie might not have Amanda's legs, or her cleavage, but she's damn sexy in a way Amanda could never get away with. When people compliment Laurie—and they do, constantly—they tell her how much they love her chic new haircut (Louise Brooks pageboy, jet black), or her fantastic taste in clothes (tonight, impossibly short jean skirt, cowboy boots). Yes, this is probably what she wore to work this morning.

If you think Laurie might treat her office like a nightclub, you should see what she does to her table at the bar. Her deflated messenger bag is strapped to the back of her chair, its contents neatly arranged in front of her. Personal cell phone on the right, work cell phone on the left. A stack of manuscripts in the middle.

"What are those?" I ask, eyes wide.

"They're for you." She slides the manuscripts toward me.

"Really?"

"Uh-huh."

I touch the pages lovingly. I was afraid to even hope Laurie might show up with her latest contraband. Usually, about once a week, she's able to sneak me out a copy of the latest book or script her boss has optioned for the film studio. Two manuscripts are a blessed rarity. I flip the top manuscript open to the first page, suddenly ravenous for new people, new places and new beginnings.

"What, you're going to read them now?"

"Of course not," I say, feeling a hot flush on my cheeks. Reluctantly, I close the manuscript. "I just wanted to see what it was."

"The top one is the new Ian Pascal—"

"You're kidding! Already?"

"The other is a translation of a German book that has been a best seller for months in Europe. No one in the States has seen it yet."

"Cool! You read it?"

"Oh, please. I don't have time to read."

She's not kidding.

Laurie's left cell phone rings. She grimaces at it.

"Shit. They're going to want me back tomorrow morning. I was so looking forward to the day off." She picks up the phone. "This is Laurie." Her eyes roll upward. "Leon, this is my work phone. Call me back on the other line." She hangs up and waits, drumming her fingers against the table. "Some people," she seethes.

Her phone rings on the right. She picks it up. "Yeah?"

Sometimes it's hard for me to remember Laurie as that bright-eyed New York neophyte I met only three years ago, back when we were both fresh out of college, working at the film festival by day, scamming our way into exclusive premiere (and after) parties at night. I'm sure that same little bon vivant still dwells somewhere inside her, popping up every now and then to tempt her with glitter eyeshadow or a pair of fishnet stockings. Maybe now her edges are a little hardened, her tone a little more gruff, but God bless her for being the only friend I have who still gets a thrill from crashing parties.

"Sorry about that," she says, snapping her cell phone shut and sliding it back into place. She reaches for one of the menus propped up at the center of the table and flips it open. I already know I'll be having the Bay Burrito and that she'll probably want to split it with me. But as long as her eyes are temporarily averted, I nudge open the top manuscript with my elbow and start reading the first page.

"So, how's the new temp job going?" she asks.

"Fine. They want me back tomorrow."

"That's a good thing, right?"

"Maybe it is." Then again, maybe it isn't.

Laurie snaps her menu shut. "Wanna split the Bay Burrito?"

"Sounds good to me."

I close the manuscript discreetly and slip it into my bag. Laurie leans forward on her elbows.

"Oh, hey! I totally forgot to tell you. Guess who I just saw in the elevator?"

"Was it Ben Stiller?"

"No."

"Owen Wilson?"

"No, okay. Stop. It was Princess."

I gasp. "*My* Princess?"

"Uh-huh."

"What was she doing in your building?"

"I think she works there now."

I gasp again. "Shut up!" I squeal. "Since when?"

"I'm guessing this is very, very recent. She acted all excited when she saw me, remembered my name and everything."

"Yeah, she must be brand new."

"She got off on the fifteenth floor."

"What's that? Marketing?"

"Uh-uh. That's not even one of our own offices. We're leasing the space to an independent film company that just lost their output deal with one of the studios. Miramax, maybe? I can't remember. Anyway, Princess says she's their new head of development."

"No way! I want to work in development!"

"I know you do."

We pause for a moment to acknowledge the presence of our waitress. Laurie places our standard order—two frozen strawberry margaritas and the burrito.

"Two plates for the burrito!" Laurie calls out to the retreating waitress. She turns back to me and smiles. "So, I think you need to ask Princess to get you a job."

"Not in a million—"

"I'll bet she'll need an assistant soon."

"Laurie, I can't go asking my old boss for a job. That's so degrading."

"Well, what other options do you have?"

I think for a moment. Real hard.

"None," I admit glumly.

"Thought so."

The waitress returns with our margaritas. It is one of the few times in my life the sight of a plastic umbrella perched atop a frosted glass does nothing to lift my spirits.

I return to my apartment a few hours later and struggle with the faulty lock on my door, silently begging it to spare me the grief. When it finally allows me inside, I freeze. The door slams closed behind me.

The sudden, and rather loud, announcement of my entrance startles Amanda.

"Jesus Christ!" she yelps, bouncing off the lap of her gentleman suitor. They disengage and dart for opposite ends of sofa. Amanda flicks an unruly blonde tendril back into place. Her confused friend cowers in his corner, looking about as inconspicuous as one of

Michelangelo's unfinished nudes suddenly appearing in the center of my living room. He crosses his hands and tucks them under his arms. If he's trying to conceal the outline of his sculpted torso—clad in a disturbingly inadequate white Hanes T-shirt—he's overlooking the fact there's no hiding the massive bulge in his pants.

"Oh, *hi* . . ." says Amanda. She turns to the man seated beside her. "Ryan, this is my roommate Sarah . . . Sarah, this is Ryan. He's the managing director at my firm."

"Nice to meet you," I mutter, brushing right past them both and into my room. I slam the door behind me.

chapter four

The very first thing I do once I arrive at Stellar Productions is sit at my desk, dial an extension, and hit speaker-phone.

"Gregory?"

"Yes?" answers the far-off voice.

"It's Sarah. I just wanted to let you know that I have a lunch date this afternoon." I flip open the new folder of deal memos. "I hope you don't mind."

"How long will you be gone?"

"It won't be longer than an hour."

"Oh." He sighs loudly, distorting the phone static. "Oh, all right."

"You sure it's okay? I mean, I usually put down an hour lunch break on my time sheet, even though I've been eating at my desk these past couple of days."

"Yes, it's fine," he concedes grumpily and hangs up.

I steal away from the office at lunchtime and arrive at the restaurant fifteen minutes late. There is no sign of Princess, so I grab a two-seater by the window and proceed to wait for another fifteen minutes.

Then my phone rings.

"Sarah, doll, it's crazy here. Just crazy! The phones, the faxes, it never ends. I will be there soon, but I can't stay long. Order me a Caesar salad without croutons, and I'll be there before it arrives. Remember, no croutons!" Princess hangs up abruptly.

In a way, her phone call is reassuring. I was worried our reunion lunch would be awkward, that there would be uncomfortable silences, futile stabs at small talk, a vague, boring catch-up conversation. I am relieved to know our relationship will pick up exactly where it left off.

When Princess finally does show up at the restaurant, she is a full forty-five minutes late. She barrels through the front door and shoots past the restaurant patrons like a high-speed locomotive—the Jimmy Choo Choo Express. Women like her who constantly defy death by attempting to run in such questionably engineered high heels never cease to amaze me.

"Sarah," she drips the vowels of my name through a tight smile. Her perfectly uniform blonde hair (I don't think I've ever spotted a dark root the entire time I've known her) has been swept up into her signature bun. Better to balance the tiara, I'd imagine.

"Lovely to see you," she says, delicately placing her foundation-caked cheek against mine. She slips into the seat in front of the Caesar salad. If she notices my turkey club is already half-eaten, she decides not to mention it.

"How've you been, Gracie?"

"Oh, good God. It's been hell." She hangs her bag delicately on the back of her chair. For the benefit of those of us who know next to nothing about fashion, Princess likes to emblazon her accessories with designer labels. Like the Kate Spade silver-plated logo above the outer tweed lining of her tote bag. And the eagle-crested, Armani-tattooed stems of the sunglasses perched above her forehead. Princess picks up a fork and sighs. "All these manuscripts and screenplays, I tell you, Sarah, there is a stack on my desk so high, I can't even see over it." She spears a piece of lettuce and holds it in mid-air. "I just started this new job . . . wait, did I already tell you about this?"

"I found out from Laurie."

"Laurie?" Princess cocks her head to the side and pretends to think. "Oh, right. Laurie. Your little friend who used to come round the office. Did I see her recently?"

"She says she saw you in the elevator."

"That's right." Princess swallows her lettuce leaf and wrinkles her nose. "Jesus. If there is anything I can't stand it is a wilted salad."

Then maybe she shouldn't let it sit at the table thirty minutes before she plans on eating it.

"And how's work going for you, Sarah?"

"Well—"

"I hear the job market is just terrible these days. I wouldn't know. I was at Paramount for a few months, as I'm sure you heard. And quite happy there, too. But you know me." She smirks. "I've never been one to pass up a better offer."

"Must be nice. These days I'd be lucky to get any offers at all."

"They'll come, you'll see. They'll come."

"No, I don't think so. It's already been six months now. And the future, well, it looks kind of bleak."

"Six months!" Princess gasps. "I had no idea it had been that long. Nothing's turned up at all? You'd think it be easy for you. You went to Yale, right?"

"Brown."

"Oh." She nods her head, as if this explains it all.

I take a deep breath. "It's funny you should bring this up, though, Gracie. 'Cause, see I was wondering, since, you know, you *are* in the inner circle and you do seem to hear of things before anyone else—"

"It's true," she agrees.

"Maybe you've heard of some potential job leads?"

"Hmmm." She places a manicured nail against her chin. "Let me think." She taps her finger. "Well, we do have a great intern pool at the office. Would you like me to recommend you for that?"

I try not to seem so stunned.

"Actually . . ." I trail off. My confidence has ruptured like a car tire, and I can hear the air seeping out in a plaintive moan. "Actually, I was looking for something more—"

"Sarah, I just had a marvelous idea!" she says, mercifully cutting me off. "This load of manuscripts I have, I am never going to get to them all. It's overwhelming! I'm so backlogged. And you, well, I've always enjoyed your coverage. Maybe you could help lighten the burden?"

"I'd love to."

"Nothing major. Just read the book, give me a one- to two-page synopsis, a few paragraphs of comments. That'd be such a blessing."

"Sounds like a great idea." I say, genuinely relieved. "It'll keep me busy in the meantime. Plus," I add hopefully, "if you ever need an assistant, people in your office will already be familiar with my work."

Princess rolls her eyes. "God, I begged for them to let me have an assistant. They said they'd look into it, but they never did put it in my contract." She must have seen my crestfallen expression, because then she adds, "But don't worry, I will definitely keep you in the loop."

"Thanks."

"Sure, sure. Now, listen, I can messenger you over a manuscript immediately. You still at the same apartment or did you have to move?"

I let her subtle jab slide. She's just being Princess.

"Yeah, I'm at the same place. But, um—"

"But what?"

"There's this silly thing with my unemployment checks. It's a real pain in my ass. It has to do with how much money I earn each week—"

"No worries. I'll be paying you with petty cash. That'll be okay, won't it?"

I smile brightly. "That'll be just fine."

"Well," Princess slides her unfinished salad aside. "I think this lunch has been very successful, after all."

"I couldn't agree with you more."

"It was so good to see you, Sarah." She pulls off her Armani sunglasses and polishes them with her unused napkin. "I am sorry I've been so rushed." She puts on the sunglasses and stands. "We'll do this longer next time, I promise. Thanks again."

It takes me a while to figure out what she's thanking me for. But when she picks up her bag and squeezes her way past the waiter, I realize he's the one holding the check. And I'm the only one left to pay it.

When I return to the office, I find a Post-it note from Gregory stuck to my computer. For a man who loves speakerphone so much, you'd think *e-mail* would be a technological advancement to make him wet his pants. Perhaps not.

Sarah,

New project coming up for Fashion Week. We're looking to spoof films that feature extended "makeover" scenes. Please help gather a list of such films.

Thanks,
Gregory

Correct me if I'm wrong, but don't all films feature a makeover of one kind or another?

I'll assume Gregory doesn't want the laundry list of forgotten eighties favorites. Does *She's Out of Control* ring a bell? No, I didn't think so. How about *Ruthless People*? Or *Just One of the Guys*? Certainly you must remember *Can't Buy Me Love*—the very film to coin the phrase, "He went from totally geek . . . to totally chic!"

But ignore those, and you're left with only the obvious choices: your Audrey Hepburn standards (*My Fair Lady, Sabrina*), your teen flicks (*Clueless, She's All That*), your cross-gender comedies (*Mrs. Doubtfire, Victor/Victoria*), basically any musical, (*Grease, Annie*), and, my all-time favorite category—when Beautiful Women with Bad Hair become Beautiful Women with Good Hair (Julia Roberts in *Pretty Woman*, Melanie Griffith in *Working Girl*, Gwyneth Paltrow in *Sliding Doors*).

I could go on forever. But luckily, I don't have to.

I am trying to add a foreign film to the list (Does *La Femme Nikita* count? Cold-blooded felon made-over into sophisticated government hit-woman? You really can't top Jeanne Moreau providing makeup tips, right?), when the glass doors to the office swing open. It is 3 p.m., too late in the day for even the surliest of employees to be coming back from lunch. I crane my head over my computer, more out of curiosity than out of any sense of obligation as a so-called receptionist.

He walks in. At first I see nothing but brooding black. Dark, slicked-back hair that grazes the smooth veneer of his forehead. Thick, devilish eyebrows that shield piercingly clear green eyes. A fine, recent sprout of stubble peppering his sharp jawline.

I expect him to waltz right by and ignore me. Just like every other employee has seen fit to ignore me before. But instead he stops and hovers by my desk. Damn my good luck!

"Can I help you?" I ask hopefully.

"Uh, maybe." He cocks me a sideways glance. It's enough to make me swoon. "What's your name?"

I can't help it. I blush. I feel like no one else has ever before asked me anything quite so intimate.

"I'm Sarah."

"Hi, Sarah." He extends a hand. "I'm Jake."

chapter five

The fact that Stellar Productions has an equipment room at all is news to me. That the room is a sprawling, high-tech lair worthy of Batman's cave is shocking. That I'm in here alone with Jake? Well, that sends a bolt of electricity down my spine so powerful I'm afraid anything I touch might short-circuit.

"This is the input monitor over here. And this is the output. You got that?"

"Uh-huh," I nod, doing my damnedest to pay attention. Not that I have any real burning desire to learn all I can about digital tape transfers. If anything, it's just another skill to add to my never-ending résumé.

The problem is I *look* interested. My body is tense and rigid, and I can't remember the last time I blinked my eyes or took a deep breath. I'm hoping my absurd posture makes me look sharp and alert, and not all hot and bothered.

"Basically you hit the button and the machine does all the work. Not too hard, huh?"

What button?

I hear a high-pitch squeal that mortifies me because I think I might just be the source of it. I'm afraid to look at Jake directly—God knows what *that* might do to me—but I catch him out of the corner of my eye, reclining against his chair and resting his hands behind his head. Clearly, he doesn't hear anything out of the ordinary. I decide the squeal must be coming from the machines.

"So," Jake turns to me with a half-smile that is frighteningly disarming. "You're the one who's going to be replacing me?"

I arch an eyebrow. "You still need to be replaced?"

"I'm thinking of going to Canada." To visit a dying grandmother? Please, please let him have a dying grandmother. "I just need some time off. You know?"

Shit. It *is* heartbreak. I bite my lip, determined not to pry. Whatever I do, I won't pry.

"Oh, yeah, sure, I know exactly what you mean. I would love to take some time off." Right. Like six months haven't been enough.

Jake stares unblinking at the screens in front of us. For a moment we watch in silence as well-practiced underwear models unhook their bras in high-speed. At this frenetic pace, their motions seem hurried and routine, and not at all seductive.

Finally, Jake looks up at me.

"Do you smoke?"

"Oh, God, yes."

Would you believe that Stellar Productions has a secret fire escape, too? Man, the things I wish I had known about earlier!

Jake helps hoist me up from the window onto the outside ledge a few feet above us. I'd like to think I accomplished the move gracefully, but the shooting stab of pain where I hit my shin against the windowpane makes me think otherwise.

He lights a cigarette and hands it to me. I feel giddy taking it. Like I'm black and white, and Bette Davis all over.

"I quit smoking a year ago," he says, firing up his own cigarette.

"Good for you."

"I just started up again this week."

Don't pry.

"I've been having a rough couple of days."

Don't pry. "Yeah, I heard," I say offhandedly, taking a long drag.

"You heard?"

I nearly choke. I realize immediately I've said the wrong thing.

"Well, Gregory told me you were having, ummm, personal problems."

"He what?"

I don't answer. Jake shakes his head incredulously. With one inhale, he swallows that entire year's deprivation of nicotine. Then he spits it out contemptuously.

"What exactly did he tell you?"

"He, um, didn't give me specifics."

We hear a rap on the window beside us. I immediately toss my cigarette over the fire escape. Jake takes another long drag and turns casually.

Jim Abbott leans out onto the escape and tilts his head upward. Even so, he can do no better than talk to our knees.

"Gregory wants to see you."

"All right." Jake exhales his last plume of smoke and tosses his cigarette over the ledge.

"No." Jim Abbott looks pointedly at my calf. "He wants to talk to *you*."

"**I** was serious when I said I thought you've been doing a good job," says Gregory. I find myself staring at him blatantly. It surprises me that he is so tiny and frail, not at all what I imagined from his thunderous speakerphone voice. "I probably won't be able to rely much on Jake for now. But he knows the equipment and he's great on set for productions, so we need to keep him on. But we still need an office manager, someone who can handle the phones and the paper-work. And you did so well with the filing—"

"Thank you."

"And we could certainly use someone to organize our budget reports. Are you comfortable handling finances?"

"Well, I really haven't done much before." 'Cause, even on a good day, I have trouble working with any multiple over three. On bad days, I lose the threes.

"What I am saying is this." Gregory folds his hands and leans forward on the desk, searing me with a look of complete serious-ness. I think I preferred communicating with him by speakerphone. "Do you think this job might be something that interests you?"

And that is the question. The one that screws me every single time.

There is a major problem with being unemployed for as long as I have. This is no longer a hunt, no longer a search, no longer a pur-suit. This is a mission. And it isn't a mission to find any old job. It is a mission to find The Perfect Job. Damn it, I've put in too much time and far too much energy to settle for anything less than utter and complete satisfaction. I want job security, growth potential, and a 401k plan I just might bother to invest in. I want my name en-graved on a gold plaque and a thousand business cards etched on steel plates. I want it all!

Because I don't ever want to have to go through any of this again.

But how I am going to explain this to my mother?

Over the course of the years my mother has begrudgingly come to terms with the fact I can't very well call her every night of the week. Nevertheless, she does expect to hear from me on a regular basis, and is sometimes even willing to schedule our phone conversations well in advance.

Today being one of my rare working days, I know she is anxiously awaiting an update. If I don't phone in by the close of the business day, she'll panic, naturally assuming I've been abducted by fake would-be employers. You know, the only-in-New-York sort of lunatic who would have the time and wherewithal to post want ads for a receptionist, hoping to entice naïve young women into wearing pantyhose and lip gloss and then luring them into the insidious domains of deserted offices in downtown Manhattan high-rises. That kind of fake employer.

I start rummaging in my bag for my cell phone as soon as the elevator doors spill me into the lobby. It usually takes me a good four minutes to locate the damn thing. Like I've said before, I'm not exactly the most organized person in the world. Just think what would happen if I were put in charge of a company's financial records.

Fifteen minutes later, I am kneeling outside the Stellar Productions office building, the entire contents of my bag spewed out in front of me. My cell phone is nowhere to be found. I can't remember placing or receiving any personal calls at the office today. Even if I did, I am not about to go back upstairs, fling open the door, and sing, "Ta-da! I'm baaack!"

No, for convenience's sake, let's just say I left my cell phone at my apartment. In fact, I'm sure that's where it is. Still, I'm due to meet Amanda at a bar downtown in half an hour. If my calculations are correct (they might not be—I know there is a multiple of three in there somewhere), there is no way I could possibly make my way uptown and back down again by then. Cursing under my breath, I shove all my crap back into my bag and do the unthinkable. I look for a pay phone.

The hard part isn't finding an available pay phone. The hard part is trying to figure out what the hell I'm supposed to do with it. What, now thirty-five cents for a local call? A couple of bucks worth of change to page the West Coast?

To top it all off, my mother isn't even home, so I end up leaving my cab fare on her answering machine. I hang up annoyed and turn on my heel, nearly colliding into the person waiting behind me. I wasn't expecting a line for the pay phone. As I slowly make my way to the curb, I try to convince myself that it really doesn't matter a complete stranger has overhead me call my mother "Mommy."

On the sign across the street, the little white walking man becomes the little red hand. I wait on the corner and try to remember if I did, in fact, say, "It's me, Mommy, just calling to say hi and I love you," or if maybe, just maybe, I said something a little more sophisticated, like, "Hello, darling, it's Sarah. So sorry you weren't at home. Perhaps I'll give you a ring in the morrow."

Red hand becomes white man again. I'm about to make my move, when I stop suddenly. I could have sworn I've heard someone call my name.

"Hey, Sarah!"

I turn. I don't believe it! A gorgeous, golden god of a man trots toward me. This is definitely a first. A thrilling first, but also a confusing one. I don't have enough time to rack my brain and try to place him. The popular guy from high school, maybe? My summer camp junior counselor? A lucky night in college I ought to remember?

He comes to a halt in front of me and bares his perfect white teeth in a dazzling smile. I suck in my gut.

"You're Sarah?"

"Yes?" I answer demurely, brushing my hair away from my face.

"Your mom is on the phone for you."

I can feel a bright shade of crimson burning my cheeks. "Oh. Thanks." I hang my blazing head and brush past him, toward the dangling phone receiver.

"Hello?"

"Sarah?"

"Mom, how did you get this number?"

"It showed up on the caller ID."

"It did?"

"Where are you, sweetie-pie? And who was that who answered the phone?"

"I don't know. Just some guy on the street."

There is a long pause. "Oh, dear," my mother whispers. "Are you calling from his . . . apartment?"

"What? No! Mom, you called me at a pay phone. Some guy just happened to answer it and he chased me down."

"Really?" Another pause. My mother doesn't grease her wheels all that often anymore. I can almost hear her stripping her gears. "Well, that was very nice of him, wasn't it?"

"I suppose—"

"I bet that doesn't happen a lot in New York. And he did have a very sweet voice. You sure you didn't catch his name?"

"Mom!" I'm pissed. Not at her. At myself. She's right. I should have gotten his name.

"All right," my mother relents. "So, tell me. How did it go with the job today?"

"It didn't take."

"What's that supposed to mean?"

I do my very best to explain it to her.

It doesn't matter how long I make Amanda wait at a bar. An hour, five minutes—I know when I find her she'll already be halfway through with her martini, tossing her hair, and laughing gaily at something the bartender just said.

She's in top shape tonight. She beams when she sees me and waves me over ebulliently. Her cheery disposition annoys me for no good reason I can understand.

"I have good news," she says.

"Me, too!" Of course I don't really. But I'm not in the mood to bask in the glow of her self-congratulation just yet.

"Oh." The twinge of disappointment in her voice please me considerably. "You go first."

"I met a boy."

She gulps. "Really? Where?"

"He's the guy I was supposed to replace at the temp job. He came in this afternoon just to show me the ropes. That was pretty nice of him, don't you think?"

"I guess." She shrugs. "Why's he leaving?"

"What do you mean?"

"Why he's leaving the job?"

"Oh. Ummm . . ."

"Don't you know?"

"Yes, of course I know," I snap. "He's, ummm, been having personal problems."

"Oh." Amanda raises an eyebrow innocently. "What kind of problems?"

"I don't know exactly," I mutter. Man, how much does it suck that even my fake good news isn't really all that good?

"I see." Amanda's smile begins to verge on the smug. "Do you get to see him again tomorrow?"

"No."

"No more ropes to learn?"

Bitch.

"It's not that." I pick up a drink menu and study it with far more attention than it really deserves. "I turned down the job."

"You did? Why?"

"Because I don't want to be an office manager."

"You're in a position to make that kind of decision?"

"Yes," I say emphatically, more so to convince myself than her.

"Okay." She shrugs. "Then when do you get to see this boy again?"

I sigh. "Probably never."

Once the words are out, I feel their sharp sting. I try ignoring the dull ache in my chest. A man I've only met once isn't allowed to break my heart.

"Oh, no, that's not necessarily true." Amanda's tone sounds infuriatingly patronizingly. Almost like she's mothering me. "You still have the number at the office, right? You could always try calling to see if he's there."

My eyes narrow. She just doesn't get it. She has no idea girls like me don't get away with calling strange boys out of the blue.

"We'll see," I place the drink menu back down.

Amanda's new pal behind the bar returns to take my drink order. Like well-practiced understudies, she and I block out our old song-and-dance routine. I ask what she's drinking. She says it's a chocolate martini. I ask if it's any good and she tells me it's delicious. I take a moment to contemplate, then decide to try it. Amanda takes a moment to contemplate, then decides to have another. The bartender commends us on our wise choice. And after the whole ordeal is over and done with, there is a moment of silence, and I know Amanda is waiting expectantly for me to say something. I take the plunge.

"Right. So what's your good news?"

She smiles coyly and polishes off the last sip of her first martini.

"I just got promoted."

I wait for the bartender to return with our drinks before I respond.

"Great." I hold up my glass to toast her. "Then I guess these are on you." Which they would have been anyway.

I think it would be nice to have the last word. But I never do. Amanda would never let me.

"Oh, by the way," she says, taking a moment to sip her new martini. "Thanks for not hanging around the another night when Ryan was over. We really appreciated the privacy."

You tell me. Is it really so wrong of me to hate her the way I do?

chapter six

Today's T-shirt celebrates the tenth annual "Greek Winter Olympics" at Dartmouth College. It features a cartoon character, head under the snow, skis up in the air. His brazen hand reaches up from under the snow bank, still proudly holding a flask of whiskey. I don't know, for some reason it feels appropriate.

I skip the candy bar for breakfast this morning. As part of Amanda's new promotion, she's been assigned to the account of a small-town Wisconsin danish bakery. It will be her job to initiate a new mail-order service to expand their product to a broader, national market. The fruits of her labors, packed into neat little squares of puff pastry, have already reached as far as our very own kitchen—and they probably will go no further. Standing in front of the refrigerator, keeping the door propped open with my elbow, I shove my face with three samples in no time flat. I don't feel even the slightest bit guilty for having helped myself to more than half my share (had I even been offered a share). I know for a fact Amanda would rather experiment with a crimped hairdo than tempt fate by mixing carbohydrates with a glucose filling.

I step away from the fridge and lick my fingers. Then somehow managing to avoid smearing sticky raspberry residue all over the kitchen counter, I fix myself a cup of quasi-instant coffee. I also pour myself a large glass of water and a smaller glass of orange juice. With all three cups balanced on everything but the top of my head, I stagger back to my bedroom and turn on my computer.

The cup of coffee has me revving up in the junk-and-spam-clotted, forgotten storage space of my e-mail inbox. The glass of water has me searching in vain for a spot in the online postings lot. But the glass of orange juice—that's where I hit cruising speed.

I've found it! The Perfect Job. It practically leaps right off the screen and cuddles in my lap, nuzzling my leg like a puppy Saint Bernard pining for snowfall.

Company	*Aspen Quarterly*
Job Title	Associate Editor
Job Location	Aspen, CO
Job Requirements	Dynamic, award-winning magazine seeks bright, creative Associate Editor to report directly to Editorial Director. Excellent research, reporting, and proofreading skills required. Ideal candidate must have prior, related editorial experience. Duties include writing and/or editing articles and generating ideas. Must be extremely organized and detail-oriented. ONLY APPLICANTS SERIOUS ABOUT RELOCATING APPLY.
About Us	*Aspen Quarterly* is a lifestyle magazine with a special interest in culture and entertainment. Our magazine provides in-depth film and book reviews and up-to-date coverage on all major media and cultural events.
Contact	Please submit résumé and cover letter to Kelly Martin at kmartin@aspenq.com.

I suppose my résumé could do with some minor tweaking. I change my last job title from "Content Development Assistant" to "Editorial Assistant," and that takes care of that.

Then I go on to blow every rule in the book.

I know, from my vast experience, that a cover letter is best when kept simple. Short, direct, and to the point. But desperate times do call for desperate measures.

Hence, I won't even bother to share this particular letter with you. After all, it's none of your business. This letter is personal, it's private—a matter between myself and *Aspen Quarterly* alone. An unrelated party might deem it wordy and excessive, whereas I find it eloquent and assured. Aggressive, you say? I'd call it passionate. How else am I going to make it plainly clear I am an APPLICANT SERIOUS ABOUT RELOCATING?

I spell-check the letter. Not a flaw. I reread it. Brilliant! But maybe I should cut it down from two pages to one?

No, no, no. The letter flows, it sings, it has charm. Editing, pasting, cutting? It'll only rob the words of their magic.

I hold my breath and close my eyes. I hit send.

When my breathing returns to normal, I peer out of one eye to squint at my computer screen. The e-mail has vanished. Yet its spell on me remains.

The grating trill of the intercom tears me from my trance-like state almost immediately. Begrudgingly, I shuffle over to my front door.

"Hello?"

"Messenger!"

"Yeah, come on up." I buzz him in.

The messenger takes his time trudging up the staircase. When he finally arrives at my apartment, I am already lingering in the doorway with my arms crossed. He balks.

"Sorry. I woke you up?"

"Huh?" I glance down at myself. I'm still wearing the college T-shirt and my Victoria's Secret boxer shorts. What, I am supposed to get all dressed up to meet the messenger? "No, I've been up," I snip, more embarrassed than angry. I make a mental note to trade in the boxers for gym shorts by noon.

The messenger hands me a manila envelope. It's much lighter than I expected. Still, I feel that familiar tingle of excitement—you know, the excitement that comes with having to open something, anything! Uncorking a bottle of champagne, peeling security strips off a new DVD, squeezing the pus out of an explosive pimple. I don't even wait for the messenger to leave before I rip into my new Jiffy sealer like it's a chocolate truffle with a rich, hazelnut center.

Miami Beach Murder? Of all the manuscripts stacked high on Princess's desk, this is what she sends me? Some breezy detective novel or, worse, a teen sex romp with a twist? I toss the manuscript with disgust on the coffee table to worry about later. I've got more important matters to attend to anyway.

I spend the rest of the afternoon exhaustively researching each and every Aspen real estate ad I can find on the Internet. I foresee no problem whatsoever with sticking Amanda with my share of the rent for the remainder of the year. She could probably afford it too, what with her lousy promotion and all. Maybe her new boyfriend could move in with her. When the lease is up, they can get married and buy a place in Connecticut and raise a family. God bless them!

It doesn't take me long to find my dream home. A condo I couldn't afford even if the asking salary for an associate editor were twice what I would expect from a similar position in New York.

Still, I let my imagination run wild and treat myself to the luxury spoils I have been unfairly denied for too long. My very own washing machine? A fireplace? A backyard?

A backyard! I could have a dog!

I click out of my real estate websites and ready my computer to launch a brand-new search for my new best friend.

I don't get up from in front of my computer until 6 p.m. And then, it's only because my doorbell rings again.

I buzz the intercom without answering, because for a split second I assume it is Amanda stumbling home drunk, claiming she can't find her keys. It occurs to me only an instant later that even though 6 p.m. is plenty late enough for someone like me to have turned one sip into five glasses, your regular working stiff doesn't start sampling the vintages until after dark.

The knock at the door is firm, and troublingly so. Nothing at all like Amanda's wishy-washy tap-tap. I keep the safety chain fastened and peer suspiciously through the crack of my door.

My darling little cell phone winks back at me. And behind it, the dark hallway brightens with the glint of Jake's mischievously charming smile.

"Hey," he says. "Forget something at the office yesterday?"

I slam the door shut. Before I unfasten the chain, I take a futile moment to brush back my hair and smooth out the bags under my eyes. Damn, damn. Of all the times for Mr. Right to come a-knocking!

I can hear Jake talking to me from the other side the door. "You left the office in such a hurry yesterday, you forgot to fill out your time sheet. I filled it out this morning for you, and your address was on it, so—"

I remove the chain and open the door, displaying myself in glorious full view. Jake's jaw drops.

"Jesus. You all right?"

The questioning look in his eyes makes it plainly clear I have not successfully hidden my tears. The gay, flimsy party mask peels off my face. The dam holding back the watershed springs a leak. I burst.

Jake staggers back a step, afraid to drown in the puddle I've just become. "Whoa. What's the matter?"

"Come in, come in," I choke between sobs.

I lead Jake through the living room and past the kitchen without offering him so much as a danish. Rather, I take him directly into my bedroom and gesture frantically at my computer.

"Look!"

Jake leans on my desk and squints at the desktop photo of a wire-haired terrier with a wet, pink tongue and forgiving eyes. He looks back at me, uncomprehending.

"I don't get it. The puppy made you cry?"

"He's abandoned."

"He is?" Jake turns back to the computer and skims the print below the picture. I slump down into the Aeron and hug my arms to keep my shoulders from racking.

"Oh, hey, no. It's okay." Jake jabs a finger at the screen. "It says here he was already adopted."

"Keep reading," I sniff.

He peers in closer. After a moment his shoulders sag.

"You finish?" I ask.

He stays quiet. Finally, he shakes his head. "I can't read anymore."

I feel the well bubbling inside me again. "You get to the part where they brought him back?"

"Yeah."

"And the part about the cigarette burns? And the broken legs? And the fact that he had been kicked in the stomach so hard, he couldn't even urinate?"

Jake shudders and clicks the picture closed. Unfortunately, there are still similar pictures, of similar victims, all lined up in a neat little row on my computer. A chain of furry snouts held high and proud for the camera.

"What the—" Jake straightens and cocks his head at me. "How long have you been doing this?"

"All day." I scoot forward in my chair. "Here, let me show you the litter of puppies they found at the abandoned warehouse—"

"No." He holds up his hand, barring me from the desk. "I think you've had enough."

He fixes me with such stern, blazing eyes I stop at once. For a moment, neither of us says a word. His expression softens, and he studies me with a sad smile. I hope he isn't checking me out. This really isn't the best time for it. I look away to pat down my swollen eyes and wipe the tip of my snotty nose with the back of my hand.

Jake clears his throat. "When was the last time you got out of your apartment?"

"Ummm, I don't remember. Yesterday?"

He nods. He was expecting as much. "You know, I passed the Loew's theater on my way over here. That new Robert De Niro movie is playing. I was thinking of going to check it out. Maybe you wanna come with me?"

I bite my lip. I am afraid any second now I may start crying again. "You feeling sorry for me?"

"A little. But I could also use the company."

"Good enough." I grab my keys from off my desk. "What time does it start?"

"Seven-fifteen."

"Great, we can get there early." I walk out of my bedroom and start looking for my bag. I find it on the kitchen counter beside the microwave.

Jake follows me toward the front door. He hesitates when I open it for him, staring at me uneasily.

"Umm . . ."

"What?"

"You, uh, want to get changed or take a shower or something before we go?"

I look down at myself. I'm still wearing the T-shirt and boxer shorts.

"Oh, right." I drop my bag to the floor. "Just give me a minute."

When the movie lets out, I get on the escalator first and Jake steps on behind me.

"What did you think?"

"It was all right," I say over my shoulder.

Jake squeezes past me and turns around. I've noticed he insists on facing me dead-on when he talks to me. It's not disconcerting. It's sweet. And when he stands on the step below me, looking up at me with an impish grin, he reminds me of the four-year-old nephew I don't have and never thought I wanted. He's adorable in a way that makes me want to show him my thumb and say, "Look, I got your nose!"

"You hated it, didn't you?" he says.

"*Hate* is kind of a strong word—"

"But still not strong enough, huh?"

"No, I guess not. I'm sorry." I shake my head sadly. "I can't lie. I thought it was terrible."

"Don't apologize. I hated it, too."

"You did?"

"Hated it so much, it makes me furious."

"Oh, I wouldn't go that far—"

"I would. Nothing pisses me off more than a mediocre movie. 'Cause, if you're going to suck, why not suck in style? Figure if things are so bad they can't be fixed, don't *try* to make them better. Make them *worse*. Throw in a dance number or something."

"Tell me about it. You notice how there are no fun-bad movies anymore? Everything's just bad-bad?"

"Paul Verhoeven. Now, there's a fun-bad director. You see *Starship Troopers*?"

"Don't you dare! *Starship Troopers* is a brilliant movie."

"What about *Showgirls*?"

"Best bad movie I ever saw."

"See? They don't make them bad like that anymore. Everything's just *kind of* bad." Jake steps off the elevator. "And don't get me started on De Niro movies—"

"Yeah, he sucks."

"No, he doesn't suck. He's just . . . not good. And that's the worse part, 'cause he used to be great. Now, he's just a caricature of himself. Him, and Al Pacino, and Dustin Hoffman—"

"And Jack Nicholson . . ."

Jake stops cold and scowls.

"Not Jack," he says evenly.

I smile in spite of myself. "You're right. I stand corrected. Not Jack. I could watch Jack read a menu." My stomach hears me say the word "menu" and does a somersault on a creaky trampoline.

"You hungry?" asks Jake astutely.

"A little."

"Any good places around here to eat?"

"Umm . . ." In my head, I run down my regular list of sushi, Thai, and Chinese neighborhood joints. But as tempting as they all sound, I'd rather not leave room for discussion. In this case, anything safe and standard would do. "There's a diner around the corner."

"Awesome. You think they have milkshakes?"

"Well, I would guess—"

"When was the last time you had a milkshake?"

"I don't know," I confess. "It's been a while."

"I think it's important to have a milkshake every now and then. Don't you?"

"I couldn't agree with you more."

I'm on my best behavior tonight. Even though I'd kill for a tuna melt, I settle for the rather disappointing Greek salad. Jake has sold me on the milkshake, though. And the side of fries.

"The problem is," he says, dipping a fry into a vat of mayonnaise. He ordered it, not me. Still, I'm pleased it's there. "Even though there are probably no good roles left anymore for actors like De Niro or Pacino, no one's really stepped up to fill their shoes. I tell you . . ." He points his drippy fry at me. "Give me the name of one young actor *now* who you could actually watch read a menu."

"You mean, other than Jack?"

"Yeah. Someone new."

I ponder for a moment. "It's tough."

"I know."

"Philip Seymour Hoffman, maybe?"

"You can compare Philip Seymour Hoffman to Jack Nicholson?"

"No, not really. You got any ideas?"

"Hmm." He chews his fry pensively. "I'd say the closest one out there right now is Johnny Depp."

"Yeah, he's easily the best actor working today. Still, he's made some pretty bad decisions. You see *Secret Window*?"

"Nope."

"Lucky you. How about Sean Penn? Or Mark Ruffalo? Oh, I know! Crispin Glover!"

He laughs. "*Charlie's Angels* Crispin Glover?"

"No. *River's Edge* Crispin Glover." I reach for a fry. Jake slides the mayo toward me. Isn't he dreamy?

"Not exactly menu-reading material. But I like your style."

Style? I don't think anyone has ever complimented my *style*. I didn't even know I had one.

"What about women?" I ask, pointing my own fry at him deliberately. "Can you name an actress you would watch read a menu?"

"An actress? Hey, I hate to be the one to say it. But actresses today aren't what they used to be. Most of them are just another pretty face. No offense."

"No offense? Are you kidding? That's the *most* offensive thing I've ever heard anyone say. There are *plenty* of gifted actresses out there who aren't necessarily all that pretty."

"Yeah? Okay. If you can name just one, I'll take it all back."

I open my mouth. I pause. I can't call up a single name.

"See?" he taunts.

I narrow my eyes. "How about Anjelica Huston?"

"Okay, first of all, Anjelica Huston was a model even before she was an actress. And secondly, you're probably only thinking about her because of the Jack Nicholson connection."

"Possibly. Cameron Diaz?"

"You're joking, right?"

"Oh, come on. She's great at what she does. And she makes excellent choices." Please don't bring up *The Sweetest Thing*. Please don't . . .

"She's still no Goldie Hawn."

"Goldie Hawn, thirty years ago maybe."

Jake leans back against the booth. "What about Sandy Dennis? Do you know who she is?"

My heart spins and stops on a dime. "I *love* Sandy Dennis! *Who's Afraid of Virginia Woolf?* is one of my favorite movies of all time. She was brilliant in that!"

"No one else quite like her, huh?"

"No one could hold a *candle* to her. Such a pity . . ." I let my voice trail off. Neither of us mentions the fact she's not around to be reading menus for our pleasure anymore.

I slurp down the last of my milkshake. For a moment, I keep the straw between my teeth. I'm heartbroken there is nothing left. The Greek salad didn't really cut it. I'm trying to remember if there is still a danish left in my refrigerator.

Jake tosses his napkin onto his empty plate. "This was fun. Thank you for coming out with me tonight."

"Thank *you* for bringing my phone back."

"No, seriously, I mean it. Thank you. I really needed this."

He sighs. I make another heroic attempt to suck down more milkshake.

Don't pry.

Jake shakes his head. "You know, I just broke up with my girl-friend."

Let the record show I didn't pry.

"We dated for five years," he continues. "I caught her cheating on me last week."

Oh, good God. Fat lot of good it does me not to pry.

"I'm sorry," I offer idiotically.

"Don't be. I'm fine now. I just know Gregory told you I was having problems, and I just didn't want you to think I was a psycho or anything."

"The thought never crossed my mind."

"Good." He pulls out his wallet. " 'Cause I really did have a good time tonight. We should do this again sometime."

Yeah, where have I heard that one before?

"Sure," I shrug.

"The new Soderbergh comes out next week. You have any desire to see it?"

"I can't wait!"

"How about Friday, then?"

Well, knock me over with a feather.

Jake and I split the check and he offers to walk me back home. We manage to avoid any of the usual, end-of-the-night awkwardness by intermittenly throwing out more names of rising young stars. I say Jake Gyllenhaal, he suggests Maggie, and we both shoot down such obvious choices. Kirsten Dunst? Too vanilla. Kiefer Sutherland? Unfortunately, too TV. Colin Farrell? He had such a promising start, but . . .

I come to a halt in front of my apartment building and turn to wait expectantly. Jake, however, keeps on going, waving good-bye to me over his shoulder.

"I'll see you next Friday!" he calls out. His pace quickens and he trots lightly down the subway steps.

How about that? No kiss on the cheek, no extended hugs, no

fond farewells? Nothing at all? I'll be damned! I turn in a huff and shove my way through the entrance doors.

It occurs to me, however, as I climb up the stairs to my apartment, that I've got no reason at all to feel so peeved. So, big deal if this wasn't a date. Big deal if Jake doesn't find me wildly irresistible. I can live with that. You know what? I think I can safely say I quite enjoyed our pleasant and painless evening together anyway.

This is good, I decide. What am I saying? This is great! I'd take a mindless conversation about movie stars over the self-pity banter of ex-jobs and ex-girlfriends any day. I like having a new friend. I especially like having a new friend who is a boy. Between Amanda and Laurie, the men I meet just get devoured. And it isn't like I can foster any thriving platonic relationships with the other sex in the workplace. I don't have a workplace. So, this is nice. This will work out just fine.

For the first time in nine weeks, I sleep in. I don't wake up until mid-morning, when my alarm goes off. I swat aimlessly at the clock on my nightstand for a full minute before I jerk upright, suddenly recalling I haven't set my alarm in months.

My phone is ringing.

I leap out of my bed and into the living room, my eyelids still sealed with dreams not ready to be dispelled. I grope blindly on the sofa for anything that might resemble a phone receiver.

"Hello?" I answer groggily.

"Hello, is this Miss Sarah Pelletier?"

"Yes, speaking." I remove the phone from my mouth and yawn.

"Hi, Sarah, this is Bob calling from Time Warner."

"Oh, hi, Bob! Thanks for calling!" Desperately, I rack my brain.

It only slides further into the sheets and hides under a pillow. I can't recall anymore which department of Time Warner I sent my résumé into. Was it HBO? New Line?

"Miss Pelletier, I'd like to talk about to you about some of our new online services—"

"Oh, of course." That would explain the call. I must have applied to AOL. "You're looking for content writers?"

"Uh . . ." Bob sounds a little confused. "Maybe. I'm not sure. I'll have to look into that. But today I'm calling to tell you about the new residential, high-speed Internet access we're offering at competitive, low rates."

Oh. Now it makes sense. Bob's not hiring. He's selling.

I hang up the phone without another word.

I suppose I should be thankful Bob pried me from my blissful slumber when he did. God forbid I waste any more time before I get cracking on that oh-so-busy day ahead of me. Some people would call my day uneventful. But I can tick off at least ten events that occupy my morning alone. I wash the dishes, check my e-mail (no word from *Aspen Quarterly*). I mop the bathroom, vacuum the living room, and check my e-mail (still no word from *Aspen Quarterly*). I put my clothes in the washer, check my e-mail, transfer my clothes to the dryer, check my e-mail, fold my clothes, check my e-mail. (Maybe I should resend my résumé and cover letter just in case?)

And somehow, in the middle of all this activity, I also manage to find the time to finish the shitty mystery novel Princess sent me. Now, because I know for a fact you'll never read the book yourself, let me just say I knew the killer was the glamorous model's deformed twin sister all along.

I crank out a quick summary of the book, add a few scathing comments, and don't even bother to reread it before I e-mail my thoughts to Princess. It does me no good, however, to remain seated in front of my computer, keenly aware that NO NEW MESSAGES are coming in for me. So, I try to devise new ways to torment myself.

Then one occurs to me.

Okay, don't tell Amanda, but I recently discovered she hides her scale in her closet behind the shoe rack. Stealthily, and on tiptoe just for the heightened drama of it all, I sneak into her room and gingerly reach behind her calfskin high boots.

I place the scale cautiously on the floor. I put one foot on, close my eyes, then add the other.

My phone rings before I can even open my eyes.

"Shit, shit, shit!" I curse, hopping off and making a buffoonish attempt to put back the scale and answer the phone all at the same time.

My caller is a frantic Mark Shapiro.

"Did you make the changes on your résumé I told you to?"

"Of course," I lie.

"Great. E-mail me the revised copy right away. I found the perfect job for you."

"You did?"

"Yup. The company is looking for a bright, think-on-your-feet kind of person. Plus, they need someone with strong writing skills. They sounded really excited when I told them about you."

"Wonderful. What's the job?"

"It's an assistant property manager position at one of the top real estate agencies in the city."

What? "Umm, okay." I think for a moment. "Why do I need strong writing skills?"

"Well, you'd be working for a man who doesn't speak English very well. He needs an assistant to type up his eviction notices."

Oh, geez.

"It's an entry-level position for now," Mark continues. "But it's got a lot of growth potential. Most of the assistants become property mangers within a year."

"But I don't want to be a property manager—"

"It pays fifty thousand a year."

"Oh." All of a sudden, it doesn't sound so bad.

"I've already set up the interview for you tomorrow."

"What time?"

"Nine a.m."

Ugh.

Early-morning rush hour. Long lines at coffee stands. Blinding light bouncing off skyscrapers, loud horns wailing from screaming-yellow taxis. Subway turnstiles chiming like Atlantic City slot machines. And stir-crazy, sleep-deprived, *New York Post*—wielding commuters packing onto the trains, clinging to hanging straps, saluting the workday with Right Guard and Secret. Headed to toil the mines with mighty axes slung over their shoulders. Well, heigh-ho, here we go!

Sarah Pelletier

121 West 68th Street, Apt. 4B
New York, NY 10023
h: (212) 555-1476 c: (917) 555-9317
E-mail s.pelletier@hotmail.com

WORK EXPERIENCE

2000–2002   *451Films.com*   *New York, NY*
Administrative Assistant to President
- Maintained and updated department databases
- Answered phones and operated switchboard
- Typed, filed, and cataloged all written correspondence
- Responsible for tracking all incoming submissions

1999–2000   *NYC Film Fest*   *New York, NY*
Administrative Assistant
- Responsible for the distribution of publicity materials
- Edited programmer notes for festival catalog
- Coordinated post-screening discussions and specialty panels
- Acted as liaison between filmmakers and festival sponsors

EXTRACURRICULAR ACTIVITIES

1997–1999   *The Brown Daily*   *Providence, RI*
Arts Writer
- Contributed film reviews
- Covered all campus-wide arts and cultural events

1997–1999   *Brown Film Society*   *Providence, RI*
Junior Executive
- Wrote film reviews
- Edited Film Series programmer notes

EDUCATION

1996–2000   *Brown University*   *Providence, RI*
BA in English
- Graduated Phi Beta Kappa—GPA 3.8

SKILLS

- Fluent in French
- Type 50 wpm
- Proficient in Word, Excel, and Powerpoint

chapter seven

On first viewing, my résumé might look exactly the same to you. There are differences, though. Subtle differences, but differences nonetheless. And in some cases, incredibly important differences. Please note:

Résumé writing is an art. It is a *precise* art. Employers look for specific words to jump out at them. And depending on exactly what kind of applicant they are seeking, they'll want to see words like "operated" or "programmed" or "created." In more common cases— my cases—they prefer "answered," "organized" or "obeyed."

Granted, most employers are going to skim over the juicy parts. If you were to write that you "were responsible for the distribution of high-quality narcotics to underprivileged children in New York City boroughs" and that "you acted as a liaison between Colombian drug cartels and organized New York City street teams," all an employer is going to know is that you can distribute and you can liaise. And that looks pretty damn good. Moreover, they may even be impressed that you choose to work so closely with kids. I highly recommend you hint at your altruistic streak as often as possible.

So, for a résumé I plan to send to a property management firm— property management being something I know nothing about and for which I doubt I am qualified—I keep my skills to a bare minimum. My employers won't need to know that I can coddle filmmakers or that I can consume mass quantities of sub-par entertainment in search of one film that could be deemed, at best, "marketable." They may, however, be impressed that I can type without looking at the keyboard.

"Content Development Assistant"? Too fancy. It's been changed to the more accessible "Administrative Assistant," which is nonspecific enough to keep everyone happy.

Under my extracurricular activities, I've also added that I was a "Junior Executive." That sounds promising, doesn't it? That I was the junior executive of my college Film Society will probably go unnoticed.

And if you're being particularly observant, you'll also notice I did, in fact, include a section for my computer and typing skills. To make room for it, I got rid of my job experiences as an intern. Who needs to know I was an intern, when already my later job descriptions have me acting like an obedient, passionless twit? You're not going to get any feistiness from me, not with this résumé. I've just painted myself as a perfectly responsible, perfectly capable little assistant. Vacant eyes, insipid smile, and all.

At 7:30 in the morning, I rub the sleep from my eyes and shuffle my way to the bathroom. The door is closed. I knock.

"Come in," says Amanda. I open the door.

Amanda and I don't usually cross paths in the morning, and I am pleased to find her in front of the mirror, skin wan, lips faded, light blue eyes hidden behind thick, dark bags. Her hair is a messy mop of curlers on top of her head. She looks almost human.

"What are you doing up so early?" she asks into the mirror.

"I have an interview."

"What for?"

"Assistant property manager," I mumble, grabbing my tooth-brush.

She unwraps one of her curlers, and a familiar, lush tendril falls into place. "Do you need to borrow any of my clothes?"

"Not unless you've got overalls and a hard hat."

She unwraps another perfect curl. "You know, that could be a really good look for you."

I make a face into the mirror.

Barb Wallace, the director of Human Resources at Cooper Union Management, is a spry little Chihuahua of a woman. Unfortunately, she's a Chihuahua in a designer navy suit. I am beginning to rethink my choice of outfit. Even though I do consider these to be my nice clothes, I am slowly beginning to understand that "nice" does not necessarily mean the skin-tight black pants and lacy halter top I saved for special occasions in college—like Homecoming or the first day of new semester classes.

Maybe it's the Chihuahua connection again, but Barb reminds me of my tiny little high school Spanish teacher who used to sit on her desk with her legs crossed. As friendly and as animated as Barb may be, she still makes me feel like a teenager without a clue. When she asks a question, she waits patiently, smiling encouragingly, as if she were ready to applaud any response I'd be willing to give.

When prompted, I assure her I am looking for a "learning experience" and that I am willing to work from the bottom up as long as the position offers, of course, "growth potential." Barb is understandably impressed with my coached and well-practiced replies.

She then moves on to stage two—The Challenge. She looks at my résumé, ponders it for a moment, then thinks of a tough question. This is what she comes up with:

"I see you've had a lot of experience in the entertainment industry. I'm just curious. Why do you no longer wish to work in film?"

It's a good question. Excellent, in fact. And the answer is very delicate indeed. Because, the truth is, I *do* want to work in film, any aspect of film. But the jobs I want don't seem to be available these days.

Luckily, I have a prepared response that is a little more, shall we say, tactful.

"Oh, I love film," I say honestly. "But I love the kind of films people don't make anymore. I love when Marilyn Monroe dips potato chips in champagne. Or when Marlon Brando lights a match off the back of his jeans. But that doesn't exist today. Now we have trilogies and remakes and Vin Diesel vehicles. I just don't want to be part of that. I'm happy to watch old movies as a pastime. But as far as work goes? I want to do something more fulfilling."

Barb smiles. She's pleased. So, moving on.

She draws me a chart. I haven't really been paying attention, but I believe the chart is supposed to depict the corporate hierarchy at Cooper Union Management. As Barb diligently attempts to distinguish an exec V.P. from an S.V.P., my mind wanders and I try to envision my future as a legitimate property manager.

I'm wearing a hard hat. I'm sitting on the ledge of a fifth-story scaffolding contraption, eating a bologna sandwich from out of a tin lunch pail. Then sure enough, the scaffolding gives out from under me. No reason. It just vanishes.

So, there I am, splayed on my back on the sidewalk. I can't move my neck. I'm paralyzed. And I am forced to look up at my former ledge, the spot that marked the height, the pinnacle, of my so-called growth potential. Then I hear the lurch. The entire contraption creaks and collapses, barreling toward me—

"So," Barb leans forward, breaking me from my disturbing reverie. "Do you think this job might interest you?"

Have I mentioned before how much I hate this question? It's not like I can say, outright, "No. The job sucks. You could turn it sideways and cram it for all I care."

"I'd be curious to explore the possibilities," I say lightly.

"Great." She stands. "Then it's time for you to meet Vladimir."

I cast a quick glance at Barb's makeshift graph and see a box labeled "Vladimir—Exec V.P." Directly below it, there is a box labeled, "You."

"Okay, do me a favor . . ." Barb implores as I rise from my seat. "Try this on?" She removes her suit jacket and hands it to me.

Let me make a couple of things clear. First, I know my pants are a little snug and my shirt a little revealing. But I resent the fact that Barb's blatant disapproval of my outfit makes me feel like a stripper ~~some impertinent office peon hired~~ for Vladimir's surprise birthday party.

And secondly, as I think I've mentioned before, Barb is a wee, little lady. Now, I'm no Amazon, but I'm certainly no five-foot-one, eighty-pound bundle of joy. Trying on her jacket is a ridiculous idea, and I am annoyed she would even suggest it. The shoulders of her sleeves don't even clear my elbows.

"Well, okay . . ." She takes her jacket back reluctantly. "Maybe if you just pull your shirt down a bit . . ."

Fighting back tears, I tug down on the edges of my shirt to conceal the inappropriate sliver of my stomach.

It comes as no surprise, then, that Vladimir gives me a critical once-over as soon as I walk into his office. I have no doubt this interview will be particularly painful. Right off the bat, he grabs his yellow legal pad, and hits me with his most obnoxious question.

"You have strengths?"

Believe it or not, I am unprepared for this line of inquiry. All of my former interviews have been conducted rather informally, more like a forum for discussion, a *salon de thé* if you will. Minus the *thé*. I consider myself above the questions regarding my strengths, my weaknesses, my most challenging experiences. Wouldn't he just prefer if I told him a little bit about myself first?

Because I have no ready response, I use my usual plan of attack. I flail and fumble incoherently, trying to regale Vladimir with some clever anecdote that may or may not be an answer to his question. Really, I'm just buying time. I tell him about Andy Edgar, a legacy of the underground film movement, who tried to develop a web vehicle to generate interest for his upcoming experimental feature film.

"Boy, was he something!" I say. "I mean, he was great. But out there, you know? He was charming and funny, and the idea was fantastic, but—wow! Guy couldn't keep a train of thought to save his life. Trying to wrestle the project into some kind of shape, that was the problem. You get a surreal guy, and a surreal project. But no one to actually make it work, right? So, of course, the project gets dropped into my lap, and I've got to find a way to hammer it out. And in the end, and I mean after *a lot* of finessing, I guess I did kind of turn it into a decent, workable proposal . . ."

Vladimir's expression remains blank. Either he doesn't understand me, or he understands me perfectly. He just doesn't like me.

"I guess what I'm trying to say is that I tend to rise to the occasion," I mumble.

Vladimir nods. I watch him write on his legal pad, "rises to occasion." He looks back up at me.

"You have weakness?"

I laugh. "Well, clearly, it takes me a long time to get to the point."

Completely oblivious to my clever witticism, Vladmir jots on his notepad, "takes too long to get to point."

After that, our interview is cut thankfully short. Vladimir is called into an impromptu business meeting, and I am asked to show myself out. Which would work if I could remember my way in. I have a bad sense of direction to begin with. And a windowless office makes it impossible for me to even use the sun as a guide to tell east from west.

I wander though the labyrinth of cubicles, skulking past the assistants who leer at my shameless display of naked flesh. A reception desk would be a welcomed sight. Instead, I stumble upon one office pantry after another. Or, most likely, I've made the same loop several times.

Instinct tells me to go left, so I go right. I finally see the double oak doors I've been looking for. I make a mad dash and hurl myself out of the stuffy office.

And into a conference room.

A sea of angry faces turn to glare at me. Vladimir, at the head of the conference table, rises stiffly. He points a militant finger at me.

"You turn around! You go to end of hall."

I turn around. I go to end of hall.

Before I return home, I stop at the bank just for the sheer thrill of checking my account balance. For a moment I toy with the idea of taking out a whole forty dollars in cash. I laugh at such absurdity and take out twenty dollars instead. Good thing, too. The ATM spits out my receipt and informs me that my remaining balance is nineteen dollars.

The good news is today is Thursday and my unemployment check should arrive this afternoon. I check my watch. It is 12:30. I have plenty of time to catch the mailman on his route and run back here to cash my check.

I crumple up my receipt and toss it in the trash receptacle on my way out. The security guard, a smiling, heavyset black woman, holds the door open for me.

"Bye, bye, sugar," she winks.

Okay, well, I suppose the bad news is I'm going to have to cash my check at a different branch of my bank. I can't very well come back here if the security guard already recognizes me. It's bad enough having to hunch over like a hoodlum in the far corners of the ATM vestibules, trying to endorse my checks with one elbow folded over the "New York State Department of Labor" logo on top of the slip. Would it be so hard for the government to adopt a direct deposit policy to make my life a little less humiliating?

I walk down a few blocks and stop on the corner to buy a cup of coffee from the street vendor. Because I don't want to break my brand-new twenty, I fish in my pockets for change and eventually cough up seventy-five cents in nickels. The vendor gives me a look. He sighs and lowers his head.

"Five, ten, fifteen . . ." He thumbs the nickels on his counter accordingly.

At 12:45, I settle down on the bench outside of my apartment building to wait for the mailman. Just before I get comfortable, however, my cell phone rings. Of course.

"Sarah?"

"Hi, Gracie."

"Hi, doll. Do me a favor. Remind me where you live again?"

"Um, Sixty-eighth Street?"

"Upper West, right?"

"Yeah."

"Great. I thought I was in your neighborhood. Can you meet me outside my gym in about half an hour? I have a manuscript I want to give you."

"Uh. Sure. Where's your gym again?"

"You know where it is, doll. It's the Equinox on Broadway. Broadway and . . . Ninety-second, I think?"

Ninety-second? How is that even remotely my neighborhood?

"Okay, Gracie. I'll see you soon."

"Bye, doll!"

Reluctantly, I hoist myself up and begin the trek twenty-four blocks north.

I find Princess standing outside, sipping from a two-dollar bottle of imported, natural spring water and shielding her eyes from the weak sunlight with her Armani glasses. She doesn't look like she's dressed for the gym. She looks like she's dressed for a costume party with a "gym" theme. It isn't enough that she's wearing the twin set velour sweat suit—a zip-front hoodie with accompanying drawstring pants. She also has the matching headband. And spanking new sneakers the exact shade as the blue racing stripe running down the sides of her legs. If you think she'd have removed her diamond earrings—or her Cartier watch for that matter—you'd be sorely mistaken.

"Hey there, doll!" She waves at me.

"You already work out?"

"Uh-uh. Bikram in five minutes." She takes a dainty sip of her water. "One hundred and five degrees and I still don't break a sweat. Loved your last coverage, by the way."

"Oh, thank—"

"Here ya go." She dips into her Kate Spade tweed tote—currently doing double duty as a gym bag—and pulls out a Jiffy sealer.

"I was going to take it home and read it myself, but something came up last minute."

I take it from her. It feels much heavier than the last one. That's a good sign.

"No problem. I'm looking forward to it."

"Great. No hurry getting the coverage back to me. Anytime next week is fine." She removes her sunglasses and blows away the nonexistent dirt before carefully sliding them into a protective leather case. "So, in case you're wondering, the reason I'm busy tonight is because I'm meeting Lenny for cocktails."

I wasn't wondering. But I raise my eyebrows and feign a curious, "Lenny . . . ?"

"Oh, Sarah, don't play coy. You remember Lenny *Hawkins*." She waits for me to be impressed. So I give it my best shot.

"Really? The writer?"

"Uh-*huh*." She winks at me. "The incredibly *gorgeous* writer, if you recall."

Uh-uh. Don't recall at all.

"Oh. Does he have a new novel he's adapting or something?" I ask, already losing interest.

"Possibly." She shrugs. "But I think we both know what this meeting is *really* about."

"Right. Have a good a time tonight."

"Oh, I will." She starts backpedaling. "Take care!"

"Bye, Gracie."

As I watch her hop up the steps to the gym, I am struck deeply with an emotion I never thought Gracie could provoke. I feel sorry for her.

I dash back to my apartment and catch the mailman just as he pulls up to my building.

"Hello, hello, 4B!" His pencil-thin black mustache curls upward in a cat-like grin. He hands me my unemployment check.

"How'd I know you'd be out here today?"

"Lucky guess?"

He chuckles and sorts through his stack of envelopes.

"You got another one, too."

"Oh, yeah?"

"A big one." He hands over a large manila envelope, surprisingly thick. "I didn't know you were going to be a hot-shot lawyer."

"What?" I flip over the envelope. Indeed, it is addressed to me. But in the top left corner, it bears the emblem of a curious sender: Columbia University School of Law.

"**M**om!"

"Yes, sweetie-pie?"

"Did you send me a law school application?"

"Yup sure did. I told you I was going to."

"Uh-uh. Never."

"I could have sworn—No. You're right. Must have slipped my mind. See, Dad and I just thought—"

"Oh, no you don't!" I throttle the phone as if it were her neck. "Leave Dad out of this. This stupid idea has your name written all over it."

"Sweetie-pie, just relax. Let me finish. Dad and I have a deal for you."

"A deal? I don't know if I'm ready to negotiate any deals. Seeing how I lack the *legal* expertise and all."

"I don't see what other choices you have. Your father and I can't continue supporting you forever."

"I've never asked you for money—"

"Maybe not yet. But how else are you going to pay for health insurance?"

"I . . . well, I . . . I'll get a job soon."

"Yeah? You sure?"

No, I'm not. I wring the phone harder.

"We'll take care of the law school tuition. It's certainly a worthwhile investment. For you and for us."

"But I don't want to be a lawyer—"

"How about an entertainment lawyer?"

I gulp back the bile rising in throat. *Entertainment* lawyer? Good God, if ever a worse combination were to exist it would probably have to include mayonnaise and pistachio ice cream.

Entertainment lawyers. These are the sort of people who keep Satan's phone number on speed dial. Because, in the end, one soul for a three-picture deal with 20th Century Fox is more than a fair-enough trade.

"We'll pay for the application fee," my mother continues, undaunted by my silence.

"I can think of far better ways for you to spend the money."

"We'll pay for the LSATs, too. There's a test next month."

"Seems like a waste to me."

"And maybe a little extra cash on the side?"

"You're bribing me to apply to law school?"

"Dad and I were thinking somewhere around three hundred dollars."

"I'll consider it."

Call waiting, thank goodness!, intercedes on my behalf. I don't even have to lie about it.

"Sarah? Sarah! What was that? You still there?"

"I've got another coming in." I don't bother to look at the caller ID. "It's important."

"All right, sweetie-pie. I love you."

"I love you too." Click.

"Hello?"

"Sarah. Mark Shapiro, here."

"Mark." I groan. "Oh, hey, Mark. Sorry, I was just about to call you. I don't think the interview today went well at all—"

"Really? Barb just called me. She said they loved you."

"You've got to be joking."

"No, no," he assures me. "They thought you were very smart and friendly. But they want to see a writing sample."

"What kind of a writing sample?"

"Nothing too demanding. Maybe a couple of paragraphs, a page at the most. Something about real estate."

"Oh, all right," I grumble.

URBAN REAL ESTATE

Nothing about who we are, what we do, or where we went to school matters much in today's downturn, understimulated, recession-era market. The true mark of success, the only testament to good standing in modern society, is where we live.

The invitation to a person's apartment is a one-way ticket into his soul. We are hence embarrassed to disclose our secret intimacies so openly. We are reluctant to admit that we are either downtown or uptown people, West Side or East Side inhabitants. The neighborhoods we live in are oversimplifications of ourselves—they pigeonhole us into limiting stereotypes, categories rife with misrepresentation. These neighborhoods, as such, are always dicey and never safe.

I should think it would better serve us to see the apartments themselves, and not their location, as the concrete, wooden, or brick versions of who we are.

We, as the citizens of Manhattan, are clusters of hermit crabs scavenging the coasts of the Hudson River for discarded shells. But we must constantly learn to compromise. The shells we choose for ourselves are often small, or chipped or colorless. In fact, the most telling feature of our apartments are not what they offer, but what they lack.

For some, the luxury of security in a doorman building is an option that simply cannot be afforded. For others, a view of a concrete courtyard overgrown with weeds, or a balcony overlooking a dimly lit alleyway, or a direct glimpse into a neighboring boudoir is considered an extravagance. Sunlight, the earth's most valuable natural resource, is often an added feature we can do well without. And so long as the apartment building itself provides easy access to nearby subway lines, laundry services, and good restaurants, the room in which we actually decide to dwell need hold nothing more than our futons.

We tell ourselves all this is temporary. With fingers crossed we anxiously anticipate the passing of estranged relatives who live in finer Manhattan domains, hoping eventually to inherit their duplexes on Central Park West. We pray for a drop in the market, a winning lottery ticket, anything that allows us to believe that our apartments, like we ourselves, will someday realize their full potential.

chapter eight

I am putting the final touches on my essay when I notice the clock on my computer—which generally tends to run a few minutes behind—already reads 6:30 p.m. I save the document to send out the following morning, grab my bag, and dart out the door. I come back a few moments later to grab my MetroCard out of the pocket of yesterday's jeans.

I manage to make good time and arrive at the Spring Street bar promptly at 7:15 p.m. As soon as I open the door, a bubbly brunette thrusts herself in front of me.

"You here for Six-Minute Match?" she chirps.

"Yup," I reply, not nearly as cheerful.

"Super!" She takes a moment to outfit me with a personal name tag, a scorecard, and a list of sample questions.

"Now, have you been speed-dating before?" she asks.

"A couple of times."

"Really? Are you interested in signing up for some of our Veteran Dating parties?"

I don't answer her immediately, because for a moment the concept of Veteran Daters makes me shudder. I picture a slovenly clan, people with mangled limbs and bandaged hearts, trading war stories from the dating front. And in the background, a fat woman is singing a karaoke version of "I Will Survive."

I take the pamphlet from the hostess anyway and offer her a mumbled thanks. Then I make haste to the bar, where I've already spotted Laurie gabbing on her work cell phone.

"Yup, no problemo. I can ask her right now." She winks at me as I take the seat beside her. "Let me call you back in five." She snaps the cell phone shut.

"You want a job?" she asks.

"Of course I want a job."

"The art department is a little shorthanded this week. The director just saw the walls for the apartment set. He hates them. They need to be repainted before we start shooting on Monday. You think you could help out?"

"For how long?"

"Two days? Three days? It's three hundred dollars."

"But I—"

"Paid under the table, of course."

"Then I'd love to."

The bartender strides past us and gives me a questioning look. I shake my head.

"You sure you don't want a drink?" Laurie asks. "I'll buy."

"Nah, I wanna do this sober."

She groans. "You're not supposed to do it sober. It's important to loosen up a bit before. That's why they tell you to show up early."

"Look, you know the rules. I let you drag me to these things 'cause you convinced me it was good interview practice. Now, until people start setting up an open bar in the reception area before meetings, I'm just—"

"Right, right, your *rules*. Sorry, I forgot. For a moment I thought you were doing this because it was *fun*."

"Fun is an expense I can't write off anymore."

"Too bad. I'm expensing this as a 'networking party.' "

"You're serious?"

"How else do you think I convinced my boss to let me out early?"

"That's so depressing."

"Wanna know something even more depressing? I checked my calendar and I can't schedule one of these events again until September. I've got to wait until September to book a six-minute date! God forbid a guy ever asks me out to dinner. What am I gonna say? 'Sorry, I'm only free from midnight to 4 a.m.'?" She tosses back half her drink. "But let's not talk about that." She leans in and whispers confidentially. "By the way, I've already picked one out. Check out the sailor in the corner."

I arch my head nonchalantly. He sits at a back table, hunching his laughably large biceps over a pint of beer. Who's he fooling with the crew cut? Even with pale blond hair, it's no secret his hairline is making a dangerous retreat.

"He's perfect for you," I say.

"Not for me, moron. For you!"

I roll my eyes.

Laurie snaps her fingers and straightens. "I remember what I wanted to tell you. That Ian Pascal book I gave you to read?"

"Loved it."

Laurie waves her hand excitedly. "Paramount just bought it. And George Clooney is already attached."

"Seriously? He's the perfect choice."

"He's the perfect choice for *anything*."

"And what about *Die Dämmerung*?"

"*Die* what?"

"That German book you gave me."

"Oh, right. You mean, *The Twilight*."

"Whatever."

"No. Nothing yet. You start reading it?"

"I've been meaning to. But I never seem to have the time. Princess has been sending me all these books to cover—"

"Whoa, whoa, whoa!" Laurie's hand shoots up again to stop me. "You've been reading for Princess?"

"Didn't I tell you?"

"No." She sneaks a furtive glance around the bar. Her voice drops to a hush. "Any chance you've come across a book called *Gideon*?"

"Uh-uh." Her secretiveness intrigues me. "What's *Gideon*?"

"It's supposed to be *huge*. We're waiting for it to slip any day now. People are saying the writer is going to be the next John Irving."

"Really? What's the book about?"

"I don't know. What are any of these books about? 'Boy Comes of Age,' probably. You'll let me know if you see it?"

"Laurie, you know I can't do that. I'd be betraying Princess's trust."

Laurie looks at me quizzically. "Geez," she grumbles. "You make it sound like we're stealing plans for a fusion bomb."

I snort. If anyone has an overblown sense of importance about the film industry, it isn't me.

"Just keep it in mind," she says.

Before I can protest any further, the bubbly brunette from the entrance steps up behind us and places her fingertips on our backs.

"Ladies. It's time for you to take your seats."

———

The sailor sits down across from me. He has a shy smile and light blue eyes that dart around helplessly. I feel awful that I've taunted his haircut behind his back. Bad haircuts can happen to anyone. I shouldn't have held it against him.

"You ready?" he asks, leaning forward a bit, but not enough to be intrusive.

I flip my hair, and then am shocked I've fallen back on such obvious flirtations. *Be professional*, I remind myself.

"Sure am."

"Good. Okay." He puts his elbows on the table. "I thought it would be a good idea if I thought of one really good question to ask. Just one. So, I've been thinking about it all day."

"And? What did you come up with?"

"Well, nothing, you know, mind-boggling, or anything. I mean, I don't care what kind of dog you think of yourself as, or, if you could be on any reality TV show, which one you'd choose—"

"Rhodesian ridgeback, and *Amazing Race*."

"All I really want to know—" He stops himself and his shy smile becomes a little less painful. "Really? *Amazing Race?*"

"I like to travel."

"Interesting," he murmurs. He bows his head. "You know, I'm actually kind of nervous. Do you mind if I just get to my question? Since I've spent so much time working on it?"

"You're absolutely right. I'm sorry. Go ahead." I make a mental note, in future interviews, to fight the urge to jump the gun and interrupt the line of questioning.

"All right." He sucks in his breath. "What is your number-one priority?"

"That *is* a good question."

"I'm glad you think so."

"But it's a little unfair."

The blood drains from his face. "Really? You think so?"

"I'm not sure I *can* narrow it down to just one. Can I pick five?"

"How about three?"

"All right." While I think, I'm tempted to chew a fingernail or toy with a strand of hair. Instead, I force myself to keep my hands in my lap. Like a little lady. "Okay, well, first of all, I have to say stability."

His eyes widen. "You're talking about commitment?"

"So to speak."

"And? Go on:"

"Second priority? Well, I know it's obvious, maybe a little cliché, but I'd have to say growth potential."

He gulps. "Growth *potential*?"

"Oh, and I also really enjoy a good challenge. And the opportunity to be creative."

"Creative?" He turns a bright shade of crimson. "What, like . . . sexual role-playing?"

Good God! Where the hell did he come up with *that*? I replay my answers in my head. Okay, yeah. Now I see what I did.

"Uh, no," I say meekly. "This has nothing to do with sex. I'm not really interested in sex."

"Not at all?"

"It's certainly not a top five priority."

He squints. "Now I'm confused. Then, why are you here?"

I try to smile. It comes out all wrong—clenched teeth, tight lips. Like I'm trying to hold back an enormous belch.

"Oh, I get it now." He leans back in his chair, the hurt in his eyes burning with new ferocity, almost enough to bring him to tears. "This is a joke to you."

"No, no, it's not that," I say quickly, feeling a minor twinge of guilt.

"What is it then?" he snaps.

I shake my head ruefully. "Can I be frank with you," I squint at his name tag, "Frank?" I pause. The absurdity of what I've just said makes me want to giggle, but I stifle the urge. "The problem is your question."

"Now all of a sudden it's not a good question anymore?"

"It's a great question," I assure him. "It's just tough. 'Cause the truth is . . ." I shrug helplessly. "The truth is, dating is not a priority for me. And finding a boyfriend? Not even remotely. I'm only here tonight because my friend Laurie convinced me it would be good interview practice. See," I swallow hard because it still pains me to say this. "I'm unemployed."

I suppose I half-expected him to leap out of his chair and shriek, "Ewww!" Instead, his shoulders lose some of their rigidity and he lets himself inch just a little bit closer.

"How long you been out for?"

"Six months."

"That's nothing. I've had friends that were out for a year. I was out for six months myself before I started freelancing."

"What do you do?"

"I'm a sound engineer."

All right, good enough.

"Hey, Frank," I beckon him with a finger. He scoots toward me and lowers his head, listening intently.

"My friend Laurie is sitting right next to me," I whisper. "She works in the film industry. Did you see *The Walk of Shame*?"

"Yeah, last Friday," he whispers back. "It was all right."

"Don't say it's 'all right.' Tell her you loved it. It's her first associate producer credit."

"Oh, okay. Gotcha."

"And if it turns out you're interested, you should invite her to a late-night dinner at Blue Ribbon. It's her favorite restaurant."

He smiles gratefully.

The whistle shrieks, signaling the end of round one. The men stand and shift seats. When Laurie turns to eye me curiously, I flash her an inconspicuous thumbs-up.

The freight elevator hoists me up and deposits me squarely in the middle of a sprawling, sun-drenched loft—the apartment set. When I think "set," I conjure up images of weights and pulleys, wooden beams, cardboard cutouts, and enormous spotlights. "Set" means fake, it means unreal. And this is, by far, the most unreal apartment I've ever seen. Hardwood floors, high ceilings, bay windows—even the walls are painted one of those colors with a fancy name. Like Sanguine Earth. Or Burnt Sienna.

"What do you think?" asks a husky voice. I crane my neck every which way around the corners of the apartment and eventually find Gisele, the art director. I can only see the top half of her, two braids under a plaid bandana, and freckled elbows propped up from behind the kitchen counter. In one hand she holds a coffee mug and, yes, in the other a cigarette.

"It's gorgeous!" I gush.

"Yeah, well, we're changing it." She exhales a smoke ring slowly and watches it vanish. "Michel wants it simple. He wants it white."

"You're going to paint the whole thing white?"

She shrugs. "It's supposed to be a boy's apartment. Michel doesn't think boys would live in an apartment painted amber."

Amber? That's a little anticlimactic. I would have called it Spicy Salsa.

Gisele takes one last drag from her cigarette and drops the butt into her coffee mug. She studies me for a moment, her eyes lingering on my T-shirt.

"You go to Princeton?"

"No."

"Okay." Like a turtle, she withdraws her head and her skinny, freckled arms behind the kitchen cabinets. "This way."

It takes me five minutes to cover the entire stretch of the loft. Eventually I find her in front of the kitchen sink, splaying the bristles of a paintbrush under the running water of the faucet.

"They have to be clean," she says. "Make sure you get every single bristle. Any trace of amber will totally fuck up the white." She hands me four large, stiff brushes. The clean one, the one she's been grazing with the hardened, callused tips of her fingers, she keeps for herself. "I'll be in the back. You can start anywhere once you have a clean brush."

As soon as she leaves, I light a cigarette and begin the thorough cleansing process. Three cigarettes later, I decide enough is enough. I pick the cleanest brush and select the wall furthest from Gisele. She has already left out a bucket of white paint for me. I dab the brush gingerly in the paint, stroke it once against the wall, and panic. The blemish is small, but not entirely inconspicuous. I am staring at a fine line of Spicy Salsa running down the center of my white streak.

I turn, stricken, and squint my eyes toward the bay windows. The most I can make out of Gisele is her tiny, dark silhouette. I breathe a little easier.

I stroke the wall anew. Now two fine lines of amber scrawl down my fresh coat of white. I grab the brush and race back into the kitchen. I don't care how many cigarettes it takes this time. I scrub the brushes raw, looking over my shoulder repeatedly, dreading the possibility of Gisele's imminent return.

But Gisele isn't my problem. My problem presents itself later, only after I've produced one entire wall of glorious, sparkling white. My problem steps off the freight elevator and stands motionless in the center of the loft, howling with fury.

"*Non!*" He stamps his foot. "*Non, non, non!*" He stamps harder.

Evidently, he has caused just enough of a ruckus to stir Gisele's attention. She turns casually from the window.

"The fuck is your problem, Roald?"

"What I'm supposed to do with thees!" he spits, cuffing his chin at the walls.

"Michel wanted it simple."

"So? You want seemple, you paint the walls *bleu*. You paint them green. You do not make them white. White, I cannot!" He spits again. He cuffs again.

It doesn't take a genius to identify My Problem at this point. This madman import, with obscenely messy hair and an affected accent from nowhere in particular, can be none other than the Director of Photography. He turns to me and sees the offending brush, slathered with white paint, in my hand.

"You! Stop dee painting!"

My paintbrush clatters onto the newspaper under my feet. Otherwise, I remain perfectly still. Gisele charges toward the center of the room and grabs her cell phone off the coffee table. The madman starts rummaging in the pockets of his suede jacket.

I've never before seen choreography timed and executed with such precision. Gisele and the cameraman turn their backs on each other, flip open their cell phones, and trade alternate screams.

"Get me Michel!"

"Get me *bleu*!"

"I need him now!"

"I need today!"

Again on cue, they snap their phones shut and swivel back to glare at each other.

"Make yourself comfortable, Roald," Gisele seethes. She marches over to me and grabs my trembling wrist, leading me away like a toddler on the verge of tears. Together we stomp further down the loft (actually she stomps, I stagger) until finally she flings me into a back room crammed with stacks of furniture. She takes a moment to readjust her bandana, angrily stuffing strands of her hair back into it.

"All right, here's the deal. We need to make this furniture look old and worn, like it's been around forever." She pulls a hammer out of her tool belt. "I want you to chip the paint a little. Nothing too drastic." She taps the hammer once against a dresser. A chip of green paint falls neatly to the floor. "You see?" She hands me the hammer.

"Yeah, I can do that."

She leaves the room and I crouch down on the floor. I hammer away at dresser furiously, shredding it into oblivion. I like the hollow sound it makes every time I give it a good whack. Bit by bit, chip by chip, I break it down and whittle it away. Like it's my dignity.

Laurie is waiting downstairs for me at 6 p.m. on the dot. She's wearing a pretty sundress and killer dark sunglasses to match her killer dark combat boots. She drops her cigarette to the cement and crushes the life out of it with a steel-tipped toe.

"Petty cash," she says, holding up an envelope. "Dinner's on us. It's an extra-special thank-you for today."

"Can dinner come in a funny glass with an olive?"

"An olive, a maraschino cherry, a lemon wedge, you name it." She slides the envelope into her purse. "Just pick the place."

"Okay, but—"

"But what?"

I drop my eyes to the ground and my voice to a whisper. "See, I told Amanda I might hang out with her tonight . . ."

Laurie rolls her eyes. Make no mistake about it, there is no love lost between the two of them. Then again, Laurie is a little wary of anyone uninspired enough to do something as tedious as math for a living. But people like Amanda—those who work too hard during the day and play too hard at night—are an altogether different kind of beast. Laurie will never be able to understand such zealots. She sees them as the corporate vampires ready to drain the life out of her otherwise bohemian lifestyle.

"Fine." She shifts the tension in her shoulders and sighs. "Tell her to meet up with us later."

"Thanks," I breathe with relief.

An hour later, Laurie and I are crammed onto a bar stool and a half in the dark, forgotten corner of a tiny West Village tavern. We chose this particular bar by default. The mad frenzy of the post-work cocktail hour is usually a standing-room-only affair, and it is a mighty tall order to ask for a firm, stiff plank on which to plant a sore, tired rear. Granted, for twelve dollars a martini you *could* buy yourself a throw cushion and cozy spot on a velvet chaise. But then you'd be forced to play coy with snooty bartenders and be graciously accepting of any group of pinstriped stockbrokers that sends a round of drinks your way. Laurie and I can do well without the cushions and trappings of such glamorous establishments. We'd much prefer to pack into the sardine tins that usually house the West Village staple of aspiring actors and screenwriters—people who don't have the means to buy you a drink, and therefore lack the approach to join a conversation uninvited.

"Who paints the walls amber? What a *stupid* idea!" Laurie giggles into her vodka collins.

"Not like white was a stroke of genius either."

"Oh, don't even get me started! I felt like a police dispatcher as soon as I got off the phone with Gisele. 'Mobilize all units to Janovic Plaza immediately!' Then everyone was like, 'What color should we get?' And, I'm like, 'I'll tell you when you get there!'"

I doubt anyone at one of those pretentious lounges would find our conversation all that funny. Yet we double over in hysterics at the sheer absurdity of colors, film productions, and people in general who take themselves far too seriously. And the tortured writer beside us, who has been hunched over his journal and eavesdropping on our conversation all evening, allows a small smile—suggesting he understands us only far too well.

All of a sudden, Laurie freezes. Her face turns ashen, as white as the controversial apartment wall. She stares, transfixed, over my right shoulder.

"Oh. My. God."

I turn my head to follow her gaze. Perched in the doorway, as always, and seemingly oblivious to the squalor she generally tends to avoid, Amanda seeks us out with a caterpillar smile and butterfly wave. But she's committed a sin considered unforgivable among single women.

She brought a date.

"That's Ryan," I whisper quickly to Laurie as they make their approach. "He's her boss. Be nice!" I'd have better luck telling my gin and tonic to be nonalcoholic.

Laurie clamps her mouth shut. I wouldn't be surprised if she doesn't say another word for the rest of the evening.

"Hey, you guys!" Amanda hooks an arm around Laurie's shoulder and air-kisses her cheek. It's such a rare display of affection, so artfully staged, Laurie grimaces and shoots me a venomous glare. I kick her stool to shake her free of the impulse to stick her finger down her throat and gag.

When Amanda makes her introductions, Laurie nods hello. When Ryan offers to buy us our next round of drinks, she smiles politely, because to refuse him would be too rude even for her. Ryan grows visibly uncomfortable under the heat of hostile eyes, so he turns to me to open up with the small talk.

"Amanda tells me you're looking for a job."

"That's right."

"Tough market out there."

"Yeah, I guess."

"You know, we're looking to hire a receptionist at the company. If you're interested you should give your résumé to Amanda. I'd be happy to put in a good word for you."

Now I'm the one glaring. Amanda refuses to catch my eye.

"What happened to your old receptionist?" I ask.

Amanda tosses her hair and shrugs. "Turns out she was a top-ranked analyst in the investment banking class she took in the spring. She's going to be replacing me."

"We're very good to our loyal employees," Ryan confirms. "We offer a lot of growth potential."

I shudder at the thought. "I'll think about it," I mumble.

Amanda pounds her palm against the top of the bar. We all flinch.

"Who wants to do shots?"

"I'm in," says Ryan.

Laurie and I exchange uneasy glances. She stands abruptly.

"I'm going out for a cigarette," she says pointedly.

"Yeah. I'll join you."

chapter nine

Here's my dilemma:

Jeans or a jean skirt?

Hair up or hair down?

Red lipstick or sheer lip gloss?

Push-up bra or no bra?

And if we're just going to be in a dark movie theater, and if this isn't even a date—definitely, not a date at all—does it even matter?

I didn't think I'd make it to the movie theater in time. A quick survey of my wardrobe led me to discover my very best jeans were dirty, so I had to run across to Urban Outfitters to buy the pair I'd been eyeing for weeks. I intended to wait for a sale, but, well, this is a special circumstance. They were worth every penny, anyway. I swear, my ass has never looked better.

While I was out, I also stopped by Sephora to try out sample lipsticks. The saleslady caught me as I was sneaking on a daring shade of come-hither red. I let her sucker me into buying an eyeliner in a grayish hue that she told me brings out the green flecks in my otherwise lifeless and unexciting brown eyes.

So you can see how the time adds up.

I run to the theater, nearly tripping over the hem of my jeans. Yes, the legs are a little long. That was intentional. I am trying to conceal the fact I am wearing old, terribly untrendy platform shoes that make me at least five inches taller.

Jake is waiting outside. When he sees me he flicks the butt of his cigarette into the street. A spray of tiny sparks dance on the curb before the filter disappears down the gutter.

"What number cigarette was that?" I ask, panting.

"Just the first."

"I'm so sorry I'm late."

"No problemo." He pats the pockets of his corduroys. "I already have the tickets. I was worried there might be a line, and my movie experience just isn't complete unless I get to watch trailers first."

"I totally understand. I only show up for the trivia questions. Speaking of which, do you know who the only person named Oscar to win an Oscar is?"

"Oscar Hammerstein?"

I gape at him, absolutely flummoxed. He chuckles at me.

"Don't look so impressed. That was one of the questions from last week. Before the De Niro movie?"

"Oh. Right."

He holds the door open for me. "Shall we then?"

I toss an imaginary shawl over my shoulder and saunter on in.

I had almost forgotten how anxious movie theaters make me on Friday nights. Fortunately, as we discovered the week before, Jake and I both prefer the middle/back sections of the theater and we manage to find the perfect seats dead center in the fourth to last row. Then a middle-aged couple waltzes in and selects the seats directly in front of us. I go rigid.

"Do you want to move?" asks Jake.

"You don't mind?"

"Not at all. How about one row back?"

"That'd be great." We pick up our bags and make our transition. "Thanks."

"Sure. People next to me were getting kinda chatty, anyway. I think they might be talkers."

"*Pfft.*" I shake my head. "Those are the worst kind." The lights go dim. Jake snuggles back into the cushion of his chair, ready to enjoy the previews. I, on the other hand, remain upright—for fifteen minutes at least—peering at the door, scowling at the latecomers who have the nerve to intrude on the show so loudly after the curtain call. This doesn't happen at the opera, I tell you. You miss the first seating, and you have to wait until intermission. Them's the rules.

Even when the latecomers stop trickling in, we still don't get to enjoy the movie in silence. We come to realize, all too quickly, there is a pair of hard-of-hearing senior citizens seated behind us.

"What did he say?" asks the man loudly. His wife tells him.

"Oh. Then what did she say?"

I crane my head around deliberately. A very obvious gesture that should be effective in and of itself. It isn't. So, I take a deep breath and project a loud *"Shh!"*

The man looks at me for a moment. Then he turns to his wife.

"What did she just say?"

The movie ends over two hours later. I step onto the escalator and turn around to face Jake.

"Bit of a letdown, huh?" he says.

"I am sooo glad you said that. I thought it was just me. I had such high expectations—"

"I know. I've been waiting for this movie all year—"

"I feel responsible. I totally build these things up. These movies couldn't possibly compare to what I had in mind."

We step off the first escalator and make our way around the corner to take the next flight down. I stop midstep.

"Wait a second!"

"What's up?"

"Look!" I point to Tom Hanks's cardboard face. "There's a movie I have absolutely no illusions about whatsoever."

"What are you talking about?" Jake scoffs. "Look at him. He's wearing a hospital gown. *And* he's in a wheelchair. That movie has Academy Award written all over it."

"We should see it!"

"What, now?"

"It started five minutes ago."

"Ooooh," Jake is beginning to catch my drift. "No, we can't."

"Why not?"

"It's just . . . not right."

"You can't be serious. Paying ten dollars for a mediocre, vastly overrated film, that's right to you?"

"I would feel guilty. I wouldn't enjoy it."

"You're not going to enjoy it anyway. That's the point." I grab his sleeve and start pulling him away from the escalator. "It's okay. It's one of the perks of being unemployed. We're actually allowed to sneak into movies."

"But I'm not unemployed."

"You can be my plus-one." I feel his arm go slack, his resistance waning. He lets me lead him into the darkened theater.

As expected, the second movie sucks even more than the first. Plus, now it has been all of four hours without a smoke break. We push our way out of the theater and set the world ablaze.

"Two for the price of one and it still wasn't worth it!"

"I know," I exhale my plume of smoke. "They just don't make movies like they used to."

"You like old movies?"

"I think the art of cinema peaked with *The Graduate* and has been on a downward spiral ever since." I pause before I take my next drag, wondering if perhaps I've just committed a major cinephile blunder. Does *The Graduate* actually qualify as an *old* movie? I'm not entirely sure.

"You know what I miss? The sagas, the melodramas. Give me Douglas Sirk any day," I add. Just in case.

"You know, they're having a Blake Edwards retrospective at the Film Forum this month."

"I love Blake Edwards!" My ears are ringing. I think I may just have squealed like Rock Hudson discovering Doris Day's mink stole. I make sure to drop my voice a couple of octaves when I speak again. "When are the films showing?"

"*Victor/Victoria* is playing on Sunday."

"We should go!"

"All right." Jake grins. "It's a date."

Do you know why Blake Edwards is a genius? I'll tell you why. In fact, I can sum it up in one scene. Julie Andrews, a poor, starving cabaret singer, is staring through a diner window, watching a fat man eating a powdered doughnut. And, I mean, he is absolutely gorging on it, taking deep, juicy bites. Julie licks her lips, getting a little woozy. The camera cuts to a close-up of the gob of sugar on the fat man's pudgy nose. Then we cut back to Julie—only now she's gone. Yet, through the window we can see a group of men run toward the diner and stoop down. When they straighten back into frame, they hoist a disoriented Julie back onto her feet and help her brush off her coat. Later, she returns to her apartment and tells her landlord she'll sleep with him for a meatball.

That's it! That's what it's all about.

Jake and I have both been so pleased with our latest movie selection we have absolutely nothing to say to each other when we leave the theater. Instead, we light up our cigarettes and smoke quietly, as if to speak would be to fully dissolve the lingering cloud of movie magic—to disintegrate the halo of the projector still scorched on our retinas, to deafen the hum of the closing song still teasing our eardrums.

"Such a lost art, huh?" says Jake, snuffing out his cigarette. And with it, the last glimmer of our star-studded haze.

"What? Musicals?"

"No. Making good movies."

I sadly nod my concurrence.

"Did you want to get dinner?"

"Nah, I'm not really hungry." I mash my cigarette under my heel. "But you know what I could really go for? A big, fruity margarita."

Jake beams. "I know just the place."

He takes me to a Mexican restaurant around the corner that is more Tijuana than Cancun. The menu is somber, without the unnecessary distractions of tacos wearing sombreros or a cowboy riding a jalapeño. And the choices are standard: *pollo, carne*, or *cerveza*. Our request for margaritas is considered such an extravagance, the bartender hoots and rolls up his sleeves, preparing the concoction with unparalleled flair.

Approximately two margaritas and a bowl of chips later, Jake suggests another round and I pretend to turn the idea over in my head for a bit before I finally agree. He signals the bartender with the universal sign for "*dos.*"

"All right," Jake says, as soon as our glasses are refilled. "I gotta question for ya."

"Shoot."

"Best movie ending ever?"

My first instinct is, of course, to say *The Graduate*. But it's such an obvious choice. I rattle my brain to come up with something more impressive.

"Oh, okay, I got it!" I take a hearty sip of the margarita. "You see *The Italian Job*?"

"Original or remake?"

I roll my eyes. "Original."

"Yeah?"

"At the end, when Michael Caine says, 'Hang on lads, I've got a great idea'? That's perfect! All movies should end that way."

"Not bad," Jake nods appreciatively.

"And you?"

"Well, I know everyone says the same thing." He shrugs. "But I gotta go with *The Graduate*."

"Sucker."

"Okay, well, what about best movie opening?"

"That's too easy. *Hudsucker Proxy*. When Waring Hudsucker steps up on the conference table and takes a running leap out of the window. Yours?"

"Hands down, *Wild at Heart*. When Nic Cage bashes that guy's head in? You know, when I went to see that movie in the theater, they were offering full refunds to anyone who walked out within the first ten minutes."

"No shit. Did they do it?"

"Walk out? Hell, yeah. As soon as the guy's brains were on the floor, the theater was totally empty."

"Some people," I shake my head scornfully. "They wouldn't know genius if it . . . if it . . ."

"Bashed their brains out?"

"Exactly."

"Tell me about it." He polishes off his drink. "One last round?"

"Sure."

Four margaritas and no dinner is never a good idea. It occurs to me, as I slurp down the last sip, that I might be sucking on the very straw that disabled the proverbial camel. I don't realize just how drunk I am until the bill arrives and I make a mad dash for my purse.

"Don't worry about it," Jake says, fishing for his wallet.

"No, no, I insist." I zip open my purse and accidentally spill its entire contents onto the floor. "Shit!"

Jake giggles. "You need help?"

"I got it!" I shriek, fumbling on the floor, trying to reel in a tube of lipstick before it rolls out of range. I manage to clumsily restuff my bag only after Jake has settled the tab.

"Here," he offers me his hand. I grab onto the cuffs of his sleeves and let him hoist me up.

There are three steps that lead down from the bar to the street. Were I left to my own devices, I would happily get on my knees and climb down. Jake, however, keeps a firm grip on my elbow and leads me to the bottom, one step at a time. When we reach the street, he tries to steady me.

"You got it?"

"Yeah, I'm okay." I straighten, wobble slightly, then find my balance. I grin with supreme confidence. "All good."

He studies me curiously. "You know, you've got great teeth."

" 'Scuse me?"

"I'm sorry. My grandfather was a dentist. I tend to notice these things. You had braces?"

"Four years," I say proudly.

"Wow." He whistles. "They did a hell of a job."

"Thanks."

"No, I mean it. You've got a beautiful smile." The edges of his grin dip unexpectedly. He leans in. Closer, then closer still. His face soon becomes a blur. My powers of observation being anything but keen, I have no idea he is going in for a kiss until his lips are upon mine. And I didn't even purse.

His mouth is warm. And surprisingly soft. To look at him, he seems like such a manly man, so strong and so tough, I half-expected his lips would feel like concrete and kissing him would be a lot like slurping ice cream off cement. Instead, it is more like sucking a milkshake out of a curly straw. I want to consume every last drop of him.

We pull apart finally for desperate gulps of air. I rub my temples, trying to thwart off a bad case of brain freeze.

"Look," says Jake, carefully taking my hands in his. "There's a question I want to ask you and I hope it doesn't, you know, freak you out."

"Don't tell me." I squint to keep his head from floating. "You want to start seeing movies with me exclusively? Sorry, but I'm not ready for that kind of a commitment."

"I want to know what you're doing this weekend."

"Does the new James Bond open? 'Cause if it does, I can't go with you. I already promised it to my friend Laurie. And, as a general rule, I don't movie cheat."

"Be serious for a moment, okay?"

"Okay."

"A friend of mine is getting married this weekend in Boston. I wanted to know if you'd come to the wedding with me."

"Yes!"

I should have paused. I should have taken a moment, at the very least, to consider the implications, to understand this isn't just an invitation to enjoy a well-deserved, getaway vacation. It's an invitation to spend an entire weekend—and maybe even a hotel room!—with an incredibly appealing man.

I shouldn't have sounded so eager.

Jake arches an eyebrow. "Really?"

"Oh, yeah. I love weddings!" I've been to two in my life. I was the flower girl for both.

"Huh." He slowly releases my wrists. "Great. 'Cause, see, my ex-girlfriend was supposed to come with me. And, well, I hadn't really given it much thought since we broke up. But, I think I put her down for the filet mignon. Do you like filet mignon?"

"Who doesn't like filet mignon?"

"Vegetarians."

Right.

He drops my hands. "Let's see if we can hail a cab." He steps onto the curb with two fingers outstretched.

A taxi pulls up at once. Jake holds open the door for me and I leap in excitedly, scurrying to the far end of the seat.

He hovers in the frame of the open door. I look up at him expectantly. This time, I'm pursing.

He heaves a deep sigh. "Good night, Sarah." He leans in and pecks me affectionately on the lips. "I'll see you on Friday."

He steps away and closes the cab door behind him.

chapter ten

Am I in love with Jake? I'm certainly in love with him this week. I love Jake because for the first time in six months, I'm busy. So exuberantly busy! I've returned to my daily gym schedule. And two days ago, Amanda handed me over a gift certificate she received last Christmas for a cut and a coloring at a new downtown hair salon (she's a fierce devotee to Bumble & Bumble and wouldn't dream of having her tresses sullied by unknown hands). And because unemployment allows for both the means and the motive for plenty of bargain-hunting, I find a fantastic Diane von Furstenberg dress off the rack at Century 21 for a steal. When I describe it over the phone to my mother (low-cut, clingy, almost sheer), she thinks it sounds perfect.

Even Laurie manages to sneak in a long lunch to accompany me to the nail salon for a quick manicure and pedicure. This is at her request, not mine. At my finest hour, I'm still a fidgety, neurotic mess with no nails left to speak of. I will have chewed off all my new nail polish before I even return home.

I'm also a little wary of having people touch my feet. Laurie, on the other hand, lifts up her foot obligingly from the basin beneath her. Her pedicurist attacks it with a loofah. Unfazed, Laurie flips through a magazine, probably hoping to see her picture under the fashion "Do" column. And fearing she might be featured in the "Don't." Either relieved or disappointed to find her photo in neither (I really can't tell), she tosses the magazine aside and picks up another.

"You want *Lucky* or *Vogue*?" she asks me.

"Neither. I don't read magazines anymore."

"Who said anything about reading? I said *Lucky* or *Vogue*."

I shake my head. "Can't do it. Magazines just make me want to buy stuff I can't afford. I'd rather not know what's out there. I'd rather have no taste, no class, and keep myself just above the poverty line."

"Take *Lucky* then. They've got specials in the back."

"Special deals on crap I don't even need? That's even worse. Then I feel obliged to buy it. Uh-uh. Hand me the *Post*."

Laurie blinks. "I'm sorry. Did you just ask for the *New York Post*?"

"Yup."

"What, you gonna do the crossword?"

"Better. The blind items."

"Ah," she grins. "A girl after my own heart."

She grabs the paper and generously folds it over to Page Six before handing it to me. "Hey, you ever figure out who the crack-smoking actress on Ludlow Street was?"

"I have my suspicions," I say coyly as I scan the print. Laurie doesn't press the issue any further. She flips open her magazine, which somehow prompts a new tangent.

"I can't believe you're missing the wrap party this weekend."

I roll my eyes. "Thanks, but I'd probably skip it anyway. I'm getting a little too old to keep crashing your wrap parties."

She looks up at me scornfully. "Old?"

"You know what I mean. I'm losing my air of mystery. By now, everybody recognizes me, and they know full well I had nothing to do with the film—"

"But, you did all the painting that day!"

"I would still feel like I'm intruding."

"You're nuts." She flips the page. "If we didn't want intruders, we'd bring a keg to the set and call it a night. The whole *point* of a wrap party is to have an excuse to invite pretty girls. I bring you, I'm actually doing everyone a favor."

I snort in response. If anyone really considers me a Pretty Girl, it's only because I meet the bare minimum requirements. I'm not grossly overweight, I have manageable hair and no major facial distortions. Even my breasts are just large enough to require a bra— but unless it's padded, I don't really see the point.

I'm a Pretty Girl when people talk in volumes. If ninety-nine scantily clad women are gyrating their hips on a dance floor, in the dark cellar of a nightclub, under pulsating lights, and I decided to join them—then, yes, you could safely say there were one hundred pretty girls on the dance floor. I am also a Pretty Girl by proximity. If I happen to stand close enough to Laurie, there's a good chance some of her sex appeal may rub off on me. If it's Amanda, I might even be able to adopt some semblance of her haughty glamor. But that's about it.

"Besides," Laurie continues, ripping a page out of the magazine and palming it in her jean jacket. "Andy Dick might be there."

"Oh, no, Laurie, please don't make out with Andy Dick. I'm not capable of helping you through a psychological ordeal of that magnitude."

"Eww!" She shudders. "I'm not going to make out with Andy Dick!"

"Thank God."

"I have my eye on Roald."

"No!" I swat at her magazine, demanding her full attention. She doesn't give it to me. "The cameraman?"

"He's not the cameraman. He's the *director of photography*."

"The German?"

"He's Flemish."

"But he's insane!"

"He's an *artist*."

"Does he even speak English?"

"Just barely." She folds the magazine over and studies the starlets on red carpets. "I think he's really sexy."

"Is it the accent? Don't tell me you've fallen for something that obvious."

"It's not the accent. It's the integrity. It's the artistic vision. It's the—" She cuts herself off and frowns, holding up the magazine to show me Jennifer Lopez's latest fashion mishap. I glance at it briefly, with no particular interest.

"It's what?" I persist.

"Hmmm?" She continues to sift through the pictures. "Oh, you know. DP's are just such bad boys. I can't help it. I just find that irresistible."

"Well, as long as you know what you're doing."

"I don't." The curtain of her thick, short bangs does nothing to hide the mischievous glint in her eye. "That's what makes it so exciting." She rips out another page. "But tell me about your guy."

"Oh, that." I squirm in my seat. The woman buffing my foot fixes me with a stern look. I hold my breath and try to stop fidgeting. "I already told you about him. He was the one I was supposed to replace at that job?"

"Right. That guy." She pauses between pages, as if her finger were stuck on a perfume sample. "Wait a second. You didn't take that job, did you?"

"No."

"He decided to stay after all?"

"I guess—"

"Because of you?"

"No, don't be ridiculous."

"Then why?"

"I don't know. He's a little confused. He's been having . . . um . . . personal problems."

Laurie blows out the side of her mouth and a wisp of bangs flutters away from her face.

"Uh-oh," she mutters. The page slides off her finger. "And what does he do exactly?"

"He . . . ummm." I tense my calf, willing it not to tremble. "Well, believe it or not, he wants to be a DP."

Laurie's eyes snap wider. "Uh-oh," she repeats.

The pedicurist taps my left foot. At her command, I lift it up and let my other foot drop back into the basin.

Laurie throws down her magazine and sighs heavily. She rolls her head around, cracking stiff muscles.

"Hey, any chance you came across that book I asked about? *Gideon?*"

"Laurie, you know how—"

"You don't have to say anything. If the answer is yes, you can, you know, wiggle your toes or something."

It takes an endless amount of self-control. But somehow or another, for an acceptable amount of time, I stop squirming and manage to remain perfectly still.

On the way back to my apartment, I decide once again to save myself the two-dollar subway fare by indulging in a leisurely stroll down Broadway. Mannequins in skimpy summer halter tops and titillating boy-cut underwear beckon from the window displays. With their demurely hidden faces and provocative stances, they seem not at all unlike the seductresses flashing their wares in a Red Light district. I suppose that would then make me the hapless tourist, my head buried in a hotel map, trying to ignore their evil temptations.

Until I stumble across an enticement even I cannot resist. And it hails from the deceptively unassuming storefront of Urban Outfitters.

S-A-L-E.

I pick up the pace and scurry on home.

When I return, I am forced to wait in an infuriatingly long line, with all the other suckers who've been lured inside. And to make matters even worse, the salesclerk who finally does offer to assist me displays no talent whatsoever for efficiency.

"When did you say you bought these?" she asks, smacking her gum and staring vacantly at the pair of jeans I've set on the counter in front of her.

"A couple of days ago. The guy said I could—"

"You remember what day?"

"Uh, no. Not exactly. But here, I have the receipt." I hand it over. She looks down at it, chewing absently.

"You remember who helped you?"

"It was a guy. He had curly hair."

"Mario!" she belts out. She shifts her gum to the side of her mouth. "Mario, can you get over here!"

We wait for a moment. I smooth out the creases of the jeans, trying to make them look as unworn as possible.

"Yeah?" says Mario, sidling up to the counter. I wouldn't have been able to pick him out of a lineup, but I recognize him now, thanks to the fact he's still wearing his manager tag.

"Hi," I say, smiling broadly. "I don't know if you remember me. You sold me these jeans a couple of days ago? You told me I could come back during a sale, and you'd refund the discount?"

"Is that right?" He holds up the jeans, hopefully noting the lack of wrinkles. "You bring the receipt?"

"Yup. I gave it to her," I nod at the gnawing saleswoman.

"Shouldn't be a problem." He turns to her. She twirls a curl of her hair girlishly. "You know how to ring this up?"

"Uh-uh," she shakes her head.

While they take a few moments to sort out the details of the transaction, I wait politely with my hands folded on the counter. And it occurs to me, in a bolt of horror, that I have now, officially, become my mother.

I've packed and repacked my overnight bag several times and something has to give. I'm going to have to decide between either the gym clothes or the pool clothes. I don't even know if the hotel will have either a gym or a pool. Besides, am I ready for Jake to see me in a bikini just yet?

I go with the gym clothes. Then that's it. I'm done. I do one last quick survey of my room to see if there is anything I've missed. The only thing to catch my eye is the stack of unopened and otherwise discarded mail on my desk. On top of it lies the Columbia University School of Law application I've been pretending doesn't exist.

I check my watch and groan. I've got over an hour to kill before Jake picks me up.

"All right, fine!" I grumble, picking up the application and ripping it open. A perfectly diverse trio of students graces the cover of the brochure. I flip the page, confronted again with more beaming young faces.

"Your parents must be so proud," I hiss back at them, turning the pages faster until I am safely in the application territory and far removed from those sickeningly beatific photos of baby-faced young lawyers.

I reach for a pen. Then, thinking the better of it, I reach for a cigarette instead. And after that, even better! My phone rings.

I balance my cigarette neatly on the rim of my ashtray and answer the phone on the third ring.

"Hello?"

"Hello, may I please speak to Sarah Pelletier?"

"This is Sarah."

"Sarah, hi. This is Kelly Martin. I'm calling from *Aspen Quarterly*?"

Now, where did I put that cigarette?

"Oh, *hi*, Kelly," I try stalling. This has got to be a joke. How is it possible? How could I have wanted something so badly—then have forgotten all about it? I clear my throat. "I wasn't expecting to hear from you by phone. But thanks so much for calling."

"I'm sorry if it's taken us a while to get back to you. We've been trying to set up phone interviews with all of our applicants. Do you have a moment?"

I should say no. I should say it's a bad time. It *is* a bad time.

"Of course." I settle back in the Aeron. My cigarette taunts me cruelly from the ashtray.

"So, Sarah, I see from your letter that you're eager to relocate. Have you been to Aspen before?"

"Oh, yes. A couple of times." Actually, I've never once been. But since I grew up only four hours away, I figure that's close enough to count. "I thought the town was lovely. Absolutely breathtaking." If you're into mountains, I guess.

"Yes, it's definitely beautiful here," she agrees. "But I should warn you. Aspen is seasonal. It can get very quiet here sometimes. It's nothing at all like New York."

"I wouldn't expect it to be."

"Can I ask why you want to leave?"

"Why I want to leave New York?"

"Yes."

Why do I want to leave New York?

"Well, Kelly, I'll be honest with you . . ." I play with the string of my blinds. The slats tilt up to reveal the pulsating neon Loew's sign across the street. "I'm kind of fed up with New York." The blue strobe light effect has become distracting. I pull my blinds back down again.

"Don't get me wrong," I continue. "I've enjoyed my experience here. But really, enough is enough. I think there is something seriously wrong with a city that has too much to offer, you know? I mean, I can see an underground, experimental film every night of the week at the Anthology Film Archives. But you know what? They're all guaranteed to be awful. And I can take my pick from any one of three weekly, so-called alternative newspapers, none of which will have anything insightful to say. Or I can torture myself every weekend by going to see a poorly acted, badly written, low rent, off-Broadway play." I can feel myself starting to ramble, so I try to shift back on track. "What I'm trying to say is that I wish I lived—and worked—somewhere where people could be a little pickier. I don't care anymore if things are new or fresh or original. I just want them to be *good*. I'd much prefer to explore those opportunities than to spend any more time wading through the crappy New York slush pile."

Perhaps, I've unloaded a tad too much?

"I see," Kelly says slowly. "Well, you know Aspen doesn't really have a lot to offer in terms of an underground film movement or alternative newspapers—"

"Sounds perfect."

"Uh-huh." She pauses. "Tell me, Sarah, are you an active person?"

"Oh, yes. Very active." After all, I've been to the gym every day this week.

"Really? What kind of sports do you like?"

"Well, I like to—" Ski? Hike? Skydive? "Rollerblade."

"Oh. I see . . ." I can hear her rifle through pages. "Just one last question, Sarah. I was wondering what drew you to our magazine in the first place. Are there any particular features or writers or columns that interest you in particular?"

"Ummm . . ." Oh, shit.

"Have you read *Aspen Quarterly*?"

Yes! Say yes!

"No," I confess. "But I've been meaning to. It seems to have sold out at all the newsstands." So much for a city that has too much to offer. "But," I add quickly. "I did ask Barnes & Noble to call me when the next issue comes in." Do they even put magazines on hold? One wonders.

"Oh," says Kelly. "I see."

After we hang up, I immediately call my mother.

"I just blew another interview."

"How is that possible? I just spoke to you half an hour ago."

I explain the phone call.

"Oh, sweetie-pie, that's just terrible! Think how perfect Aspen would have been. You would have been only four hours away from us. You sure you can't call them back? Maybe you could reschedule an interview for a better time?"

"I'm not sure that's how it works."

"Damn! That's such a shame. We could have visited you on the weekends. And you could've come home whenever you wanted to . . ."

Hmm. I hadn't thought of it that way. Suddenly the loss doesn't seem quite so devastating.

"Okay, Mom, well thanks for putting things in perspective."

"You know, sweetie-pie . . ." I can sense her trying to broach a new subject tactfully. Which is never a good sign. "If you're really serious about leaving New York, maybe you *should* just come back home for a couple of weeks?"

"But, Mom, I *don't* really want to leave New York."

She sighs. "That's what I thought."

We hang up. I reach over to salvage what little remains of my dying cigarette. It strikes me as oddly amusing: Aspen, with its fancy resorts and condescending mountains and its exclusive little upscale community had sounded like the perfect oasis. I never thought of it as actually *going home. Blech!* The very idea makes my skin crawl. Thank God that disaster was so artfully averted.

Jake calls me on his cell phone from downstairs an hour later. I scurry breathlessly down four flights and meet him at his car. He takes my overnight bag from me and tosses it into the backseat.

"That's all you brought?"

"Yeah, I like to travel light." Big, fat lie. The reason I have only the one bag is because I don't want him to think I'm too fussy. If I've learned anything from over a decade of trying to impress boys, I've learned that I'd much rather have them discover all my major character flaws slowly, and over a good length of time.

Jake helps me into the car and then trots around to climb into the driver's side. He fastens his seat belt and waits. I turn to find him looking at me, smiling in a way that makes me want to bat my eyelashes.

"I really like your highlights."

"Thanks."

He peers in a little closer. "Did you lighten your eyebrows, too?"

"No!" I say, indignant. Of course I lightened my eyebrows. But he's not supposed to notice *that*.

He starts the car. Soft, ruminating music wafts from his speakers, and a dry male voice croons a melancholy tune.

Uh-oh.

"You can change the CD if you want," he says, pulling into traffic. "The case is under your seat."

"No, no. This is fine," I insist, trying hard not to panic.

I am so unbelievably stupid. A downright idiot. It should have occurred to me earlier that I am in no way, shape, or form ready to be going on a road trip with Jake. Traffic getting out of the city is guaranteed to be a tense, nightmarish ordeal, at best. And conversation will most likely be strained. But all that I can deal with. What I cannot deal with are the tests, the pop quizzes—because at some point or another, Jake is going to ask me to pick a radio station, or suggest I select one of his CDs, and I'm either going to have to play dumb or finally break down and confess that I have terrible taste in music.

How do I know my taste in music is so atrocious? Well, I'll tell you. I once dated a guy in college who tried desperately to indoctrinate me into the cult of Bob Dylan. One night he played "Lay, Lady, Lay" for me. I cried.

Ever since then, I've had it with the weepy, heartaching stuff of the chronically miserable. I don't like it when a song knocks me in the chest and shatters the steel plate of cynicism I spent a good many teenage years trying to construct. If music can make me feel remotely human, if it provides me with any sense of communal understanding, I want no part of it.

From what I gather, there are some people who hear songs like Simon and Garfunkel's "America" and they get nostalgic—misty-eyed, even—for the flower-scented, bygone years of the sixties. What do I know of the sixties? I hear "America" and I get nostalgic for Cameron Crowe's *Almost Famous*. And frankly, that's just how I prefer it.

Jake merges the car onto the expressway and collects his ticket from the tollbooth. Five minutes later, the moment of truth descends. The CD stops. Jake ejects it from the player and hands it to me.

"Do you mind putting this back in the case?" he asks.

"Yeah, okay." I reach under my seat and pull out a massive black tome—weighted down even more so by its threat to expose all my inadequacies.

I take the CD from Jake's outstretched hand and quickly find an empty slot in the album for it.

"See anything in there that looks good to you?"

Crap, crap, crap.

"Ummm," I flip through the sleeves, dismayed to discover I don't recognize the name of a single band. "Anything you like is fine with me."

"I like them all. They're *my* CDs. What do you like?"

"Uh, mostly I like sound tracks," I say, hoping that will at least buy me some time.

"Sound tracks, huh?"

"Yup."

"Okay." He thinks for a moment. "Which sound tracks?"

Oh, goddamn him!

"Hmm . . . I really liked *High Fidelity*."

Jake nods appreciatively. "All right. Put in the Beta Band. It's on the first page."

I pick out the disc and slip it into the player. Within seconds, the speakers begin to purr a rather catchy song. I cock my head to the side, listening intently.

Jake watches me out of the corner of his eye and grins. "It's 'Dry the Rain.'"

"Huh?"

"You know. When John Cusack is at the record store and he says, 'I will now sell five copies of the Beta Band?' This is the song he plays."

"Oh, yeah!" I lean back in my seat, letting the music warm me over and take me back. And I fondly recall just how much I love Jack Black in those goofy sidekick roles.

I am disappointed when the CD ends.

"What next?" I ask Jake eagerly.

"How do you feel about *The Royal Tenenbaums*?"

"Loved it."

"Great. Put in Nick Drake."

I do as requested. And I am thrilled that I recognize the first song immediately.

"Hey, this is from that car commercial!"

Jake sears me with a reproachful glare. My heart stops. Only when he cracks a devilish grin do I realize he's teasing me. I breathe a little easier.

The wedding ceremony is perfect in the way all ceremonies should be. It's short. Minimal hymns, a brief, funny anecdote by way of the priest, only one reference to a "holy union," and a slight rough patch as the groom stutters his way through a set of generic vows. The service concludes with cheers from the audience—not because we've borne witness to such a moving tribute to love everlasting, but because it is now officially time to get rip-roaring drunk.

We all file out to the reception area where two options present themselves. Long line for the restroom or long line for the bar. Jake and I skip both and duck outside behind the church for a cigarette break.

It doesn't take long for our fellow smokers to join us. Like most social pariahs, smokers are drawn to one another—either psychically or chemically, one can only guess. Without even a glance, or a secret handshake, or any verbal exchange, we tend to seek each other out, meet at clandestine headquarters staked just outside the doors that bar our entrance, and we huddle together, as if by campfire, letting our burning filters warm our hands and our hearts.

The first of our comrades to find us is the best man, a tall, wiry surfer or skateboarder type with shoulder-length brown hair slicked back with goop for the occasion. Hot on his heals trails the token fat bridesmaid.

"Yay! More smokers!" she squeals. "I thought we'd be the only ones."

"Yeah, we're a dying breed," Jake quips.

"If I ever get married, I'm going to insist on smoking and non-smoking sections at my reception," she giggles.

"Jake!" The best man slaps him on the back. Jake responds the same. "Long time no see. How've you been, man? I got that last e-mail you sent. Pretty sweet."

Jake looks confused. "What e-mail?"

"You know, with the girl? And that butterfly tattoo? Ouch. That's gotta be painful, putting it . . . down there."

"Eww!" the bridesmaid gasps.

Jake smiles at me and shakes his head. "He's joking."

"Or am I?" The best man winks at me. "Hey, I don't believe we've met."

"Oh, sorry," says Jake. "Skeeter, this is Sarah. Sarah, this is Skeeter."

"And I'm Rachel!" says the bridesmaid, fumbling to light her cigarette.

"Sarah." Skeeter takes my hand and plants an exaggerated kiss on my wrist. "So you must be the girl we've all heard so much about."

My heart flutters. I look up at Jake in awe. He *talks* about me?

"Ah, no," says Jake. "She couldn't make it."

All of our jaws drop simultaneously.

"I mean, we broke up," he corrects himself quickly. "A couple of weeks ago. This is Sarah. She's a friend."

We all remain silent. The door behind us swings open and the wedding photographer, with a guilty cigarette clenched between his teeth, stands in the portal. Because his hands are otherwise occupied, he thrusts up his head by way of a greeting.

"I wondered where you guys were hiding."

Skeeter leans in to offer him a light. To shield the flame with his hands, the photographer sets down his camera and tripod. Jake peers over to admire it.

"That medium format?" he asks.

"Yeah. Hasselblad." He sizes Jake up out of the corner of his eye. "You a photographer, too?"

"I dabble."

"Oh, yeah, that's right!" Skeeter snaps his fingers. "You wanted to make movies or something, right? How's that been going for ya?"

Jake shrugs. "Just waiting for the big break. Right now, I'm still at the same ad company, shooting commercials."

"Which company?" asks Rachel.

"Stellar Productions?"

"Sure, I know Stellar. I'm in advertising too. J. Walter Thompson."

Alarm bells start ringing in my ears. Well-honed instinct tells me this is the part of the conversation I'd best steer clear of. I make a big display of noticing my cigarette has petered out and look for an appropriate place to dispose of it. I tiptoe to the bushes.

"And what about you?" I hear Jake ask Skeeter. "You were at Toyota the last time we spoke, right?"

"Honda," Skeeter corrects.

"No kidding? You've got that new hybrid coming out now, don't you?"

"A couple of them. And, oh man, let me just tell you. *Fifty-two* miles to the gallon."

Jake whistles. "Nice."

Thinking it's safe to return, I step out from behind my fortress of bushes. Unfortunately, the question I had been so keen to avoid still awaits me.

"And what do you do?" Rachel asks me pleasantly, dropping her cigarette to the ground and tapping it out daintily with her blue dyeable shoe.

"Um," I cast a sideways look at Jake. He nods at me encouragingly.

"I'm unemployed."

Now, maybe I just imagined it, but I could have sworn I heard a gasp. And I'm sure I saw Skeeter and Rachel exchange a look of panic.

"Shit," Skeeter says, grimacing with compassion. "That sucks."

"Fucking economy," the photographer adds helpfully.

Rachel shakes her head. "The market is still so terrible these days. I feel like everyone I know has lost their job." She sighs. "I guess some of us just got lucky."

The door behind us lurches and we all swivel gleefully to welcome another diversion. Under the awning, an oafish usher wipes the sweat from his brow and smears it on his tuxedo lapel.

"You guys," he gasps. "They're doing the speeches."

"All right." Skeeter smooths down his greasy, lubricated head. "It's showtime."

I hardly fare any better once indoors. As luck would have it, we've been seated at a table next to Lindsay and Colin, both investment bankers. They, too, hail from New York, but from where they're perched, in penthouse suites with rooftop gardens and wraparound terraces, it's an entirely different city. They couldn't be more foreign to us if they were tourists sporting Panama hats and slathered in multiple coats of white sunblock.

Across the table are Phil, the lawyer, and his girlfriend, Maribella, an Italian sculptor from Italy. They met on the Internet through a dating service. She doesn't speak a word of English. I wish I had thought of such a clever excuse. Instead, I manage to avoid actively participating in the conversation at hand by repeatedly flagging down the waiter to refill my wineglass.

The couple to our right introduces themselves next, but I don't catch their names. I am numb with dread, realizing it's only a matter of time before the circle completes itself. Jake and I are the only ones at the table yet to entertain our viewers with the *TV Guide* episode recap of our lives:

Heartbroken boy with a great eye for photography invites lonely, unemployed girl to a friend's wedding in hopes of staving off her suicidal tendencies.

"Excuse me," I say quietly and to no one in particular. I stand and carefully skulk away from the table.

A sudden hush falls over the trees when I step outside. It is as though I've interrupted them in the middle of their catty gossip—the elm having just snootily remarked how terribly unclassy it is for girls to forgo pantyhose on even a sultry summer night. The shrubs perhaps wondering why slips are no longer so popular.

I light up my cigarette. The leaves shake their heads and mutter, "Tsk, tsk."

"I can't believe you abandoned me like that!"

I turn. Jake emerges from the shadows, holding two flutes of champagne. The tapering pink light from the entrance dances in the bubbles.

"What abandoned? You looked like you were having a fine time with that Italian artist."

"Maribella? You kidding me? She's got no sense of humor. Didn't laugh at a single one of my jokes."

I look at him cock-eyed. "She doesn't speak English."

"So? I was talking very loudly." He holds out one of the flutes. I take it from him. "You're having a terrible time, aren't you?"

"No, not at all." I take a small sip. "I just forgot how hard this would be."

"Is it because you don't have a job?"

"Let's put it this way. The last party I went to was a pink-slip party. I just feel like I had more in common with that crowd."

"Look, I don't know why you're letting this get to you. You've seen how impressed people are when I tell them what I do, and you know my job is crap—"

"That's different."

"Let me finish. All I'm saying is, those people in there bragging about their wonderful jobs? They're *lying*. Because you don't know any better. I don't know any better either. But I can tell you one thing. *Nobody* likes their job. And that's a fact."

"So, what am I supposed to do? Go back in there and start lying, too? Pretend I have a job?"

"Why not?

"Because I can't imagine anything more pathetic." I stamp out my cigarette effectively.

"Fine. Then don't talk about it all. You don't have to." He spreads out his hands. "I just came out here to tell you there's nothing to worry about anymore. The band is playing now." He pauses. "And I wanted to know if you'd dance with me."

I fold my arms over my chest.

"*Can* you dance?" I ask.

"Ha! Please." He offers me his elbow. "Don't insult me."

We catch the tail end of the opening number—the timeless crowd-pleaser, "Twist and Shout." To continue the rocking tempo, the band transitions into a passionate rendition of "Tutti Frutti."

Jake leaps onto the dance floor and executes a flawless spin, the unbuttoned flaps of his suit jacket fanning out behind him. He halts himself with a nimble toe and holds out his hand.

"Come on!"

I grab his wrist. Off we go.

He's a remarkable dancer, much to my relief. Graceful, limber—and most importantly, he displays an excellent sense of rhythm. Now, see, I can chassé, jeté, and pas de bourrée with the best of them, mind you, but I am also the first to admit my timing is a bit shaky. Ask me to fling alternate kicks to the beat of "New York, New York" and I've got a fifty-fifty shot at getting it right. The odds drop sharply, though, as soon as a boy grabs my waist, when he reaches around and places a firm hand on my back. That's when anxiety sets in and my ear for the music goes stone-deaf. If I'm lucky, I'll just spend the rest of the song playing catch up with the beat. If I'm unlucky, I'll hit the ground and take my partner with me.

With Jake, I find myself dancing to a different tune. When he twirls me around, I feel like I'm sailing on linoleum, flying with champagne wings. And when he lifts me up from a playful dip, I'm so overcome with giddiness, I reach up and plant a quick peck on his lips.

Jake's eyebrows shoot up. "Wow." He touches his lips self-consciously. "I wasn't expecting that."

"I'm not going to apologize," I say coyly, wrapping my arms around his neck. "I've wanted to do that all evening."

"Yeah?" He grins mischievously. "Know what I've been wanting to do?" He slides his hands from my waist down to my rear and squeezes hard. Just as I'm about to gasp, he plunges his tongue deep into my mouth. The kiss is so electric, I see a blinding flash of white light.

I blink my eyes a few times to regain my sight. The wedding photographer, not three feet away from us, lowers his camera and clucks his tongue.

"That's it," he says. "That's the money shot right there." He shrugs good-naturedly and struts off.

"Hey, hold on!" Jake calls after him, letting go of my waist. Just as I feared, I nearly drop to the floor.

The photographer turns and waits. Jake dips into his jacket pocket and retrieves his wallet.

"What are the chances I could ask you to send me a copy of that picture directly? If I give you my e-mail address?" He holds out his business card. "I'll pay you for it."

The photographer takes the business card but waves away the cash.

"I'll see what I can do," he says.

There is a discernible shimmy in Jake's step when he returns. By the time he reaches me, he's already in full swing. Grinning from ear to ear, he takes me by the hand and twirls me around. And when I stop spinning, he's ready to scoot seamlessly into a shuffle.

"You're so good!" I say.

"My mom was a dancer in the Miami City Ballet. She made me take dance classes when I was little."

"You're joking!"

"Of course I'm joking." He spins me again with such panache, I do wonder whether or not he's telling the truth.

I fall back into his arms breathlessly. Yet the strong grip I expected to engulf me goes limp. I look up at him questioningly, afraid to find his features contorted in pain.

"Did I just step on your foot?"

"No." He leans me backward and nuzzles his face close to my ear. A delicious ripple travels down from my arched spine to my pointed toe.

"I think my high school girlfriend is heading over," he whispers. "When I pull you back up I want you to start dancing over to the end of dance floor, okay?"

"'K," I say.

"Quickly!"

He lifts me up—and plants me directly in front of a raven-haired pixie in an inappropriately short red dress.

"Jake?" She pulls back the silky drape of her hair with a long fingernail. "Jake Bleecker? No way!" She wraps her lithe arms around his neck.

"It's been a long time, huh?" She pats his stomach approvingly. "You look good."

Jake wiggles out of her grip. "Yeah, you, too." He shoots me a look. I shuffle from foot to foot. I'm in that awkward position. I'm not dancing and I'm not yet included in the conversation. I'm just the idiot standing in the middle of the dance floor.

"Sarah, this is Tina."

"Nice to meet you," I say.

Tina nods curtly in my direction and turns back to Jake. "So, what have you been up to lately? Last I heard, you were at an advertising company?"

"Yeah. Still there. You?"

"Didn't you hear? I just left *Marie Claire*. I'm now the new fashion editor at *Charm* magazine."

"Oh, wow!" I say. "That's fantastic." I look at Jake to see if he's as impressed as I am. He isn't.

"Yeah, it's not so bad." She angles herself toward me slightly, the greatest effort she's made yet to acknowledge my existence. "So, are you, like, a photographer, too?" she asks.

"Oh, no. Not me."

She raises an eyebrow. I say nothing.

"What do you do?" she asks.

"I'm a Rockette."

Her eyes widen. I wait expectantly for her to start guffawing. But instead, her smile dips and turns quizzical. She tilts her head to study me carefully—the dark hair, the five-foot-four frame, all torso, short legs. She must know I'm lying.

Doesn't she?

Oh my God. I've hit gold!

Tina's expression goes from blank to distant. "Oh hey, you guys, sorry, you'll have to excuse me." Her eye wanders aimlessly over the crowd. "I think Sammy is on his fourth glass of champagne. I want to say hi while he still recognizes me." She tosses us an unapologetic flip of her hair and dances off to the music.

"Sheesh." Jake chuckles. "I'm sorry. I had no idea. Here I

thought taking you to a party to go dancing would be fun. But it must be just like another day at work for you, huh?"

"No way. I've always hated having to perform other people's steps. This is great. It gives me a chance to really be creative and try out all those new moves I've been working on."

"Yeah? Like what?"

"Nothing I'd dare try without proper stretching."

The music stops abruptly. For a couple of seconds, the band struggles with an awkward transition. I realize, with a slight twinge of horror, that they've segued into the eighties portion of the program.

"Yes!" Jake's fist shoots up in the air in a classic end-of-the-movie freeze-frame. "Karma Chameleon!" He bobs his head excitedly. I can't quite match his enthusiasm, so while he crisscrosses the room with ecstatic little hops, I entertain myself by trying to execute a complicated pirouette.

Much to my surprise, I stick the landing perfectly. Half-expecting a smattering of applause, I turn to face the crowd. Jake, however, is nowhere to be found. Instead, I am facing a pink-faced girl in a green satin dress. She stares at me wide-eyed.

"Are you the Rockette?"

"*Former* Rockette," I correct her as I continue dancing. "They cut me this month 'cause I didn't make the weight requirement. Can you believe it?"

Her brow furrows. She's not sure what to believe.

"Here," I offer, hiking up my skirt. "Wanna see my high kick?"

With that, I let loose with a kick that would put the entire rag-tag team of dollar-a-day hoofers in *A Chorus Line* to shame. It's a kick that isn't part of the show—it *is* the show. Perfectly arched foot, pointed toe, taut thigh. A long, lean leg fueled with such passion it reaches up for the sky—

And keeps on going. I watch in panic as it soars clear over my head, the folds of my dress catapulted behind it. The next thing I know, a sharp stab of pain hits my tailbone. And all is dark.

I scurry to yank my dress down to a less compromising position. When I remove the fabric from over my eyes, what should I see but Jake—sweet, darling Jake—holding my shoe and howling with laughter. I glare at him furiously.

"Do you mind helping me up?" I stick out my hand. "I think I pulled something."

"I'm sorry." He wipes a tear from his eye, his shoulders still jerking with convulsive giggles. "Here." He hands me my shoe and hoists me up. "You okay?"

"Yeah. Fine," I snap, as I replace the slipper. He wraps an arm around my waist and helps me hobble off the dance floor.

"I think we should get you back to the hotel."

"We can't leave now. They haven't even cut the cake."

"We'll get dessert from room service."

"I want to stay," I insist.

"Wouldn't you rather order pay-per-view?"

"No. I'll be okay in a couple of minutes. I promise." I try to pull away from him, but my knee buckles. He hoists me closer to his hip.

"Come on. Let's get you out of here." He carts me off limping. And in my weakened condition, it's not exactly like I can resist him.

Once I've painfully succeeded in arranging myself into a flat, prone position under the covers, I can start to feel the sore muscles in my back relax and a warm wave of pleasant inertia spread over the rest of my body. I nestle my head against two thick pillows and close my eyes, listening to Jake's voice drifting toward me from the other side of the room.

"Yes. Hi. I'm in room 312. I'd like to order strawberry short-cake and . . . what do you want?"

I roll over and open one eye. "Chocolate," I murmur, rubbing my cheek against the satin pillowcase.

"Chocolate mousse?"

"Mmm. Sounds wonderful."

"And a chocolate mousse," he says into the telephone. I struggle to prop myself up against the headboard and pick up the remote control on the nightstand beside me. I click a couple of buttons. Nothing happens.

"Here," Jake takes it from me. He hits a few more buttons and the TV finally turns on. "You know what you want to watch?"

"What's on?"

"There are all those pay-per-view movies. Or . . ." He flips through the channels. "Hey, check it out! *Tootsie* is on!"

"Oooh! Let's watch that." I snuggle deeper under the sheets.

Jake puts down the remote. He's still fully dressed, perched on the end of the bed as far away from me as possible. I peer out of the corner of my heavy eyelids and watch him slowly unthread the tie from around his neck.

I am fast asleep before room service even knocks on the door. But just before I slip into unconsciousness, I do remember smacking my lips and thinking that chocolate mousse will make an excellent breakfast.

chapter eleven

I have no idea how long our drive to Boston might have taken. I simply never bothered to check the time. Because even if we were stalled in heavy traffic, at least our conversation flew at lightning speed, often punctuated with quick interruptions and gleeful cries of "me too!"

Our ride home is different. I count each brand-new minute as it flickers once and becomes a steady green unit on the radio dial. The seconds I have to imagine on my own—*tick, tick, tick.*

Jake and I have exhausted our entire reserve of movie quotes, and creating an altogether original conversation is an effort we can't quite muster. Right now, I am just tired and cranky enough to dare assert myself.

"I'm turning on the radio," I announce, fangs bared, ready to attack if he even tries to argue with me.

Jake shrugs. "Fine with me."

I lean forward and eject the CD, thus silencing the husky-voiced boy who has been whining about being misunderstood for the last half an hour. It pleases me to no end that I can stick him in a sleeve and slide him under my chair, where he can rot and fester with the rest of his unhappy, self-pitying friends.

A quick scan through the radio stations, however, does nothing to lift my spirits.

"You ever feel like listening to the radio is like trying to pick a movie from the video store when all the good stuff has already been rented?" I demand.

"Hey, turn it back."

"What? To this?" I flip back a station and tilt my head, trying to place a familiar song. "Wait a second. This is Elton John. You can't be serious."

"You don't like Elton John?"

"Does anyone?"

"Yeah. I do. That surprises you?"

"No."

"It does, doesn't it? You don't think it's cool enough."

To be honest, that's exactly what I thought. I've never paid much mind to Elton John one way or another. I had just assumed I wasn't *allowed* to like him.

"What do I know from cool?" I say grumpily. Still, I turn up the volume, feeling generous enough to give the song the benefit of the doubt.

"Hold on. Did he just say 'sugar bear'?"

"I believe he did," Jake says cheerfully.

"Well, that's a little sappy, isn't it?"

"You hear what you want to hear. But obviously you're not paying attention." He turns up the volume. With his eyes half-closed, his hands gripping the steering wheel, he belts out the lyrics with the kind of emotion I never imagined him capable of. I shake my head ruefully.

"What are you grinning at?" he demands.

"You. I never figured you for a love song kinda guy."

Jake groans. "You really disappoint me, Sarah. This isn't a love song. This is a big fuck-you to a woman he's leaving at the altar. When he says, 'sugar bear'? He's being facetious. There. Does that make you feel better? Now that you can keep your oh-so-cool cynicism intact?"

I feel my face burn. Not because he's proven me wrong. But because he's figured me out so right. I listen intently to the lyrics, trying to find a way to save face.

"Okay, fine." I say suddenly. "So it's not a love song. Then who is the 'someone' who saved his life tonight?"

"I thought that was obvious." He grins. "It's you."

Is he being facetious? It's so hard to tell these days.

I don't know how much credit Elton John—or, more specifically, "Someone Saved My Life Tonight"—is due, but when we finally enter New York City, when the glittering George Washington Bridge raises its arm over the horizon and waves us on in, Jake and I sigh contentedly, the miseries of a long, slow car ride all but forgotten.

It feels good to be home.

Jake pulls off the West Side Highway and coaxes his car a few blocks further before we finally come to a halt in front of my apartment building. I reach over to the backseat and pull up my bag.

"Man, I don't envy you having to go back out in that traffic."

"No. It'll be miserable."

"How long's it going to take you to get back to Brooklyn?"

"With traffic like this? An hour? An hour and a half?"

"Eeck."

"I know."

Then it falls upon us. The thick, dead weight of the pre-farewell silence. The car fills with fumes of dread.

"You know," I say lightly. "You don't have to go back if you don't want to. You're welcome to spend the night at my apartment."

Jake stares hard at his steering wheel. I can feel myself starting to falter.

"I mean, it's not like we haven't shared a bed before," I add. "Last night wasn't so bad, was it?"

"I don't know. You've got a pretty powerful snore."

My mouth drops open. I'm mortified and I don't even bother trying to conceal it. Jake breaks into his impish grin and laughs.

"I'm just kidding. You were fine." He nods pensively. "All right. I'll stay. You go up and I'll park the car."

"That's ridiculous. We'll both park and go up together."

It takes us close to another hour to find a spot.

Tired, spent, and ravaged by an entire day's worth of traveling, we shuffle into my apartment only to find Amanda sitting cross-legged on the sofa, in the thoughtful process of selecting the very best Cheetos from out of the bag. She looks up and smiles guiltily.

"Whasshup?" she asks, trying to sound nonchalant. Her slur gives her away.

I drop my bag to floor with a thud. *Of course* she would be home tonight. I fold my arms over my chest, not pleased.

"Where's what's-his-name?" I ask her.

Amanda frowns. "Early conferesh meeting tomorrow. He couldn't stay. But . . ." she points her bare, blue-polished toe at the expensive wine bottle on the coffee table in front of her. It's empty. "He sends his apologies." Amanda squints her eyes, finally noticing Jake standing behind me. "Hey, who are you?"

"I'm Jake." He casts me a sideways glance.

Amanda looks him over. "I'm sorry. Where are my manners?" She yawns and stretches her arms over her head, exposing the soft, supple hollow below her rib cage. "Do you wanna drink? I think there might still be beer in the fridge." She tosses her blonde locks. "You look like a beer drinker to me."

Whether or not Jake knows it—whether or not Amanda knows it—this is definitely a test. And he better pass it.

"I'm good," says Jake. I exhale with relief and grab his elbow, leading him to my bedroom.

"Good night, Amanda," I say deliberately. I close my bedroom door behind me.

Jake turns his back and unloads the contents of his pockets onto my desk. He pulls out car keys from the front pocket, a cell phone from his back pocket. He fishes out a handful of change from yet another pocket. Then it's assorted credit cards, more coins. No wonder boys don't carry purses. How deep do those pockets go?

"So." He stacks his quarters into a neat little pile. "Where'd you meet her?" he asks, jerking his head at the door.

Great. Amanda. My favorite topic of conversation. I kick off my shoes and sink down on the bed, waiting for Jake to join me. He opts for the Aeron instead.

"Oh, you know. We knew each other in high school. Vaguely. Then we bumped into each other one fateful day at Starbucks, summer after college. Found out we'd both be moving to the same city . . . and, well, one thing led to another—"

"Sounds romantic."

"Doesn't it?"

"How long you been living together, then?"

"I dunno. Three years?"

He whistles. "Wow!"

"What? You don't like her?"

"I'm sorry. I know I judge people too quickly. Does that offend you?"

Offend me?

"No, no," I say. "I'm the same the way. It's just that, I mean, a lot of guys think she's cute—"

"Seems to me *she's* the one who thinks she's so cute. But I can see how some guys would fall for that. Most men will believe anything a girl tells them."

"But not guys like you?"

"Definitely not guys like me."

He doesn't like Amanda!

Right then and there, I decide to sleep with him.

Of course, it's never that easy, and we don't actually sleep together. Sure, I lean over to kiss him and he not only meets me halfway, he leaps out of the chair and onto my bed and crawls on top of me. We giggle and wiggle, and somehow or another, I end up on top of him, and in the process, we kick over the sheets and the pillows fall off the side of the bed.

But before the belt is unfastened, I stop. I roll away from him with false modesty and fling a troubled arm over my eyes.

"We shouldn't be doing this."

"What?" Jake straightens. The look of panic in his eyes almost makes me want to laugh. I bite my tongue. "What's the matter? Did I do something wrong?"

"No," I sigh. "It's not that." I remove my arm from over my forehead and try to look troubled. "I just worry that this might be wrong for you. I mean, obviously you've had a pretty traumatic breakup, and well . . ." God, I hope I sound even remotely sincere. "I just don't want you to feel like I'm rushing you into anything you might not be ready for."

"Hey," he says, brushing his lips lightly against my shoulder.

"Hey, look at me." He tilts up my chin and kisses me on the nose. "I'm fine. Really."

And so, I unfasten his belt. More kissing and groping ensues.

But before the bra is unhooked, he stops. He rolls onto his back and stares at the ceiling. I clutch the sheets around my chest and sit up.

Now what did I do?

"What's wrong?" I ask.

He sighs. "I hate that you said that."

"What? What did I say?"

"I hate that you think you're pushing me. I don't want you to be worried about this in any way. If you don't think the time is right—I mean, for either of us—then maybe now's not the time to do this."

"No, no, no. I'm okay now."

And so, more kissing, more groping. More hesitation and more indecision. By four o'clock in the morning, we're both so exhausted, we decide to smoke one last cigarette and go to sleep.

I wake up in the morning and blink until my sight starts to rack into focus. I can make out Jake's form perched at the edge of the bed. Seconds later I can tell he's fully dressed and cradling a phone receiver in the crook between his neck and his shoulder. And then the garbled words of his conversation gradually begin to make sense.

"I'm just running a little late . . . I had problems returning the rental car. It's all taken care of now . . . I'm on my way." He hangs up.

I stretch my bare arms skyward and yawn loudly.

"You leaving me?"

Jake turns. "I woke you up?"

"Nah, I was up anyway."

He smiles and crawls toward me. "I'm not leaving just yet." He runs his finger down the line of my arm. I shiver.

"You cold?" he asks.

"Yeah, a little," I lie.

He pulls the sheets up to my chin and rubs my shoulders. "Better?"

"Much."

He leans down to kiss me, a kiss without urgency, a kiss without the fury and panic of impending sex. Just a kiss.

I don't know how long the kiss lasts. It falls into that strange span of time that is both endless and not long enough. We pull apart sadly and lick our lips. I reach for my discarded shirt on the floor.

"I'll show you out."

We linger in the foyer, still kissing. As far as I know, we've kissed our way over here. Jake reaches around his back and opens the front door. Reality walks in, tips his hat, and makes himself at home.

We pull apart for good. I'm afraid to ask when I'll see him again. I'm afraid I'll sound like too much of a girl.

"Listen," Jake rubs my arms. "I can't see you tonight."

I swallow the lump forming in the back of my throat. "Okay."

"I have to go back to Brooklyn. I need to feed my cat. But I'll call you later."

I nod. He kisses my forehead.

And then he's gone.

I close the door on an empty hallway and feel myself slowly deflating. The entire stretch of an empty day looms before me. I don't think I've ever felt this alone.

Fortunately, though, like Snow White lost in the forest, I do find solace in the form of seven diminutive companions—Lysol, Pine-Sol, Windex, Tilex, Clorox, Pledge, and Swiffer. The plight of a lonely housewife is becoming all too real for me, and it makes me slightly queasy. Or maybe I should stop inhaling toxic cleaning supplies.

True to his word, Jake calls me when he gets to the office just to say hello. His faraway, disconnected voice only serves to make me feel lonelier.

And then, on top of it all, I get an unexpected phone call only a few minutes later.

"Hello. May I speak to Sarah, please?"

"This is Sarah."

"Sarah, this is Jeanie. I am calling from Dr. Cohen's office?"

My heart sinks. Great. As if things weren't bad enough, now someone is calling to tell me I'm dying. I should have known.

But then I remember—I no longer have health insurance. I haven't seen a doctor in years. So, for the time being, at least I can rest assured that even if I were dying, no one would be calling to tell me so.

"Oh, hi, Jeanie!" I vamp. "Thanks for so much for calling." But what for?

"Sure, Sarah. No problem. I would have called sooner, but Dr. Cohen has been very busy lately. He has an opening tomorrow afternoon, though, if you'd like to set up an interview."

"Tomorrow is fine." I think. I think real hard. "Where are you located again?"

"We're on Sixth Avenue between Fifty-sixth and Fifty-seventh Streets?" Jeanie reminds me. I hate to tell her, but it doesn't sound at all familiar to me. "Oh, and can you e-mail me a copy of your résumé?"

"Of course," I say. She gives me her e-mail address and we hang up. For a moment, I stare off into space, waiting for my memory to trigger some inkling of recognition.

Dr. Cohen?

The phone still dangles in my hand. I stare at it for a moment. Finally, I suck up the nerve to dial the dreaded number.

"Hello?"

"Hey, Mom. Do you know anyone named Dr. Cohen?"

"Nope. Let me check with Dad . . . Steven!" She shrieks directly into the phone. "Do we know a Dr. Cohen?!"

A third phone line clicks open and enters the fray.

"He's Carl's cousin. Remember? At the biomedical firm? He needs a new secretary? How could you have forgotten? Carl pulled so many strings to get you that interview!"

"I'm sorry," I say, assuming he's talking to me. "That was a long time ago. It must have slipped my mind."

"What about getting health insurance? Did that slip your mind too?"

"Dad! I can't talk now! Dr. Cohen is expecting my résumé." I hang up. On both parties.

Any good interviewee will tell you that you don't go in cold for an interview. Even the bare minimum of background information is absolutely essential.

Once, in an interview for a job at a print magazine, I told my would-be employer that I was thrilled to be moving out of the field of online media. Using material I had rehearsed for hours the night before, I launched into a spiel about the emptiness and insignificance of online content—how the written word was always slave to the format. I said I was excited to finally pursue a job that was more intelligent and serious in nature. New media had always struck me as vastly unoriginal, and I was looking forward to working in an environment that would be both more structured and more creative. In fact, I had always felt stifled working for a website.

My interviewer waited for me to take a breath. I sensed I had expressed myself quite sufficiently when she finally put down her legal pad and stood.

"I think you've been misinformed," she said. "This *is* our online division. We're setting up an adjunct to our print magazine."

So, now I know. I've learned the hard way that you must cram for an interview the way you would for a final exam, for a class you're failing, for the last credit you need in order to graduate.

For my meeting with Dr. Cohen, the extent of my research is as follows:

I access the official, Pharmateque corporate website. I read the company profile. I call my mother.

"What's a hedge fund?" I ask her.

"I don't know. Let me ask your father. Steven!" She shrieks, again, *directly* into the phone. I hear muddled words in the background. "Something about risk . . . risk management . . . huh?" She gives up. "Hold on. I'm putting him on."

"No, don't—"

"It's like hedging bets," says my father, his babbling now somewhat more comprehensible. "It's a way for investors to pool their resources for investments that may seem risky. That way, if it pays off, it pays off big, but if it fails, you don't lose too bad. You get it?"

"Well, no. But thanks anyway."

We both abandon the conversation willingly before things get out of hand.

Sarah Pelletier

121 West 68th Street, Apt. 4B
New York, NY 10023
h: (212) 555-1476 c: (917) 555-9317
E-mail: s.pelletier@hotmail.com

WORK EXPERIENCE

2000–2002 *451Films.com* *New York, NY*
Administrative Assistant
- Created & updated databases to log submissions
- Researched & tracked competitive development through industry trades
- Provided fact-finding skills to research the validity of subject matter in project proposals
- Answered phones & operated switchboard
- Responsible for department scheduling, traveling, & expense reports

1999–2000 *NYC Film Fest* *New York, NY*
Assistant Programmer
- Responsible for the distribution of publicity materials
- Scheduled screenings & coordinated discussions and specialty panels
- Acted as liaison between filmmakers & festival sponsors

Summer 1998 *The Late Night Show* *New York, NY*
Office Intern
- Managed all aspects of daily office operations
- Assisted show producers with production needs
- Maintained & updated department databases

EXTRACURRICULAR ACTIVITIES

1997–1999 *The Brown Daily* *Providence, RI*
Writer
- Researched & covered campus arts events

EDUCATION

1996–2000 *Brown University* *Providence, RI*
BA in English
- Graduated Phi Beta Kappa
- GPA—3.8

SKILLS

- Type 50 wpm
- Proficient in Word, Excel, & Powerpoint

chapter twelve

You've been fooled again, haven't you? Still looks like the same damn résumé. But, *au contraire*! This one has the distinction of being my "Financial Résumé." Because I happen to be severely lacking in financial savoir faire—both professionally and in life—I've had to resort to a subtle trick. A trompe l'oeil, if you will. (Incidentally, my tendency to borrow so heavily from the French language is due, in part, to the fact that I've chosen to omit my skill as a fluent French speaker from the résumé at hand.)

But while we're on the subject of fancy words and phrases, let me try another one on you. How about *ampersand*, that funny little "&" symbol? If you'll notice, I've used it quite liberally. Such a dependence on funny little symbols suggests, albeit falsely, that I am comfortable working with numbers and equations. To wit, my GPA, a *3.8*, has now earned its own line. And my prowess at typing, a whopping *50* words per minute, is the first skill I've listed. I also toyed with adding my SAT score—1,510, if you really must know—but relying on the results of a test I took almost a decade ago seemed more of a liability than asset.

In all honesty, I can dress up my résumé with a thousand numbers, accessorize it with a million little symbols—but I will never be analytically chic. Don't believe me? Let the record show that there are several numbers I've neglected to include on my résumé, none of which have ever worked in my favor.

Total Number of Years of Higher Education: 4
Total Number of Years in the Workforce: 2
Weekly Gainful Employment Check: $567.50
Weekly Unemployment Check: $284.00
Total Number of Minutes in Daytime Cellular Plan: 400
Overage of Allotted Cell Phone Minutes: 82
Total Number of Résumés Sent Out: 27
Total Number of Job Prospects Therein: 0

I had originally imagined the Pharmateque Capital Headquarters as a blinding white clinical facility equipped with oxygen masks and rows of pressurized radiation suits. It's actually far worse than that. The office is located on the fifty-ninth floor of a midtown high-rise and has been fastidiously outfitted with marble floors, Brazilian rosewood furniture, and original artwork in gilded frames. I most certainly do *not* feel as though I belong here. I feel like an impostor in Amanda's Banana Republic suit.

While I wait for the busy Dr. Cohen to do me the dubious honor of pretending to interview me, I browse through the reading material in the lobby. Nothing really appeals to me. I select the *Financial Times* only because the pages are pink.

Moments later, a dazzling ray of white light crisscrosses the unread headlines of the page on my lap. When my eyes adjust to the unexpected flare, I see an outstretched hand in front of me, an enormous diamond ring reflecting light from off the glossy walls.

"Hi, Sarah. I'm Jeanie."

I shake the ring awkwardly, trying to deflect the beams away from my sensitive eyes. Jeanie's cherubic young face comes into focus.

"Dr. Cohen will see you now." Her sparkling finger beckons me hither.

I see now why Dr. Cohen might be in need of a new secretary.

The good doctor is startled by Jeanie's rap on his door. "Dr. Cohen?" Her tiny face disappears into his office. "Sarah is here to see you."

"Oh. Oh, right!" I hear him say. "Come on in." The magnetic pull of Jeanie's ring guides me into an office that seems to span the entire stretch of the city. A bank of wraparound windows makes it difficult to tell where the office ends and where Central Park begins.

Jeanie motions for me to sit and pulls back a matching chair for herself. Across the desk, Dr. Cohen straightens his glasses.

"Okay." He looks first at Jeanie, then at me. "So, um . . . how do I know you?"

I cast a glance at Jeanie. The geography of the office allows me to assume, perhaps incorrectly, that she's on my side. Jeanie nods her head at me encouragingly.

"Your cousin Carl is my father's business partner?"

"Right, right." Dr. Cohen nods. "You . . . um . . . have a résumé?"

I balk. I almost always bring an extra copy of my résumé just in case. Naturally, the one time it turns out I need it, I show up empty-handed.

"You have her résumé," Jeanie informs him, only a split second before I'm about to bolt and run. "It's in your left-hand in-box."

"Really?" Dr. Cohen shuffles through a stack of paperwork. He produces the elusive document and scans it thoroughly, as though this were the first time he has ever laid eyes on it. "Where'd you go to school?" he asks eventually.

"It should be on the bottom—"

"It's on the second page," says Jeanie.

Dr. Cohen gives me an admonishing look. It's the same look my mother gives me when I stub my toe and instinctively start screaming obscenities. It's the how-could-you look.

"You know, your résumé should really be on one page," he tells me.

My eyes narrow at the mere suggestion. Like I don't already know that. Like that isn't the first, most sacred rule for jobseekers.

I feign a gasp. My eyes widen in terror.

"It isn't on one page?" I ask, appalled. "It should be! It's on one page on *my* computer. The margins must have shifted when I e-mailed it to Jeanie." Thus I throw her the ball, letting her shoulder this terrible blame. After all, we're teammates, right?

"It's entirely possible." Jeanie waves her glittered hand dismissively. "My computer could have formatted it differently."

Dr. Cohen nods, appeased, and flips the page. I remain silent but smug, waiting for him to get a really good look at what school I went to. It won't be long now before he starts apologizing, truly sorry for having questioned my highly reputable, if not outrageously overpriced, education.

"Oh, okay. Brown. Phi Beta Kappa. Not bad." He folds his hands over my résumé, not too terribly impressed. "So, what exactly are you looking to do?"

"Well, I do have excellent communication and written skills. I'd be happy to put those to good use."

Dr. Cohen raises an eyebrow. "You know this is a finance firm, right?"

"Well, yes," I blush. "I know you deal with hedge funds and . . ." Don't say it. *Don't* say it. ". . . stuff." There, I said it. "But I know I am more experienced working with written documents, letters, memos . . ." I trail off. Is it, in fact, possible that Dr. Cohen has never had to write a single memo in his life? Is there a language I don't speak that communicates only in numbers, symbols, and double helixes?

"Jeanie," Dr. Cohen interrupts, bored with my litany of useless skills. "Do you know anyone in the office who might need a writer?"

"Uh." She stares down at her lovely, twinkling hand. I can feel her slipping away from me, our united front severed. "Not at the present time."

"I'll tell you what." Dr. Cohen puts my résumé back on top of his left-hand in-box and instantly forgets it ever existed. "How about if Jeanie gives you the names of our top headhunting agencies? We only use the very best. Would that help?"

"Thanks." I turn to Jeanie. "That would be great," I tell her icily. Traitor.

The doctor stands and extends his hand.

"It was good to meet you."

"It was good to meet you, too."

The interview concludes with one effective pump of a hearty handshake.

Fifty-nine floors later, I exit into the lobby and toss my list of the Very Best Headhunting Agencies into the trash can by the elevator. What good will it do me anyway? I know I will never be one of those pretty, bejeweled young corporate secretaries in sheer stockings who say things like, "It's in your left-hand in-box, Dr. Cohen," or "You mailed that out yesterday, Dr. Cohen," or "Your glasses are on top of your head, Dr. Cohen."

Who needs it, right?

On my way out through the rotating doors, I fish in my purse for my cell phone. I have no intention of calling my mother—I'm not ready to disappoint her just yet. Instead, I call Jake. Yes, I already have his work number programmed.

"Well, that's another job lost," I say into my shoulder, balancing my phone awkwardly while I light a cigarette.

"I'm sorry."

"Don't be. It's no big deal." I pause to summon up my best impression of a coo. "I want to see you tonight."

Jake sighs deeply into the phone.

"That was a loaded sigh."

"I can't tonight. I have to go back to Brooklyn."

"Why? To feed the cat? You fed him yesterday. How often does the damn thing need to eat?" Maybe it's a little too early in the relationship to let on to the fact I am not a cat person. Perhaps later on I'll blame my aversion to the vile creatures on allergies (which is only partly true).

"No. It's not that. She's coming over. She wants to pick up the rest of her stuff."

She. He still can't even bring himself to say her name.

chapter thirteen

"One more round?" I ask.

Laurie glares at me from across the table. Her bag is gripped tightly on her lap, where it has been ever since she got here. I think her hand might be tucked into her purse, ready to toss out a tip at a moment's notice.

"I think you've had enough."

"Oh, come on. One more glass of water won't kill you. You know you're supposed to have eight a day."

"Yeah. I know."

I flag down the bartender to order another round. This will be Laurie's fifth glass of water. And, because I've managed to keep up with her shot for shot, this will be my fifth margarita.

An hour later, I find myself teetering in the middle of my apartment, sensing that something—although I'm not quite sure what— is amiss. When I finally stop swaying, I realize the apartment is quiet. A little too quiet. It's empty.

Oh, such ecstasy! An entire evening all to myself! How long have I waited for this very moment? And what do I do now that it has finally arrived? I strip off my clothes—and crawl straight into bed.

What, you thought I'd dance around naked? Bathe myself in champagne? Search for a Zalman King series on cable?

Just knowing that no one, not a soul, can poach on my territory is enough for me. I tuck myself into my sheets and bask in the warm glow of my night-light and the ephemeral world of *Die Dämmerung*. Or *The Twilight*, rather. Granted, I find myself rereading each sentence twice before it makes sense, but within a few pages, I have drifted peacefully to a place that, right here and right now, exists only for me.

The sudden ring of my telephone yanks me back down to the stiff coils of the mattress. I nearly bounce right off my bed.

I grope for the alarm clock on my nightstand and check the time. It's one o'clock. One o'clock in the morning is a downright terrifying time to receive a phone call. It's emergency time, somebody-has-been-in-an-accident time. The reason Amanda isn't home time?

"Yes, hello!" I breathe fearfully into the phone.

"Sarah?"

"Jake? What's wrong? You okay?"

"Yeah. Well, no. It's been a bad night."

"Why? What happened?"

"She just left. She took her stuff. It's all gone."

"Oh. Oh, right." The pounding in my chest begins to ease.

"I want to come over."

"Here?"

"Is that all right?"

"How long will it take you?"

"About an hour."

I look at my alarm clock again, even though I already know very well what time it is. I listen to the tick of the clock, the patter of my heart, and dig deep for a little nugget of self-control. It's hard to come by. I'm still suffering the consequences of five cocktails.

"It's a little late," I say quietly.

"I know."

"Maybe it's not such a good idea."

"Okay. I understand."

"But, how about tomorrow night?"

"That would be great."

"All right. Well, good—"

"Oh, hey, Sarah? Can you give me your e-mail address?"

"My e-mail address?"

"Yeah. There's something I want to send you."

"Ummm, okay. You got a pen?" He pauses a moment to find one. I give him the address. "Good night, Jake."

I replace the phone in its cradle. Feeling strangely content, I nestle deeper into my pillows and flip the page of my manuscript.

The first thing I do the next morning is leap out of bed to turn on my computer. Because it's only 9:15 a.m., I don't expect to find a whole batch of new e-mails. In fact, there is only one.

It's from Jake, subject heading: *Hey, Sugar Bear.* I click it a million times because it won't open fast enough.

Appallingly, there's no text to the message. I feel utterly humiliated. How dare he get my hopes up like this, make my heart beat so ferociously I could easily lapse into a seizure right here on the Aeron, only to—

Oh, wait. There's an attachment. I open it slowly this time, lest I fall prey to another one of his not-so-funny practical jokes.

Am I just a glutton for punishment? The sweet, warm gush of

blood in my veins runs suddenly cold. I feel as though I'm inhaling razor-sharp icicles through my nostrils.

He sent me a picture. Not a sample of his work, not something he felt brave or open enough to share with me. No, this is a picture of *himself*. And there he is, so smug and so shameless, in heated lip-lock with a knockout brunette. I'm supposed to get a kick out of this?

I crack my knuckles and ready my response. "Hey, Scumbag"? "Hey, Shit for Brains"? A whole slew of choice phrases comes to mind, and it's hard to pick just the right one. I glare at his self-satisfied grin for inspiration.

"What the—" I grip the desk and peer in closer, because I have this weird feeling that the knockout brunette in the picture might—just might—be me.

It *is* me! I recognize the dress. I recognize the dance floor of the wedding reception. But those amorous doe eyes and full, parted red lips—those are *mine*?

Man, I don't know what they were paying that wedding photographer, but it couldn't have been nearly enough. I don't know how to say this, not without sounding like an obnoxious, faux-sincere Best Actress award recipient—ah, to hell with it! I'm beautiful! Gorgeous and sexy and positively radiant!

Maybe the girl in the picture isn't really me after all. Certainly not the me I know. Not with that hazy glow on my face, not with that dreamy look in my eye. She's a creature spawned by a split-second flash, with just the right lighting to cast harsh lines into shadows, just the right angle to gloss over the imperfections. By luck of a camera, she appears once. Then she vanishes forever.

Or does she?

———

I could spend all day staring at that picture, imagining who I could send it to, wondering if there were a way I could doctor it somehow and use it next to my byline when I become an award-winning newspaper columnist. I know these thoughts are no good, unhealthy even, poisonous daydreams that will, at best, turn me into a useless sap and, at worst, crush me when I must come to terms with life's harsher realities. It is thus with heavy heart that I grab the *Die Dämmerung* manuscript and force myself to retreat to the living room.

While rereading the very same passages I struggled with the night before, it occurs to me that reading for pleasure is a luxury I can't afford. Is it just me, or has Princess been a little slow fanning the flames of my ardent literary burn? Come to think of it, it would also help if she fed the fire a few more chips—preferably the crisp, green kind printed by the U.S. Treasury.

On an impulse, I pick up the phone. On another impulse, I slam it back down. Has it really come to this? Must I really beg, grovel, plead?

You bet I do.

I shift in my seat—better to accommodate the tail between my legs—and start dialing. She answers on the first ring.

"Hi, it's Sarah." I have to force myself to sound bright and chipper.

"Sarah?" Princess asks innocently.

"Sarah Pelletier," I say, fighting to keep the irritation out of my voice. She knows damn well who I am.

"Sarah, doll, of course! So sorry. Somewhere in all this mess I must have misplaced my mind. It's been so busy here, you know."

"That's a good thing, right?"

"Pfft," she snorts.

"Anything I can do help out?"

"Oh, doll, that's so sweet of you. But really I think I'm all caught up with the manuscripts—"

"It doesn't have to be just manuscripts. Is there any chance you've started looking for an assistant to lighten the load?"

"God, I wish! Crap . . ." I hear her phone bounce off the desk and topple to the floor. Part of me thinks she may have dropped it on purpose.

"I'm back. Sorry about that. Tell you what, doll—" Since when has she started calling me doll? It's beginning to irk me. "I'm looking at this book on my desk. I've been meaning to read it myself, but I never seem to find the time. It's very hush-hush, though. Can I trust you with it?"

"Of course."

"Great. It's right up your alley."

"What's it called?"

"Hmmm? Oh, let me see. Damn. I know I'm going to butcher this, but I think it's pronounced *Die Dämmerung*?"

Somehow I find the strength to suppress a maniacal giggle. How hush-hush can a book be if *I* already know about it?

"Yeah, sure, I'll take a look at it," I say, sounding mighty charitable indeed.

"Fabulous. I'll messenger it right over."

By mid-afternoon, I've taken to waiting in my living room for the messenger to arrive. So imagine my surprise when it is Amanda who walks through the front door instead. She's caught me staring at a blank TV screen, an unused piece of floss wrapped around my index finger. I do a double take. I'm not so good with the days of the week anymore, but as far as I know, it's either a Wednesday or Thursday. Or maybe a Tuesday. Suffice it to say, I do believe it's a weekday and I wasn't expecting her intrusion.

"Must have been some night last night, huh?" I say, snapping off the string of floss.

Amanda throws her bag on the sofa, narrowly missing me, and walks by without a word. I take it as an invitation to continue baiting her.

"You call in sick? Feeling a little hot? A little . . . peaked?"

She wheels around, eyes narrowed, nostrils flared.

"You disapprove of me, don't you?"

"What? No, of course not."

"You think the only reason I got promoted was 'cause I was sleeping with my boss."

"I don't think that. And who cares, anyway? If I had a hot boss, I'd be all over him, too. I think it's romantic."

Amanda laughs once. A harsh, bitter laugh. "It's not romantic," she scoffs. "It's hell and you know it."

She disappears into the kitchen and starts slamming drawers. I abandon my floss and follow her.

"What is your problem?"

She grabs a cup from the dish rack and points it at me furiously.

"Do you really think you're better than me?"

Yes. "No!" It comes out a little funny.

Amanda grimaces into the coffee mug in her hand. "Would it kill you to make sure you get the coffee grounds out of your cup?" She throws the mug into the sink. "I am sick of cleaning up after your mess."

Okay. Now it's getting personal.

"You clean up after me? Are you insane? What do you think I do all day?"

"I don't know. What *do* you do all day?"

"Well, for one thing, I take out the garbage. I've been meaning to explain this to you. Taking out the trash does not mean you tie up a full bag and leave it *next* to the trash can. You have to take it *out* of the apartment for it to actually count."

"Oh, yeah?" Amanda pulls herself up to full height, reminding me just how short I am in comparison. "And there is something I've been meaning to tell *you*," she seethes. "I know you've been sneaking into my bedroom to use my scale. I want you to stop. One of these days, you're going to break the fucking thing."

I am struck absolutely dumb. I know there are a million equally cruel things I can say right back to her. I just can't think of a single one.

Amanda doesn't give me the satisfaction of coming up with a lame response anyway. She flips her hair and stomps angrily toward her bedroom, slamming the door behind her. Because I refuse to be upstaged by her yet again, I stomp off to my room and slam my door, too. Harder.

I spear a pan-roasted potato and pretend it's Amanda's heart. The teeth of my fork sink in a little deeper and I feel instantly gratified. I move on to stab another potato, then another, and soon I've amassed a pleasing assortment of wounded spuds.

"You're not hungry?" asks Jake, swallowing a piece of my salmon.

"Nah," I continue to pulverize my side dish. "I'm just out of it."

"You seem a little down."

"I'm fine." I give my limp fish a hard whack.

"You wanna hear a joke?"

"I'm not really in the mood for—"

"Did I ever tell you the one about the ignoranus?"

"Huh?" My fork is wedged in salmon. I give up on trying to yank it out. "Uh, no, I don't think so."

"Okay. What do you call a person who is both stupid *and* an asshole?"

I peer up at him, over the upright utensil stuck in my entrée. I have no idea what he's getting at.

"An ignoranus?" I ask.

"What? How did you—" His eyes narrow. He looks hurt. "Why didn't you tell me you already heard that one?"

I stare at him closely and realize he is completely serious.

I laugh. I laugh and I laugh and I laugh. Even my fork finally collapses. The waiter returns to our table while the tears are still streaming out the corner of my eyes. Jakes smiles at him apologetically.

"Can you wrap up the salmon? She'll take it to go."

Ever the gentleman, Jake pays the check, carries out my doggie bag, holds open the door, and lights my cigarette while I struggle with the daunting task of trying to pull myself together. I wipe away the last of my tears.

"I am sorry. You've been so wonderful tonight. Thank you for putting up with me."

"I don't put up with you. Believe it or not, you're fun to hang out with. I didn't think anyone could laugh like that."

"I sounded like such a girl, huh?"

Jake shrugs. "In a good way." He snuffs out his cigarette. "Where to now?"

"Hmm, I don't know." I wrinkle my nose as I survey my options.

The restaurant was Jake's choice, an unexpected little East Village gem. But, to tell the truth, this neighborhood isn't really my scene. The East Village is the place where rich people come to pretend they're not. And by claiming destitution, they think they have the right to complain. So complain they do. Loudly: Drinks are too expensive, bars are too crowded and the music sucks. (All true, by the way.) But that's not the point. The point is the people of the East Village have created a cult out of their dissatisfaction. The neighborhood movie theaters play crappy, low-budget independent films, the music venues book mediocre bands, just so people can pay ten dollars to have something to bitch about later at the bar around the corner.

Jake senses my hesitation. "You wanna just grab a bottle of wine at the liquor store and go back to your place?" he suggests.

Oh, boy. I cringe visibly.

"You hate that idea."

"Well . . ."

"You want to just call it a night?"

"No, no. It's not that. It's just . . ." How do I explain Amanda to him? How do I tell him she brings out all that is vile and petty and spiteful in me? How do I put it, decisively, that I don't want him to see me that way? That I don't want her to reduce me to claw-scratching and fang-baring in his presence?

"My roommate has PMS," I tell him. "She's been complaining about cramps all day. I think she wants to be home alone tonight with a cold compress."

"Well, then," Jake spreads out his hands. "Do you want to come back to Brooklyn with me?"

Brooklyn. That, I have to think about for a moment. For even though it lies just beyond the span of a river, Brooklyn could just as well be Brigadoon for all I know. A small forgotten village in the mist, where, by one account, Hassidic Jews light candles and read aloud from the Talmud, and by another account, liberal arts college grads dye their hair pink and write poetry. Every image I have of Brooklyn—mostly garnered from books that were foisted on me in high school—paints an entirely different picture. Am I ready to embark into a world so vast and so strange?

Yes.

"Yes," I say.

We stop first at a liquor store tucked in between an all-night Japanese toy store and a Mexican restaurant featuring live music. The wine is my treat, so I pick a nice, but relatively inexpensive bottle of cabernet. The clerk clucks his tongue and shakes his head when he rings up my selection.

See what I mean about the East Village?

At Jake's insistence, we splurge for a cab ride that transports us out of the petulant city and over the noble Brooklyn Bridge. Not only is this the first time I've crossed the bridge—it's the first time I ever been made fully aware of its awesome presence. I feel like I've been cupped in Atlas's palm, and when I look over my shoulder, I see the rest of the world lies firmly on his back and I have nothing to worry about.

The cab comes to a stop at the end of a pretty, tree-lined street, which seems oddly disquieting. I scan the block for late-night drug deals on the corner, a private investigator asleep in a dark sedan in the middle of a stakeout. I wouldn't even be surprised if down the street, Spike Lee were walking toward us, dribbling a basketball. And from the other side, John Travolta were strutting in a white leisure suit, clicking his heels to the tune of "Stayin' Alive." And then, somewhere in the middle, a fat man smoking a cigar would throw open his window and jut out his beer belly, yelling at us all to "get the fuck out of hee-ah." Downstairs, his middle-aged spinster daughter—tired but still strangely seductive—would give us a long hard stare, more curious than cross.

Of course, there is nothing of the sort. Only your typical sub-urban block, with your typical lampposts and typical cherry blossoms. The neighborhood is completely ordinary in an altogether fascinating way.

Jake leads me up the stoop of a real brownstone, to a door that is made of wood, not steel. Inside, we amble up a crooked stairway that creaks.

People really live like this? Not the people I know.

On the third floor, at the end of the last flight of stairs, Jake opens the door to his apartment. I walk in and find myself, again, dumbfounded. The place is charming. It's a decent size, bright and airy. And almost completely empty.

"Nice place," I say. "It's very . . . spacious."

"Yeah, sorry. It used to be nicer." He points to the center of the living room. "She took the coffee table. Great table. Round? The kind that spins?" He points to the bare wall. "The bookcase, too. And obviously all the books." He grabs the bottle of wine from my hand and steps into his adjoining kitchen. "Make yourself comfortable."

I sink down on the futon and cross my legs, angling myself toward the kitchen so I can admire Jake's strong, stunning back as he pops the cork. When he reaches to open the cupboard doors above him, his shirt pulls up and I can catch a glimpse of the top of his boxer shorts. Calvin Klein. Boxer briefs, maybe? Hopefully? A delighted shiver runs down my spine.

"Shit." Jake slams the cupboard drawers shut.

"What's the matter?"

He turns to me, his eyes downcast. "I forgot. She took the wineglasses." He studies his barren kitchen for a moment and picks up two discarded plastic cups by the microwave.

"Is this okay?" he asks, handing me a cup.

"It's perfect."

He pours the wine. "Cheers."

"Cheers."

We sip our wine quietly for a few moments, staring at our reflections mirrored in the black void of a Sony TV screen at the center of the room. How is it that, even when a TV is turned off, it is still the focus of any aimless eye?

Jake picks up the remote. "You mind if I turn it on?" he asks.

"Yeah, go ahead."

He flicks it on and hands me the clicker—a downright gracious gesture that loses its impact almost immediately. He only gets four channels. Two are in English.

"*You* don't have cable?" I ask, shocked.

"I did. It was in her name. I told her to cancel it."

"Why on earth would you do that?"

He shrugs. "I didn't think I was sticking around for much longer. Thought I'd be in Canada by now."

I decide not to ask why he isn't.

"Well, we can still find something to watch," I say, lightly. "You have any movies?"

"Some."

"Hey, you got any movies you've made? I'd love to see your stuff. I wanna find out if you're really as talented as I think you are."

"No," he says adamantly.

I decide not to ask why not.

Jake heaves himself off the futon and toys with the rabbit ears for a few minutes. We finally get somewhat clear reception for NBC, which suits us just fine because Conan O'Brien is on, and we're both big fans, even though we can't remember the last time we actually watched his show.

"This reminds me of college," I say.

"I'm sorry."

"No, I meant that in a good way." I put down my wine and scratch my arm. When I realize I am rubbing my skin raw, a thought occurs to me.

"Oh, hey, where's your cat?"

"Yeah, well." Jake picks up his cup of wine and stares at it. "She took the cat." He takes a deep swig.

On the TV, the studio audience erupts into laughter, so we force ourselves to join in. Soon, laughing gives way to giggling, giggling gives way to yawning, and—if I think I've heard correctly—yawning gives way to snoring. I look over to find Jake's head tilted at a funny angle on the back of the futon, his mouth hanging slightly open. I poke him gently.

"You tired?"

"Huh?" He snaps his head up and blinks. "Oh. Yeah." He turns off the television and gets up, leaving me stranded on the futon. A door swings open behind me and I assume he has retreated to the boudoir. I haven't exactly been invited, but I don't think it would be out of line to join him.

"So," I say, sneaking in and closing the door behind me. "This is the bedroom."

"What?" Jake's T-shirt is halfway over his head. He peeks out from under it and searches for me with sleepy eyes. "Umm, yeah."

I follow his lead and remove my own shirt.

"You have a side of the bed you prefer?" I ask, coyly flinging my blouse aside.

"Umm, I guess I usually sleep on the left."

I drop my skirt to the floor and gingerly step out of it. Thinking I'm being rather seductive, I sink languidly onto the right side of the bed and prop myself up on my elbows.

Jake's tired eyes linger on me. It occurs to me that I've just given him the perfect opportunity for comparison. How easy it must be for him to imagine me literally taking his ex-girlfriend's place.

"You know what? I think it would be better if you slept on the left."

I recoil as if slapped and quickly withdraw to the other, safer, side of the bed.

chapter fourteen

Jake's lips graze my forehead. I struggle to open my eyes.

"I have to go to work," he says.

"So?" Grumpily, I grab the pillow and roll over on to my stomach.

"I left a set of keys for you on the dresser so you can lock up after you leave. But . . ." He plants sweet kisses on my shoulder. "You don't have to go if you don't want to."

I open my eyes again and blink at the alarm clock: 7:45 a.m. Ugghhh.

I don't remember closing my eyes, but when a car honks outside I am jolted back into consciousness. Jake is gone and the alarm reads 9:15. I am wide-awake. And I don't really see much point in staying.

Waking up in a strange bed is a peculiar experience, mostly because it is a practice I don't engage in regularly. But this bed is made stranger still. I slither out of the sheets as if afraid of waking a sleeping ghost. If I strain hard enough I can hear her snoring. Loose strands of her hair probably still cling to the pillowcases. I collect my clothes and tiptoe into the bathroom.

She follows me there, too. The crème de corps, the lavender

shower gel, berry lip gloss, and sugar shea butter—these all must have been hers. I find it hard to believe Jake is a man accustomed to keeping his hands soft and his lips sun-kissed. I rip off a sheet of *her* toilet paper, flush *her* toilet, and rinse my hands with *her* antibacterial hand soap.

And here she is now, in the living room. Her absence, quite literally, has left a big gaping hole in the middle of the apartment. And where her coffee table once stood, now lies my colossal messenger bag, almost irreverent in its casual disarray.

I've never been one for a purse, and people like Jake who can cram their wallets into their pockets and head out the door utterly amaze me. Me, I don't go anywhere without a wallet, keys, cell phone, an extra pack of cigarettes, a journal, my hairbrush, and assorted chapters of whatever manuscript I'm still reading. And then there are the just-in-case items: an umbrella, a change of socks, half a bottle of tepid water, and a prescription for birth control pills I never bothered to fill. Shamefully, almost apologetically, I repack my items and clear the bag out of the way.

And the keys Jake left for me on the dresser. Did these once belong to her, too? I shove them into my pocket and head out the door, fishing for them only when I need to lock up behind me.

That bloody apartment—by daylight, a rather intrusive examination of all of Jake's most savage, open wounds—may be all well and good behind me. But now there's the rest of Brooklyn to contend with. Bright, sunny Brooklyn with blue skies and scattered clouds so long and thin they stretch like arms in an open embrace. I shield my eyes and curse the fact I've forgotten my sunglasses.

The only sign of traffic is a bus that lurches down a nearby avenue. No taxis, of course not, that would be asking too much. I stop a man loading crates into a restaurant and he mimes directions to the nearest subway.

"Gracias," I tell him.

The further I stray from the apartment, the less it continues to haunt me. So there's a coffee table missing from the living room. So there's an abandoned kitty litter box in the corner. Big deal. But the wineglasses—just thinking about those evil vessels makes me cringe. Because somewhere in the deep recesses of my fragile ego, I think I just might be their plastic cup replacement. Cheap, functional, and disposable.

Now, where the hell is that subway?

Luckily, like Manhattan, it turns out Brooklyn has a grid system of its own. So, even though I don't know where I'm going exactly, at least I know I've made progress. I've gone from Fifteenth Street to Eleventh on a particularly quaint little avenue lined with boutique clothing shops and home accessory stores. If you want to bring a subway to a major hub of activity, my guess is this would be the place to do it.

I pass a deli, which is another good sign. After that, a newsstand, even better. Then I stop dead in my tracks. In the window of the Park Slope Animal Clinic, a yellow flyer presses its cheek against the glass and whimpers plaintively.

His name is Sleeve. He is a beautiful pit bull and Labrador mix with a goofy grin. His coat is all white except for one little black leg. It is as if someone tried darning him a black sweater and gave up only after the first few stitches.

"ADOPT ME!" the flyer begs. My throat constricts and a dull pain in my chest starts throbbing. Then I peer in closer to read the fine print.

"Volunteers welcome! Come in and say hi!"

Need I say more?

———

Okay, so not that I have a thing for Julie Andrews or anything, but the rest of my day is a page right out of the *Sound of Music* libretto—starring me as the impetuous nun Maria, of course. I've embraced the role so completely that soon I find myself twirling gleefully on the greens of Prospect Park, with my head tilted upward and my arms outstretched. I've even assumed the massive undertaking of teaching my charge how to sing.

"Doe!" I command.

"Doe!" he responds.

"A deer! A female deer!" Ray, a drop of golden sun.

"Me!" I shout.

"Woof!" he agrees.

"A name I call myself!" I toss him a branch and watch him gallop after it. Far—a long, long way to run.

It's been a long time since I've enjoyed a good frolic. Years, even, since I thought to turn a cartwheel. I wish someone had clued me in on the secret of Brooklyn's existence before. Who needs the recycled air of a stuffy office environment when outside there are flowers to smell and rumps to be sniffed? I think Sleeve and I can concur—there is nothing like the tree-filtered light of a blazing afternoon sun to burn the abandonment blues right off our sweaty backs. I'll bet the most rewarding job at the most reputable company couldn't grant me half the satisfaction I feel today.

A warm patch of grass and a dog's head in my lap. Reading a book and dozing off for a nap. A phone in my pocket that never once rings.

These are a few of my favorite things.

I return Sleeve by sunset and leave the clinic smelling distinctively like dog. Which doesn't bother me so much, but it might not be a prospect so enticing to my fellow subway travelers. An unfamiliar jangling in my pocket reminds me, however, that an inviting shower is a mere five blocks and a twist and a shove away. And a climb up three flights, another twist and a shove—well, you get my drift.

I don't emerge from the shower until well after my fingers are pruned and my toes are pickled. The bathroom heaves a deep, steamy sigh of relief. And then, just as soon as the aloe-scented cloud kisses the mirror, it is sucked right back out of the room as if through a vacuum.

The door has opened. Jake stands motionless with a guilty hand still on the knob.

I'm sure his mind is a flurry of witticisms, charming apologies, a gracious word or two. But the only one he can think to voice is a rather panicked, "Oops!"

Modesty being my first instinct, I grab a towel from the rack—and shriek.

The door slams shut, concluding the shrill pierce of my scream. I clutch the towel securely around my body and wait. A moment of incredibly awkward silence ensues.

"Jake?"

"Yeah?"

"It's okay. You can come in if you want."

The door reopens a smidgen. He pokes in his head.

"I'm sorry," he says. "I didn't—"

"No, *I'm* sorry. I went to the park today and I came back to take a shower. I didn't realize you'd be home this early and—"

"It's all right." He pushes the door open a little wider. "I just wasn't expecting you. I mean, I'm glad you're here. I wanted you to be here. I didn't think you would be, but I was hoping . . ." his voice trails off.

I smile at him. A brilliant, dazzling white smile. But I doubt he even notices it. Because, at the same time, I also let my towel drop to the floor.

Sleeve pounces a pile of leaves and looks up at me, wagging his tail beseechingly.

"Good boy, Sleeve," I assure him from my perch under a nearby tree. He rests on his haunches, eyes wide and earnest. I grab a twig by my knee and toss it to him.

"Go get it, boy!" He races beneath its floating arc.

Sleeve and I have become fast friends over the course of the past couple of days. I like him because he doesn't judge me and I hope I offer him the same. I don't care that he comes from a broken home or that he's suffered from poor upbringing. In return, he is willing to overlook the fact that my clothes are wrinkled and that my English major in college is a bit ineffectual.

Sleeve trots back with the twig between his teeth and drops it in front of me. Then he settles back and cocks his head sideways.

I ignore the twig. I've got a better plan.

"Hey, Sleeve. Where's the—DUCK!"

And he bolts off again, racing a couple of yards down toward the lake, where he plants his little mismatched feet in the water and peers down his snout, seeking out that elusive bird. Begrudgingly, I return my attention back to the final chapters of *Die Dämmerung* spread out beside me.

It would be so easy to slip into a blissful lull, to enjoy the sunshine and the puppy love and to take the time to appreciate a good literary denouement. But my coverage for this book is long overdue, and I'd be a fool to believe Princess would be inclined to further extend her goodwill. Even if she had no designs on this material

at all, she'd still be expecting no less than a prompt and thorough report on it.

It is with much resentment that I then force myself to skim
through the final few pages. Already the gist of my synopsis and impending comments begin to take shape in my head.

A buzz in my pocket startles me. It takes me a while to realize
my phone is ringing. Thank God. The damn thing hasn't rung in
ages. I was beginning to think no one cared. I mean, really—I've
been in Brooklyn for almost a week. Don't you think *someone* on the
isle of Manhattan would have noticed I've gone missing?

"Hello?" I answer.

"Hey, so you're all set! I got you the interview. You still have
the address, right?"

"Ummm, I don't think—"

"Wall Street, remember? Are you wearing the suit?"

Huh? "No."

"But you said you were going home to change!"

"I did?"

"They're expecting you at Livingston, Gainor, and Price in half
an hour!"

Whoa whoa whoa. Who, What, and Where?

"Mark?"

"Yeah?"

"Mark Shapiro?"

"Yeah, what?"

"I can't go to an interview in half an hour. I'm in Brooklyn."

"How is that possible? You just left my office fifteen minutes
ago!"

"No I didn't. I haven't talked to you in weeks."

He pauses for a moment. "This is Sarah Gill, right?"

"Uh, no. This is Sarah"—come on, say it!—"Pell-tee-ay."

"Oh. Sorry." He hangs up abruptly.

I close my phone and lower it against my chin, thinking. It figures. The one time my headhunter has found me a job that sounds even remotely respectable, it wasn't even for me. Maybe I should have just played it off—half an hour is plenty of time to get dressed and head out for an interview in Lower Manhattan. Or maybe I should call back Mr. Mark Shapiro and demand a little more loyalty on his part. After all, what could another Sarah possibly have that I don't?

My chin starts to vibrate. I check the caller ID on my phone and see Mark Shapiro has taken it upon himself to smooth things over. Well, damn right.

"Sarah?"

"Yes?

"Sarah Pell-tee-ay?"

"Yes, Mark, it's me."

"You still interested in that property management job?"

"That's still available?"

"Yeah. They just called. They *loved* your writing sample."

"You're kidding."

"I can schedule a second round of interviews if you're still interested."

I take a moment to think about it. But only a moment.

"Mark, I told you. I'm not really interested in real estate. Has anything come up yet in publishing?"

"Ummm. Not really. But I'll let you know if I hear of anything."

"Thanks. I'd appreciate it."

After we hang up, I stuff my phone back into my pocket, right where it belongs. Out of sight, out of mind. Sleeve yelps and a duck splays its feathers and darts across the water. Mission accomplished. The happy puppy trots back to me and nods his confirmation. It's time to go home.

We follow the wooded path back to civilization, past the corral where the first horseback-riding lesson of the season is in full swing. A beautiful brown mare hangs her long neck over the gate and fixes us with a big, watery eye. Sleeve balks and stops short. With his little black leg held in the air, he turns and tilts his head at me, wondering, perhaps, if I've ever seen a dog quite so big.

We return to the clinic where a dumpy caretaker in an unflattering set of scrubs leads Sleeve back to his kennel. She's worn the same name tag four days in a row, so I think it would be safe to assume her name is, in fact, Julia.

"You been spending a lot of time with him lately." She says this as if it were a bad thing.

"Well, yes. I thought he'd enjoy it."

"Why don't you just adopt him, then?"

I feel my face go flush. How dare she! What kind of a person makes a *volunteer* feel guilty?

"I . . . I can't adopt him."

"Oh, yeah?" Her beady black eyes glint at me. "Why not?"

"I don't have the time to look after him."

"Seems to me you got plenty of time."

"I have a job."

"Oh?" She raises an eyebrow, not convinced. "You do?"

"Well, no, not now. But I'll have one soon."

Her eyebrow drops back into place. "Uh-huh," she grunts, turning to hang the leash up on the wall. "I see."

I march sullenly out of the clinic and stomp my way back to Jake's apartment, feeling slightly rattled and terribly resentful. For moments like these, there is only one cure. A little bit of shopping might be the very thing to cheer me up. So I stop in a liquor store on my way home.

While I'm studying the overwhelming rows and columns of voluptuous bottles, a saleslady sidles up beside me.

"Red or white?" she asks pleasantly.

"I was thinking maybe red?"

"You have a price range in mind?"

"Well, I didn't want anything too expensive."

She pauses to survey her options. "Have you tried the Coppola?"

"Coppola? As in the filmmaker?" I ask.

The woman smiles politely. "Yes, I believe so."

"Great, I'll—" I stop myself suddenly. "Wait a second. Sofia or Francis Ford?"

She selects the bottle from the shelf. "Francis Ford, of course." She shows me the label to prove it.

"I'll take it."

She leads me to the counter to ring up my purchase. As I wait, I peer around the store nonchalantly. The window display out in front catches my eye.

"How much for the wineglasses in the window?" I ask.

The woman looks up and frowns at the display. "I think it's twenty-eight dollars for a set of four."

I gulp. "Would it be all right if I just bought one?"

She smiles kindly. "I don't see why not."

The attack from the rabid animal clinic caretaker still has me unnerved the following day. So, I do what any evolved, mature adult would do. I take it out on the poor, defenseless animal and decide to forgo our afternoon jaunt in the park to stay home and wash the dishes instead.

I'm in the process of lathering up the new wineglass with cleansing suds when I suddenly retract my hand as if scalded by the running hot water. The glass slips from my grip and shatters in the sink.

What am I doing? Like *hell* I'm going to wash a man's dishes just because I am unemployed! I turn off the faucet and sit down on the couch, leaving the shards of glass untouched in the sink. I twiddle my thumbs, pick at my split ends, and let my eyes wander about the apartment, taking note of the fact the hardwood floors are in desperate need of a Swiffer and the rug could use a good vacuum. But, no, damn it! I cross my arms over my chest.

By three o'clock, I decide it's okay to turn on the television. Of course, there's nothing worth watching. I click it back off and toss the remote aside with disgust. I've got a full two hours left before Jake comes home. What could I possibly do with that much time all to myself—in a relative stranger's apartment?

And that's when a terrible thought occurs to me.

Up until this point, I've considered it a blessing that Jake has welcomed me so wholeheartedly into his home and allowed me to shape it into my own mini Brooklyn oasis. But now my gratitude has officially run its course. Mired in boredom, I've allowed myself to succumb to the one vice I've been desperately trying to keep at bay.

I start snooping.

Within minutes, I find exactly what I've been looking for. In the very back of Jake's video cabinet, wedged behind his David Lynch collection, is a stack of VHS cassettes with handwritten labels. I pop in the first tape, which turns out to be a reel of generic commercials for soda brands. Eject. The second tape, labeled "Suggestive Service," sounds infinitely more promising, but it is not as provocative as I had anticipated. It is a collection of corporate videos preaching the lost art of subtle sales tactics—suggestive service, if you will. Eject, eject. Finally, I stumble across a tape labeled "Jake's Short: Untitled." Fast-forward through the credits . . . and here we go.

It's a beautifully shot film, expertly crafted with an artist's flair for obtuse angles and exquisite lighting. Not much by way of a story, but then again when do short films ever have a powerfully moving plot?

The film is good—great, even—but that doesn't surprise me. I had been expecting to be impressed with Jake's talent. If anything, the film is disappointing because it just isn't—what's the word I'm looking for?—*juicy* enough. No wicked perversions, no deviancy, no dark fears laid bare. Not even a hint of misogyny or any other discrepancy I could possibly hold against him later.

No, this simply will not do. If I really want to snoop, I've got to do this right. I put down the remote and duck into the bedroom.

Believe me when I say no stone will be left unturned. There isn't an inch of this apartment that is safe from my meddling hands. Not the sock drawers, the filing cabinets—even curiously labeled folders on his computer are fodder for my obsession.

An hour later, I still come up empty-handed. I try to tell myself I should be thrilled. Jake is perfect. He has absolutely nothing to hide.

I feel so defeated.

And herein lies the problem with snooping. It would be bad enough to find some incriminating evidence that would expose Jake as anything less than ideal. But the fact that I haven't found anything even remotely upsetting is far worse. Perhaps I haven't tried hard enough.

At four o'clock, I decide it's okay to start smoking.

I grab my pack of cigarettes off the kitchen counter. As an afterthought, I also grab the stack of Jake's mail and take it with me to the futon. I light the cigarette, turn on the TV, and with half-hearted interest, I casually flip through his mound of bills.

And there it is. Tucked in between the latest issue of *Time Out New York* and a pre-approved credit card application. It's a J.Crew catalog. But it isn't addressed to Jake. It's addressed to her. To "She."

To Simone Anderson.

Now, why does that name sound so familiar?

Of course! I lunge for the remote and rewind the tape in the VCR. Holding my breath, I hit play.

Her name appears almost instantly, earning its own title card under the caption "Writer." And then it appears again, seconds later, the only name listed under the heading "Special Thanks."

I leap up and turn the place upside down trying to find my cell phone.

"Simone? Give me a break," says Laurie. "What kind of a name is that?"

"I'll bet it's French," I whisper. My side of the phone conversation takes place underneath Jake's desk. I figure I can't be too safe. There's always a chance he'll come home early and overhear me. Never mind that if he does walk in right now, I'd have a hard enough time explaining what I'm doing under the desk.

Laurie groans. "Come on. With a last name like Anderson? So not French. Pelletier. See, that's a real French name."

"Hardly."

"Sarah, do yourself a favor. Forget you ever heard the name Simone Anderson. And stop snooping!"

Oh, if it were only that easy.

I realize now my prior method of ransacking had been doomed from the start. Before, it had been aimless and unfocused. But this time, I know what I'm looking for. I crawl out from under the desk and pull open the top drawer. The little black address book I discovered—and ignored—earlier lies comfortably on neat little rows of staples and paper clips. I carefully remove the book without disturbing any of the other items and flip it open to the first page.

Hello, Simone Anderson.

There are two phone numbers listed for her, one under Home, the other under Work. I retrieve my phone and duck back under the desk. I dial Work.

"Hello, Regal Bookstore?"

Downstairs, a door swings open. I hang up quickly.

Jake is home.

chapter fifteen

Julia is all smug smiles behind the counter when I return to the clinic the following day. Her droopy eyebrows make a concerted effort to lift up by way of greeting.

"Still no job?"

"I'm here to pick up Sleeve," I remind her curtly.

"Uh-uh." She shakes her head, jiggling the loose flab under her chin. "He's not here. He was adopted yesterday."

My jaw goes slack. "Really?"

"Yup. A couple came by in the afternoon. They have a garden apartment out in Bay Ridge. Plenty of room for him to run around in. He couldn't have gone to a better home. He's one of the lucky ones, you know?"

I can't believe it. I should force myself to smile, pretend to be happy. But I can't bring myself to say a word. Julia glances back down at her clipboard. I doubt she even notices when I leave.

Still reeling once I'm outside, I find myself walking the wrong way, down a stretch of Brooklyn I've never been to before. I could lie to myself and claim I am just wandering around, trying to walk off the shock. But the truth is, I know exactly where I'm going.

The Regal Bookstore is a quaint little shop, right down to the artfully arranged book displays and the inviting, plush armchairs tucked into hidden corners. It's the sort of place I could lose myself in for hours. But not today. Today I have a mission.

I establish my stakeout at the Bestseller table and assume my undercover identity as someone with a passing interest in the new fiction titles. Thus, the extent of my master-spy skills. Subsequent sleuthing in Jake's apartment turned up no discarded or even mangled photographs of my perp—can I even call her that?—so I have no idea how I plan to make this Simone Anderson. I don't even know if she is working today.

I circle to the far end of the table and pick up a book. While pretending to read the blurb on the back cover, I look up over the spine to study the clerk behind the counter. He's a boy—and not a very appealing one at that. Years of raging hormones have taken their toll on his complexion and his less-than-stellar physical coordination. When the phone beside him rings, he fumbles to pick it up and then drops it. After a few seconds of total pandemonium, he is finally able to clutch the receiver in a grip of panic. He mumbles something quietly as he straightens the frames of his glasses. Then, lowering the phone against his chest, he lifts up his head to address the entire store in a shrill voice.

"Simone! Phone for you!"

Well, how about that? I swivel around to see what happens next.

I know her immediately. In fact, I think I'd know her anywhere. She is stooped in front of a young girl, her skirt tucked over her smooth, bare knees. She murmurs "Excuse me," and stands, handing the girl a paperback—*A Tree Grows in Brooklyn*. The choice is a little obvious if you ask me.

She brushes right past me. I can smell her hair as it grazes my shoulder. Vanilla? No, almond.

That luxurious blonde hair glides, it swims, across the store, taking long easy strokes. She reaches the counter and cradles the phone receiver against her ear, tossing that magnificent mane over her shoulder to reveal a dainty, patrician nose, full lips, and a small, sharp protruding chin. If those delicate curves weren't enough, her chest obliges by rounding out her form, with hips to match. She listens intently to her caller and the heel of her sandal lifts and drops to the floor methodically, triggered by the pulse and contraction of her long taut calf.

My God. She's beautiful. And I am so relieved!

Does my relief surprise you? It surprises me. I hadn't realized until this very moment that my one true fear would be that she look *exactly* like me. I suppose I had imagined myself a poor man's substitute for her, an imperfect replica. Now I can rest assured. I'm no substitute. I don't even compare!

I approach the counter and shoot the acne-scarred boy clerk a deadly look. He trips over his feet in his haste to scurry away from me.

"Uh-huh," says Simone into the phone. "It came in this afternoon. I have it here waiting for you." I prop my elbows up on the counter. Simone looks up and offers me a sweet, apologetic smile. I shrug back and indicate there's no need for her hurry on my account.

"Great. I'll see you then." She hangs up and straightens. I see now she's a good few inches taller than me. And much thinner. My relief rapidly begins to fade.

"Can I help you?" she asks.

"Uh, sure. I was wondering if you had a pub date for *Die Dämmerung*?"

She blinks at me through a veil of long, blonde lashes. "I'm sorry. The what?"

"*Die Dämmerung*. It's been a German best seller for months. I wanted to know when the English translation comes out."

"Umm, okay." She places her fingertips on the keyboard in front of her. "How do you spell the title?"

I spell it for her far too quickly. Her fingers make a heroic attempt to catch up.

"D-A-M . . ." she repeats hopelessly.

"You sure you haven't heard of it before?"

She shakes her head and waits. "The computer doesn't recognize it. Do you know what the title would be in English?"

"*Dämmerung?*" I raise my eyebrows in disbelief. "It means 'twilight.'" Duh. "*The Twilight?*"

She types it in.

"No, I'm sorry." She squints at her computer screen. "It's not in our database."

"All right. Well, what about the new Ian Pascal?"

"Oh, that!" She grins broadly, ever so eager to please. "*Moments of the Day?* It's in our New Paperback section."

"Nooo," I let out an exaggerated sigh. "I mean the *new* Ian Pascal. The book Paramount just bought? George Clooney is set to star?"

"Oh." Her smile dips. "What's it called?"

I give her title. While she types it in, I lean on the counter and try to peer at her screen.

"You a fan of Pascal?" I ask.

"I liked his last book."

I roll my eyes. "Personally, I think he's in desperate need of a good editor. He's not as sharp as he used to be, dontcha think?"

She hits her enter key and watches wordlessly as the information scrolls up. I drum my fingers against the counter impatiently.

"That book doesn't come out until November," she says.

"Aw, man, you're kidding me!"

She looks up and fixes me with a hard stare. Her sweet, angelic smile has all but vanished.

"I'm sorry. Is there anything you'd like to buy *today*?"

Blindly, I reach for a magazine from the rack below the counter. I slap it down and stamp it with a winning smile.

"Just this," I say.

I keep the magazine tucked under my arm on my way out the door and down to the corner. While I wait for the light to change, I decide to take a good look at my latest, and rather frivolous, new purchase.

"Oh my God!" I gasp.

You're never gonna believe this. I'm holding the latest issue of *Aspen Quarterly*.

Isn't that just always the case?

I think it might be time to leave Brooklyn.

The subway ride back to my apartment in Manhattan should take no less than forty-five minutes. And clearly the trains aren't at full capacity on a midday journey from the outer boroughs into the city. I manage to find a good seat and settle down with my very own issue of *Aspen Quarterly* spread across my lap. I read it cover to cover. It's a good magazine. Probing. Insightful. Smart. Witty.

I would have fit in perfectly.

To: Kelly Martin
From: Sarah Pelletier
Re: Associate Editor Position

Dear Kelly,

I am writing to thank you again for taking the time to call me the other day. I thoroughly enjoyed our conversation and I hope we will have the chance to speak again soon.

I also wanted to let you know that I did finally find a copy of the latest issue of *Aspen Quarterly*. Of course, just as I suspected, the magazine was a delightful read. In fact, I couldn't put it down! I thought the film reviews were insightful and articulate, and, in some cases, more entertaining than the films themselves. And I happen to wholly agree with Julie Watson's piece on the growing demand for intelligent documentary films. The documentary on child prodigies she mentions sounds particularly fascinating. I can't wait to see it!

So, thank you again. If nothing else, at least you've turned me on to a fantastic magazine I will enjoy reading for many years to come.

Best,
Sarah Pelletier

chapter sixteen

It is no big secret that a well-crafted thank-you letter is a job hunter's trump card. It is the sticky adhesive that stamps a brilliant résumé to an employer's forehead and says, "Hey! Remember me?" It is also the varnish that glosses over the rough edges of a rather standard interview. Or, in my case, it can be the corrective fluid that erases mistakes and allows me to start anew. Or so I hope.

I step away from my computer to let the letter sit for a while, allow it to breathe. I need a moment for myself anyway before I summon up the courage to send it. So I light a cigarette, which is always a surefire way to get my phone to ring.

And ring it does.

"Hello?"

"What's wrong?" Jake's voice comes in quick and panicky.

"Nothing's wrong."

"Then why did you leave?"

"I had to come home to feed my cat."

"Are you upset with me?"

"No." Well, yes, but not in a way I can justify. I look at the flickering letter on my computer screen and sigh.

"That was a loaded sigh," he says.

"I just needed to come home. You understand that, right?"

"I guess."

When I hang up the phone my hands are shaking. It is amazing how hard it was for me to be so curt and unfeeling to Jake. What was I trying to prove, anyway?

Poor Jake. Poor, unsuspecting Jake. He has no idea how much I want to hurt him. And, to make it worse, he hasn't an inkling how much he's hurt me. How dare he have a beautiful ex-girlfriend he never talks about! How dare there be any part of his life that doesn't belong to me.

And why should I care? Because for reasons I can't even begin to fathom, I need Jake. And more importantly, I need him to need me. Someone out there has to.

There were moments in Brooklyn—times when he'd graze his stubbled chin against the back of my neck, times when he'd stir in his sleep and reach out to pull me closer—times when it occurred to me that we might truly be fated to be together. Because the alternative—that we were drawn to each other only because we needed to be, only the way two desperate, lonely people can be—is simply too awful to consider.

I feel a sharp sting against my fingers. My cigarette has burned its way down to the filter. I toss it into the ashtray and take a deep breath. Enough time elapsed. I squint my eyes to reread my thank-you letter to Miss Kelly Martin at *Aspen Quarterly*. On an inspired whim, I decide to attach my real estate writing sample as well.

And that takes care of that.

In the past few months I haven't accomplished much worth celebrating. So finding the courage to send an impromptu e-mail certainly warrants a toast. Not that there's any wine left in the kitchen. I wouldn't expect there to be, not when I've left Amanda to her own devices for a full week. Instead I help myself to a bottle of beer that's been in our refrigerator for ages. I think it may have come with the apartment. I unscrew the cap, turn on the TV, and light another cigarette.

So, of course, my phone rings again.

"Sweetie-pie?" Shit! I mash out the cigarette and wave away the lingering smoke as if she could smell it.

"Oh, hi, Mom." She hasn't even said two words, and already I feel the creeping of a guilty conscience her voice always provokes.

"Where've you been? I haven't heard from you in ages!"

"The phone works both ways, you know." Wait a second—was it really *me* who just said that?

"Tell me, sweetie, did you ever fill out that law application?"

"Yeah, actually, I did."

"Oh, good. You know, I don't know if I ever told you, but I worked as a paralegal myself right of college. It was so much fun. Best time of my life."

She has indeed told me this before. And let me set the record straight: my mother's love of law lasted just about as long as it took her to snag a proposal from my father, a budding young assistant district attorney at the time. Then I suppose her passion for him surpassed all else. A year later, she traded in the bar for a baby, and an eighty-hour workweek for extended luncheon dates with the wives.

"You know you can always work at Dad's firm when you're out of school."

I groan. "Why do you do this?"

"Do what, sweetie-pie?" she asks innocently.

"You know what. Mom, you know I love you guys, but—" Okay, this is delicate. I want to say, *but I don't want to be you*, but she might take that the wrong way. Instead I opt for, "But I want my own life."

"I know *that*. You can always practice law in New York. I was just saying."

"Fair enough."

"You'll let me know when you pick a date for the LSATs?"

"Yes, I promise I will."

"Good. Love you, sweetie."

"Love you too, Mom."

We hang up.

A key rattles against the front door and I leap off the sofa with joy. Never have I been so thrilled to see Amanda. I skip to the door to greet her as she walks in.

"Oh, Jesus!" She steps back, her hand clutched to her chest. "You scared me! I wasn't expecting you."

"Sorry."

She inches the door closed behind her. "Where've you been, anyway?"

"Brooklyn."

Amanda wrinkles her nose, not very impressed, and throws her bag onto the sofa. She stares at it for a split second, then looks up at me guiltily. "Sorry about the place."

I glance around the apartment and pretend not to notice it is in a rather violent state of disarray. "The place looks fine."

"It's a shithole."

"Yeah, well . . ." My voice trails off. I'm not ready to launch into another petty squabble. The truth is, I'm spent. I've exhausted my entire reserve of pettiness for the day.

I can sense Amanda feels the same. She lowers her head and runs her foot down the line of the filthy rug. "You know," she begins. "I'm really sorry about the other day—"

"Oh, please. Don't worry about it. That was so long ago."

"Yeah, okay." She looks up. "Thanks."

Great. We've agreed not to fight. Now we're tapped out.

"So," I grin broadly. "What you up to tonight?"

"Ugghh." She removes her suit jacket. "It's been a long day. I was seriously looking forward to hitting the sheets and just going to bed."

"Oh." I'm crestfallen.

"But I'm not busy tomorrow," she says. "You wanna hang out?"

"Sure!" I bet she has no idea she's made my day. "Maybe we could rent a movie?"

"I'd like that." She smiles and heads to her room.

I climb into bed a few moments later feeling all different shades of happy—the yellow that brightens, the orange that warms, the pink that tickles. But night is soon to close in, washing away my temporary bliss with a dark, heavy gray. The smile slips from my lips and wilts. And my room grows heavy, bloated with the threat of another night of sleeplessness.

Damn Jake! I damn him when I kick my sheets and search desperately with my cold toes for his warm, bare leg. I damn him when vague sepia-toned dreams elude me and become, instead, the face of Simone. I damn him when the phone wails from the living room, because I want so very much for it to be him and I know it will be.

"Hey," he says.

"Hey," I say.

"I just called you."

"I know."

"But I'm calling you again."

"I know."

"I shouldn't say this—"

"Say it."

"I can't sleep without you." My heart soars. "I don't ever want to sleep without you again."

"Me too."

"You in bed?"

"Yeah," I draw the sheets up to my chin to prove it. "You?"

"Yeah. I wanted your voice to be the last thing I heard before I went to sleep."

I say nothing.

"You know, if you don't talk, that's not going to work."

"I'm sorry. I just didn't realize how tired I was until you called."

"Yeah, me too. One quick question before I let you go to sleep, though. Do I get to see you tomorrow?"

"Well, I—"

"No I take that back. It's not a question. I want to see you to-morrow."

"I can't tomorrow. I promised Amanda I'd hang out with her."

"Oh." The twinge of disappointment in his voice is unmistak-able.

"Tell you what, though," I offer quickly. "How about you pack yourself an overnight bag on Friday? Throw in enough socks to get you through a couple of days. And, oh, definitely some of those cute little boxer briefs you own—"

"The red ones?"

"Damn straight the red ones."

"Am I planning a weekend trip?"

"How do you feel about Manhattan? I happen to own and operate a lovely little bed-and-breakfast on the Upper West Side. You'll love it."

"Hmmm, I don't know. I try not to travel during the height of tourist season."

"Oh, come on. There's great shopping in the area, and you'd be just in time for all the summer sales. Plus, there are tons of fabulous restaurants, and we're really close to all major transportation—"

"Yeah, but how's the service?"

"Excellent. You'll be treated like royalty."

"And if I want to extend my stay?"

"The dates are totally flexible."

"Then, I guess it's a deal."

"Super. I'll see you on Friday."

"All right." He stays quiet for a moment, letting all things left unsaid speak for themselves. "Good night, Sugar Bear."

"Good night, Jake."

$8.74. I have $8.74 in my bank account and that's it. Am I even allowed to have as little as $8.74 and still call it an "account"?

The worst part about $8.74 is that I can't even withdraw it. I suppose I *could* cough up twelve dollars, deposit it in my account, and then retrieve the minimum twenty dollars from the ATM. But if I had a whole whopping twelve dollars on me, I wouldn't need to drop by an ATM at all now, would I?

Okay, let's see—there's *got* to be a way to work this out. Do I dare face a flesh-and-blood bank teller and ask her to close out my account? Good God, how mortifying! I'd prefer to just hold up the place instead. At least in jail, I'd be able to enjoy free room and board. Not to mention the fact most prisons come equipped with high-speed Internet and cable TV. Sounds like a pretty sweet deal to me.

Then again, I'd have to get a gun. And although I have no idea what the going rate for firearms are these days, I've got a hunch they'd cost more than $8.74.

"Wait a second!" I gasp out loud. The people waiting in line behind me groan and throw up their hands. A second is far too long to make them wait at all.

I pay no heed. For despite the faulty wiring in my brain, a light-bulb has unexpectedly switched on.

Princess! She still owes me over a hundred dollars for my book coverage. And didn't she say she'd pay me in petty *cash*?

I may not have enough money to hail a cab, but using nothing more than my own two feet—and a perilous bolt of adrenaline—I clear twenty city blocks faster than I ever have before.

I push my way past the teeming hordes of Times Square tourists, trot impatiently through a revolving door, dash into the lobby, sail through the metal detectors unscathed and sign my name in the visitor's log with a flourish. Just before the elevator lurches closed in front of me, I stick out my foot and let the doors bounce off my thigh. The people inside narrow their eyes and suck in their guts, providing just enough room to let me slink in. The elevator shoots up. I hold my breath.

When the doors open up on the fifteenth floor, the tempest resurges and propels me down the hall. A polite receptionist points me toward Princess's office. Her extended index finger is a cannon that fires me off once again. And when I finally hit my target, what should I see but a pretty, young girl seated primly at a small desk. I stop cold.

"Who are you?" I demand.

Her large brown eyes widen.

"I'm Crystal," she says, smiling hesitantly. "I'm new here."

"What do you do?"

"I'm Gracie's assistant."

"**S**arah, doll, you didn't really want this job."

"What are you talking about!" I fume. "I kept telling you, over and over again, that I wanted it."

"Oh, come on, doll, let's face it." Princess flings her arm casually over the back of her chair, flaunting the ample chest she acquired only a couple of years ago. "You're overqualified. You would have been miserable here."

"No, I wouldn't—"

"Shhh!" Princess nods her head at her closed office door and gestures for me to keep my voice down. "Sarah, this isn't exactly a growth position, if you know what I mean. I don't even need an assistant."

"Then what is *she*—" I jerk my head at the same door—"doing here?"

"Let me finish. I was telling you that I don't need an assistant. What I really need is a secretary. Crystal's young. Fresh out of college. And she's hungry. She'll do anything I tell her to." She uncrosses her orange fake-tan legs and leans forward. "Now, I'm not proud of myself. But I'm also not going to apologize for my needs. I want to be able to ask someone to get me a cup of coffee. And I *don't* want to feel guilty about it. You? Doll, if I asked you to make me coffee, you'd—well, you'd give me that look of yours."

"What look?" I seethe.

"You know. That *look*. Like you're so above it all. And I'm not saying you're not, but . . ." She pauses. "Honestly, Sarah, I know I'm not telling you anything you don't already know—but you make terrible coffee."

"That's why you didn't hire me? Because I make bad coffee?"

"No. Not at all. I didn't hire you because you're too old to be making coffee. You deserve better, Sarah." She places her hand against her inflated chest in a ridiculously phony gesture of concern. "I really, truly mean that."

Her hand drops. But that phony display of concern? No, that stays.

"I sincerely hope you won't let this ruin our relationship," she continues, her voice oozing sugar. "You know how crazy I am about your coverage. You do excellent work, doll, you really, really do. In fact," she lowers her voice confidentially. "There is a *major* book I just got my hands on. Definitely, no talk, no trade. The agent isn't even going to officially submit it to film companies for another two weeks. He just happened to give it to me last night as a thank-you for—" She stops herself. "Well, let's just say as a thank-you. Anyway, you'd be so perfect for it. I couldn't trust anyone else."

With that, she leans back, permitting me a moment to fully absorb her rare confidence. And despite myself, I blush at the faint praise and prickle with a twinge of excitement.

"Yeah?" I say, careful to remain guarded. "What's the book about?"

Princess groans and flutters her hand in the air. "The same thing they're all about. 'Boy Comes of Age,' I suppose."

Uh-huh. Not to be confused with Girl Comes of Age. A different genre entirely.

"It's called *Gideon*," she adds.

I swallow a gasp and try to keep myself in check. But if my face has registered any of the shock tickling my spine, Princess doesn't notice. She picks up her phone and dials an extension, drumming a French-manicured nail against her desk impatiently.

"Crystal?" she barks into the receiver. "You remember that manuscript I made you hide in the bottom drawer of the filing cabinet?" Princess swivels in her chair. With her back to me and her head bowed, she continues speaking in a hush. "I changed my mind. We're going to let Sarah have it instead."

She hangs up the phone and spins back to me. "So." She smiles brightly. "Don't I owe you some money?"

She gives me two hundred dollars in an envelope. The manuscript she puts in a padded sealer, wraps in tissue paper, and stuffs in a Bloomingdale's shopping bag. I hold out my hand to receive the package. Instead, Princess stares at the bag for a moment, thinking.

"You're headed uptown, right?"

"Yes," I say cautiously.

"Excellent." She reaches under her desk and pulls out yet another shopping bag. "Can you swing by Bloomingdale's on your way? Sheila at the Lancôme counter gave me the Resolution night treatment for dry skin when she knows full well I only use the one for normal skin. If you tell her I sent you, she'll know exactly what I am talking about."

I balk. "You're serious? Bloomingdale's is all the way on the East Side."

"Oh, Sarah." She laughs. "You make it sound like it's in a different *borough*. It's only another couple of blocks." She stuffs the smaller bag into the bigger one and hands it to me. "Thanks, doll, I appreciate it. I'll have a messenger come by your place tomorrow."

Fuming, I snatch the bag from her hands. If any part of me had been even remotely flattered that Princess considered me more than just a personal assistant, that part knows better now.

I march out to the hallway and wait for the elevator to arrive. When the doors open, a hefty man in a light suit cocks an eyebrow at me.

"Going down?" he asks.

"Uh-uh." I shake my head. "Going up."

"Now, you sure you want to do this?"

Normally, if *Laurie* is the one to voice any reservations at all, I should know I am encroaching on dangerous territory. But this time, my mind is made up.

"I'm sure."

"Okay." She stares uneasily at the manuscript pages on the copier tray. "I'm hitting copy."

"Fine." I shrug. "Hit it."

She does as told. The machine sucks in the first page. The small, dark room soon becomes an orchestra of white light and electronic purrs. I turn my head because I cannot bear to look. Laurie smiles at me.

"Must feel good to be bad."

"Sure," I lie.

chapter seventeen

The following week, at 4 a.m. on a Tuesday morning, I can be found in front of my computer, wearing flannel pajama bottoms and my favorite Brown sweatshirt. My desk is lost under the remains of an Amazon rain forest—several trees at least which now serve as disorganized manuscript pages and hastily scribbled notes. To jab my finger even deeper into the wound of Earth's imperiled ecology, I've also been using several Diet Coke cans as makeshift ashtrays.

The first light of dawn forces its way through the slats of the window blinds. And still I push on, swallowing another swig of soda, inhaling another hit of nicotine, and trying to ignore my heavy eyelids.

I haven't pulled an all-nighter since college. There is something so wholeheartedly romantic about it. Like I am eighteen years old again, tired but determined, beaten but not even close to broken, welcoming the new day like it belongs to only me.

Of course, I do not force myself to stay up all night by choice. The official submission date for *Gideon* is only three days away and Princess has insisted I turn in my coverage no later than 9 a.m. this very morning. I finish up my synopsis by 6 a.m. But by then, I am too tired to think clearly. I've already entertained an hour's worth of daylight. I'm entitled to a quick nap. I set my alarm for 7:30 and slide under the sheets. Not even a minute later, I dream of comments that include such inspired observations as "well-crafted," and "ingenious use of structure."

By 8 a.m. I consider myself refreshed enough to type up the rest of my coverage. I sit down at my computer and turn off the screen saver. Much to my disbelief, I see I've received a new e-mail. And even more startling, it has been sent from Variety.com.

A FRIEND THOUGHT YOU MIGHT BE INTERESTED IN THIS ARTICLE.

YOUR FRIEND'S MESSAGE: CHECK IT OUT! MY NAME IS IN THE LAST PARAGRAPH!

I click it open.

And then a bloodcurdling scream lodges in the back of my throat.

The *Gideon* acquisition makes the front page. It beat out the new developments in the Academy screener ban scandal *and* the official announcement that an esteemed New York independent film company has declared bankruptcy. Above the text, there is a picture of Laurie's boss, dazzling the camera with a buffoon-like grin. I read his generic statement with openmouthed horror—although I'll admit to feeling a momentary stab of pride when he says he thought the book was well-crafted and employed an ingenious use of structure.

When I reach the final paragraph, my stomach lurches. I had been warned in advance, and yet I still wasn't prepared. Not for Laurie's full name and title. In bold.

I am too shaken to move. I debate sending my coverage to Princess anyway, but in the end I decide I don't even want her to *associate* my name with that book. I turn off the computer and fire up a cigarette.

I tell myself that if I don't hear from Princess by noon, I'll be in the clear. There is no logical connection between me and Laurie. Laurie could have gotten that book anywhere. She knew all about it well before it came to Princess's attention. I can prove it—although I'd better not. No, there is no reason—absolutely no reason at all—for Princess to even fathom that I was the one who handed over that cursed manuscript.

I just have to wait until noon.

The phone rings at 10:30 a.m. I light one cigarette off another and let the machine pick up the call.

"Sarah, it's Gracie. It is extremely urgent that you give me a call as soon as possible. I will be in the office all day." The machine clicks off abruptly.

I hack on the cigarette fumes and crush out the filter with revulsion.

Her second call comes in at 1:15 p.m.

"Sarah!" She hisses on my machine. "I cannot stress how terribly important it is for you to call me back. I am stepping out of the office now for lunch. Call me on my cell. 917–755—"

I switch off the machine. In a sudden fit of furious energy, I toss off my bathrobe and slip into yesterday's workout wear, shove my keys in my pocket, and head out the door.

I return two hours later, a dripping, soppy mess of frizzy hair and aching muscles. I hobble painfully over to my answering machine. The panic button blinks a fierce glowing red.

There is one new message.

I grimace and hit play.

"Fine, Sarah." Her voice is ice cold. "This is the last message I will leave you. Frankly, I don't care if we ever speak again. However, I would like to warn you. You might want to consider leaving my name off your résumé. If people start calling me for recommendations, you may not be pleased with what I have to say."

Click.

During the many months of my unemployment, I've been lazy at times. I've been despondent. I've been bitter. But never before have I truly dedicated myself to a long stretch of good, solid self-loathing. As it turns out, I'm quite good at it. I can mope and kick myself for days on end. There's nothing to it. I lie in bed for the most part. When that gets old, I get up and lie on the sofa in the living room. And if recent incidents have ceased to make me cringe and shudder, I have a backlog of plenty of other painful memories I can call upon to do the trick. Like the time I poured out my heart to Andy Finklestein in the fifth grade by secretly slipping a mix tape into his schoolbag. He returned it a day later, snidely remarking that he'd had a bad reaction to Bon Jovi's "Bad Medicine." For weeks after, boys would come up to me in the hallway, singing "Let's play doctor, baby cure my disease." (And maybe *that* explains my current repulsion for music.)

So steeped am I in my nirvana-like state of self-pity not even the most tempting of wordly pleasures can rouse me from my trance.

"How about we all go out for dinner? Sushi, maybe?" Jake suggests.

I shake my head. "Not hungry."

"Wanna go to a bar? Have a couple of martinis?" Amanda prompts. "It's on me."

"Blah."

"This is impossible!" Amanda turns to Jake and rubs her temples. "She's been like this for two days. All she does is watch reality television."

"I see it's done wonders for her vocabulary."

I narrow my eyes at him. "Blah," I repeat, with more feeling this time.

"What is it, honey?" Amanda reaches for my hand and strokes it gently. "Isn't there anything you want to do?"

"How about we rent a movie?" Jake asks.

"No, I don't wanna—" I stop my head in mid-shake. "Movie?"

Oh, it sounded like a good idea at the time. But as we make our way to the video store, the weight of our impending decision clings heavily upon my shoulders and throttles my neck. I've always hated making decisions. I have a knack, in fact, for making particularly bad decisions. And the one that still awaits us is destined to be tough.

For some time now, Jake has been angling fervently for the Kieslowski trilogy that was finally released as a Special Edition DVD. But Amanda hates the "readers," and even though she claims to speak French fluently, I know she'll need her glasses for the subtitles. And she really hates to wear her glasses in front of boys.

No, Amanda will probably be reduced to tears if I don't at least *consider* letting her rent the new Reese Witherspoon flick. Although I have a sneaking suspicion that Jake might be a huge Reese fan, I doubt he's ready to admit that just yet.

Woody Allen is always a safe standby, of course. But he's not as safe as he used to be. I'd suggest some of his earlier films, but Amanda still hasn't recovered from the shock that *Manhattan* was shot in black and white. I remember her turning to me, her eyes wide and her mouth agape, when she said, "Just how old *is* Diane Keaton, anyway?"

Then there's Jake, Mr. Saw It, Hated It, Saw It, Own It. Is there any middle ground for people like that?

"Who's Guy Richie?" Amanda asks, studying the back of a DVD case in her hands.

"Madonna's husband."

"Eeck!" She makes a face and returns the box to its rightful place on the shelf. She trails a finger down the row and stops, quite predictably, when she sees Adam Sandler's goofy grin on display.

"Oh, I love him!"

"Great!" I grab the DVD and make a mad dash across the store toward the Classics section.

"Okay," I tell Jake, still panting. "How do you feel about watching Adam Sandler take a stab at serious drama? I heard he was surprisingly good in this."

"Oh, yeah!" Jake jabs his finger at the box. "He was awesome! I saw that in the theater. You guys should definitely watch that some time. You'll love it."

"Right." I lower the DVD. "Thanks."

"Hey, what about this?" He hands me the case for *How to Succeed in Business Without Really Trying*. "Robert Morse is really funny. He's like an early Jim Carrey."

"I'll give it a shot." And I'm off again, hurdling the displays on my way back to the New Releases.

"Amanda," I gasp for air. "Remember how much you liked *Moulin Rouge*?"

"Oh, yeah. Nicole Kidman was fabulous in that!"

"Okay, well, then how about we get a musical? And I mean a *real* musical." I hand her the box. She studies it, her nose pinched.

"Sarah, this was made in 1967. We weren't even born then!" She holds the offensive video case away from her with two fingers. "Tell Jake I'm okay with classics. But they can't be older than 1980."

"Right." I take the movie from her, tuck it under my arm, and charge.

Yellow flag! Illegal cell phone on the field. I flip it open.

"Yeah?"

"Sarah?"

"Yes."

"It's David Morton."

"David . . . ?"

"David Morton? From Ponderosa High School?"

I come to a screeching halt. "Oh, David." My stomach churns the sudden, excruciating recollections. David Morton's thick tongue plunging down my ear canal, his sweaty fingers painfully pinching and twisting the flesh on my thighs. His rough hands sneaking up under my bra no matter how many times or how hard I try swatting them away.

"Been a while, huh?"

I cast a glance at my surroundings. I'm in the Horror section. Safe. I crouch down low and whisper into my mouthpiece.

"Yeah. Wow. This is really unexpected. How did you get this—"

"I called your house and talked to your mom for a pretty long time. She gave me your number."

"Great." It doesn't sound as sarcastic as I mean it.

"So, I hear you're in New York."

"That's right."

"Yeah? And what have you been up to?"

"Well, I . . ." Am seeing someone? Have a boyfriend? Am finally having good sex? "Haven't really been up to much at all. You?"

"Well, that's the funny thing. I'm in New York too tonight."

Oh God. "You are?"

"Last-minute business trip. And, see, I'm just here for the one night and I was wondering if, maybe if you weren't busy, we could grab a drink?"

"Oh, gee, David, I'm sorry. I'd love to, but—"

"No, it's okay. Don't apologize. I thought you might already have plans. Just wanted to check."

"I appreciate—"

"Hey, your mom says you're living with Amanda Reubens. For real?"

"Actually, I—"

"Any idea what she's up to tonight?"

"No," I snap. "I haven't the foggiest."

"Yeah. That figures. Tell her I say hi, okay?"

"Sure, will do." Fat chance.

"And if you're ever in Denver, give me a ring. I'd love to catch up."

"Sounds super. I really got to go now, David."

"Okay. Talk soon."

"Bye."

I hang up my phone not a moment too soon.

"There she is!" I hear Amanda say. I grab a movie from off the shelf and pray it isn't *Caligula*. When I turn, I find Amanda hovering directly above me. Jake's head pops up over her shoulder.

"What are you doing in the Horror section?" he asks.

"I don't know," I mumble. "I thought it might be fun to watch a scary movie."

"But we already made a decision," Amanda pouts. Jake holds up a DVD case.

Tootsie. Now why didn't I think of that before?

I cock an eyebrow at Amanda. "You sure you're okay with this?"

"I've never seen it before." She shrugs. "I heard it was funny."

"Great." I stand up and brush off the knees of my jeans. "Then let's do it."

We leave the rental store just as the sun begins its descent. The windows in the sky draw their pink curtains and the streetlights slip on fuzzy, little orange hats. The air is crisp, crackling with electricity. And I am suddenly overcome with the urge to skip.

Skipping, I daresay, is a tragically neglected art. It is the perfect combination of both gleeful abandonment and utter lunacy—or are they the same? At any rate, it is just the sort of public display of hedonism people should partake in more often. Think how much happier we'd all be if we decided, *Never mind the subway! I think I'll skip to work this morning instead!*

I cannot convince either Amanda or Jake to join me in this bunny-hop parade. All the same. If you don't feel the urge to skip, it really can't be forced upon you. And so I forge ahead, leaving it up to them to keep up the pace.

"Are you sure you're all right?" Jake asks warily.

"Never mind me!" I pant between hops. "Just a little bout of Manny-D."

"What's Manny-D?" Amanda asks.

"Manic—" Hop. "Depression."

"Oh God," she mutters. "Only you would have a cute little nickname for your psychological disorders."

With one resounding last hop, I land squarely in front of our building. Then I straighten and go rigid.

Huddled in the corner of my front step, and furtively smoking a cigarette, is one of the saddest and most forlorn creatures I've ever seen. And when she lifts up her head and peers through her bangs with red-rimmed eyes, I gasp.

"Laurie?"

With trembling fingers, she tucks her hair behind her ears.

"I . . ." Her voice catches. She starts again. "I need to talk to you."

I turn to Amanda. She quickly fishes for her set of keys.

"We'll see you upstairs." She and Jake carefully sidestep the despondent heap on the front step and disappear into the building.

"What's the matter?" I ask finally, crouching down beside her.

Laurie's lip quivers. "I got fired."

"Oh." I pause. "Is that all?"

"No, Sarah, I'm serious. I'm not going back." She blinks furiously, holding back a flood of tears. "He called me fat."

"He did not!"

"Yeah, he did." Again, her voice cracks. She takes a moment to clear her throat. "This morning he got so angry he threw his cell phone out the window. So I get on the elevator *immediately* and I run downstairs, and I pick up all the million fucking pieces. And then he's screaming at me to put it all back together. And by some fucking miracle I get it to work." She coughs to hide the threat of another sob. "But, by then, he finds out he missed an important phone call from some director in London. So he throws the phone again, this time at *me*, and he says he never would have missed the call if I had just moved my fat ass faster."

"Laurie, that's unacceptable!"

"I think it is, too," she sniffs.

"Come here." I wrap my arms around her. "It'll be okay. You wanna come in?"

Laurie shakes her head. "I can't. I have to work on my résumé. Oh God!" Her cigarette slips from her fingers. She buries her head in her hands. "My résumé!"

"I know, I know," I say, patting her gently on the back. "Don't worry. I'll help you. I've gotten really good at résumés lately, you know?" I stand up and fetch my keys.

"I really can't stay." Laurie hoists herself up. Calmly, she brushes back her bangs and smooths out the wrinkles on her skirt. It amazes me how unflappable she can be. If it were me, I'd be a flailing, sobbing mess. Maybe Laurie's experience has taught her how to maintain composure. But I think the truth is, it's a gift. She takes one deep breath, closes her eyes, and shakes her head. Poof! The brief bout with emotion ricochets right off her.

"I need you to do something for me, though," she says, slipping her hand into her bag. She pulls out her cell phone and looks at it longingly. "I know I won't be able to keep it off. I'll turn it on to check my voice mail, and there will be a message from the office telling me to come back. And I won't be able to say no." She hands me the phone. "Take it. I need you to return it to the office for me tomorrow. Please?"

"So that's it? You're not going back at all?"

"Never. I'm going home now to file for unemployment. Then I'm going to start looking for another job."

I hold out the phone to her. "I think you should go back to the office yourself. I think you're entitled to tell that asshole off. And you should demand a severance."

"Uh-uh." She waves her phone away. "If I go in asking for severance, he'll just offer me my job back. Then I won't be able to collect unemployment. And I should be getting at least $400 a week."

"Wow." I raise my eyebrows. "You've really thought this out, huh?"

She straps her bag tightly around her shoulder. "Sarah, I've been thinking this out for three years." She kisses my cheek and strides down the street. She may not be skipping exactly, but there is a definite spring in her step I haven't seen in a long time.

There are a few movies—and I mean, really a handful—that if you see at the right time, when you're in the right place, can say it all. I'm talking about the movies you see when you're young, when you're perched at the edge of that awkward transition into adulthood, and you're just about to discover this crazy, magical thing called irony. And then you hear a witty line of dialogue, or see an unexpected gesture, and it takes you aback because it's just so clever in a way you never fully understood before.

Out of all the scenes, in all these movies, the one that has stuck closest to my heart throughout the years is a brief moment in *Tootsie*. If you've already seen the movie, you know exactly what I'm talking about. It comes during the montage, the Depression montage, if you will, when Dustin Hoffman wanders the park ruminating on a life of failure. A job lost, the woman he loves gone. His hands are in his pockets, his chin is tucked to his chest. Then he stops and looks up. A mime is trying to balance on an imaginary tightrope, with one leg aloft on a curb. Dustin watches him struggle for a moment. Then he walks up—and pushes him over.

Isn't that just a kicker!

You know what else I love about rewatching old movies? It's an experience that provides the all-too-rare opportunity to rediscover a fundamental truth that's been lodged in your rattled, disorganized mind for years but that you just didn't have the Dewey Decimal number needed to call up.

And the truth I've uncovered tonight? Well, think about it. *Tootsie* is the story of a down-on-his-luck actor who can't get work to save his life. Sound familiar to you? I'll bet it sounds familiar to a heck of a lot of people. But see, Michael Dorsey (aka Hoffman) is so fed up he does the unthinkable. And we're not talking about a little padding of the résumé. We're talking a little padding of the bra. The man actually becomes a *woman* to get a job!

I guess sometimes you just gotta do what you gotta do.

When the movie is over, and Amanda's remaining bottle of wine is sucked dry, we all bid our sleepy good nights. Amanda retreats to her bedroom. Jake and I duck into mine.

The door closes. Jake slips out of his jeans and into a new pair of boxer briefs. He folds his clothes and places them in a neat little pile on the floor. I pull on a large college T-shirt—Harvard this time, possibly obtained during the Head of the Charles regatta—and climb into bed. He crosses over to the other side and nestles in beside me.

It strikes me as overwhelmingly tragic that we no longer have to fight to keep our urges in check. Blouses don't rip at the seams, buttons don't pop off unexpectedly. Tongues don't seek each other out with a burning hunger, and hands don't dart down to secret, dark places. Instead, we let our noses probe gently into the crooks of shoulders and necks. Our fingers are loosely interlaced in nothing more than a prolonged handshake.

Some people might yearn for exactly this kind of comfortable affection. But snuggling to me is like the swill of a fine vintage wine when all I really want is a tequila shot with a spicy kick.

Jake flings a lazy leg over my hip and rests his palm on the hollow of my stomach. I wait eagerly for his hand to circle in one of two ways—up or down. Instead it remains put.

His leg grows heavier, pressing into my thigh like dead weight. His hand goes limp. I am bitterly disappointed to feel him slipping into a peaceful slumber.

"Hmmmm," I murmur, turning to brush my lips against his ear. His relaxed body spasms with a sudden shiver.

"Jake, can I ask you a question?"

"Uh-huh," he yawns.

"How come you never talk about your ex-girlfriend?"

He groans and rolls over on his side, withdrawing both his leg and his hand from my yearning body. "I really don't want to talk about this right now."

I reach around his waist and try to pull him back to me. He won't budge.

"That's unfair. There's never a good time. You never want to talk about her."

"Of course I don't want to talk about her. She's a horrible, horrible human being. I hate her."

I freeze. " 'Hate' is a strong word," I say slowly.

"So what? It's true. I despise her."

"Well, I don't think you should hate her. I think she should be a nonissue."

Jake flips back toward me, his eyes narrowed. "She *is* a nonissue."

"No, she isn't," I insist. "Not if you still have feelings about her, one way or another."

"What feelings? You're the one who brought her up." He fidgets restlessly under the sheets. "Would you really prefer it if I were still friends with her? I can call her up right now and ask her to coffee tomorrow. Would that make you feel any better?"

"Of course it wouldn't!" I snap.

"Then why are we even discussing her? It seems to me like you're trying to pick a fight. Is that what you're doing?"

"No."

"Then what is it?

"Don't you see?" I shrug and smile at him innocently. "I'm jealous. *Crazy* jealous. Aren't you flattered?"

"Yeah," he grumbles. "That's wonderful." Still, he wraps his leg around me again forgivingly.

"And I want—" Okay, now how do I put this? "I want more of you."

He puts his hand back on my stomach. My flesh tingles with relief. "Sarah, I'll give you everything. Anything. You just name it." He rests his head against my shoulder. "What do you want?"

"Well," I toy with the strands of his silky smooth chest hair. "How about sex? For starters?"

His head jerks up. After his features adjust to the initial shock, his expression softens into the sweetest grin.

"Sugar Bear," he cups my chin in his hand. "You never have to ask for that."

Even unconsciously, Laurie has always been a master planner. I've got to hand it to her—that girl runs a tight ship. And she couldn't have picked a better day to walk the plank.

It's Friday—blessed Friday!—day of the Sabbath, the only day of the week to earn a capital "Good," and a day of worship for even that secular clan of Hamptonites—the latter of which would include Princess, of course. No, there's no chance at all of me finding her at corporate headquarters today. For as long as I've known her, Princess has never put in a full workweek during the summer. On Fridays, she is out of the office by noon, cursing at drivers on the Long Island Expressway by three, and enjoying the sunset from her beachfront patio in Southampton by seven. Big Ben couldn't keep time more precisely.

Thus it is with not a shred of doubt, not even a whimsy of fear, that I cruise down to Times Square this afternoon, Laurie's cell phone jangling in my pocket.

I always thought it was absurd that Laurie would have an emergency work cell phone. I mean, let's face it. Her job was to make movies—and a movie won't exactly have a coronary on the golf course. But Laurie never took her job lightly. She seriously believed that she was the one expected to "rescue" a project whether it threatened to "die" of its own volition or the L.A. office had ruthlessly decided to "kill" it.

If I have any doubts that filmmaking is a life-or-death profession to rival that of law or medicine, I need only to step into Laurie's office building to be convinced otherwise. Usually, I make it through the metal detectors without much to-do, but today I create more than a minor stir. Security bells and whistles—and other assorted trimmings—shrilly announce my arrival. Chagrined, I shuffle over to a checkpoint where a guard sorts through the debris in my messenger bag. (Thank goodness I've already finished and discarded all of Laurie's pilfered manuscripts.)

"Ah," says the guard, triumphantly holding up the *Tootsie* DVD I plan to return later. "One of the classics. Bill Murray as the roommate? Cracks me up every single time."

"He's spot-on, isn't he?"

"That part when he says he wants to put on shows in theaters that are only open when it rains?"

"Or how he doesn't like when people say they liked his play? He likes it better when they come up to him afterward and say, 'I didn't get it'?"

"Exactly."

The guard repacks my bag and hands it to me with a smile. "You're free to go."

"Thanks!" I beam, continuing on, only to be impeded a few yards later at the front desk.

"ID, please!" barks a stern woman in uniform. I sigh and sort through my reshuffled bag to find my purse. I hand over my driver's license and, in return, I'm given a sign-in sheet to fill out.

When I've completed the form to satisfaction, I'm given a gold star. Only it's not a star. It's a sticker that says "Visitor." The woman in uniform narrows her eyes and watches me closely to make sure I wear it correctly.

And even that is not enough. The elevator opens up on the twenty-third floor and puts me squarely in front of a shielded door. I flag down the attention of *another* woman behind *another* desk and eventually she buzzes me in.

"Can I help you?" she asks.

"I'm actually here to return a phone."

"Oh?" The receptionist cocks an eyebrow. "Whose phone?"

"It belonged to Laurie—"

"Oh, there you are!" cries a voice from down the hall. Caught off guard, I wheel around to find a woman in perilously high-heeled Mary Janes prancing toward me, a heavy stack of papers clutched to her chest. I don't recognize her immediately. But only because I wasn't expecting her.

"Thank you soooo much for bringing that back!" Laurie gushes, her wide eyes pleading with me to remain silent. "I don't know how I would have gotten through the rest of the day without it." She motions to the reception desk with her elbow. "Just leave it there. I'll walk you to the elevator." She takes two steps toward the security door and stops.

"Hey, Sonya?" she calls over her shoulder. "You mind?" The receptionist obliges by pressing the buzzer. The security door swings open. I follow Laurie out into the lobby. Behind us, the door vaults closed again.

"What are you doing here?" I ask through clenched teeth.

"You don't have to whisper. They can't hear us through that door."

"Well?"

She sighs. "Sarah, I can't be unemployed. It's just not in me. I'm not strong like you."

"You don't have to be strong to be unemployed. You just have to be out of work."

"You know what I mean." She hits the elevator button. "But listen, I found out about a job lead yesterday that I think might be good for you."

"Oh, yeah?"

"Yeah. There's an opening at the WCA talent agency. Marianne Langold is looking for an assistant."

"Who's Marianne Langold?"

"Don't you know? She's only one of the top talent agents in New York. You wouldn't *believe* who she reps." Laurie ticks off a list of actors I haven't even dared to fantasize about.

"And? What's she like?"

"Oh, she's a raging bitch."

Figures. "Okay. And what about the job?"

"I'm not going to lie to you. There's a high volume of calls."

"What's that supposed to mean?"

"Phone calls. You'll be answering a lot of them. And when you're not answering them, you'll be making them."

"It's a start."

"Send me your résumé when you get back home. I'll get it over to her office ASAP." She doesn't spell it out. She actually says "ay-sap."

The elevator doors open in front of us. I step on.

"Oh, hey, wait!" Laurie checks over her shoulder. "Take this." She removes the top half of her stack of papers and hands it to me.

"What's this?"

"It's a historical romance."

"Oh, no," I groan.

"No, no. I think you'll like it. Meryl Streep is already attached to star. I'll talk to you later?"

"Sure." The elevator doors slide closed between us.

I use the time wisely as I go down in the elevator reorganizing my bag. I pull out the case for *Tootsie* so I'll have it in my hands and remember to return it on my way home. And yet, as I stare at Dustin Hoffman's lovely dolled-up face on the cover—his glossy smile, his feathered wig—a small germ of a thought takes root in my head.

Two facts become crystal clear to me all at once. First, *everyone* lies on their résumé. And second, no one wants to hire somebody who is *overqualified*. So, I ask you, then: how wrong is it, really, to lie on a résumé to make yourself seem less qualified? What if I were to shave a couple of years off my age (employers aren't allowed to ask how old you are anyway)? And what if I were to revert to an earlier, older version of my résumé?

And if my résumé were, in fact, an *accurate* representation of my former, younger self—is that really a lie at all?

Sarah Pelletier

121 West 68th Street, Apt. 4B
New York, NY 10023
Phone h: (212) 555-1476 c: (917) 555-9317
E-mail: spelletier@hotmail.com

EDUCATION

1998–2002	*Brown University*	*Providence, RI*

- BA in English, Minor in Modern Culture and Media
- Graduated Phi Beta Kappa, GPA—3.8

2000–2001 Université Lumière, Lyons, France

- French Language and Cultural Studies, Junior Year Abroad

RELATED EXPERIENCE

Summer 2001	*NYC Film Fest*	*New York, NY*

Festival Intern

- Responsible for the distribution of publicity materials
- Coordinated post-screening discussions and specialty panels
- Acted as liaison between filmmakers and festival sponsors

Summer 2000	*The Late Night Show*	*New York, NY*

Office Intern

- Managed all aspects of daily office operations
- Assisted show producers with production needs
- Maintained and updated department databases

EXTRACURRICULAR ACTIVITIES

2000–2002	*The Brown Daily*	*Providence, RI*

Arts Editor

1999–2002	*Brown Film Society*	*Providence, RI*

Executive Member

2001–2002	*Art Forum*	*Providence, RI*

Director of Student Film

SKILLS

- Fluent in French. Avid reader. Proficient in Microsoft Word, Excel, and Power-point.

chapter eighteen

Even though my WCA interview isn't scheduled until 11 a.m., I am up at the crack of dawn to catch Amanda before she leaves for work.

"You in there?" I pound against the bathroom door.

"Just a second!" The toilet flushes. She opens up the door a crack and pokes out her head, the end of her toothbrush jutting out between her teeth. "What's up? You need to come in?"

"I need to know what you think." With one hand I hold a black turtleneck sweater against my chest, with the other, a wool skirt to my hips. "Well?"

"Jesus! It's like ninety degrees outside. You're gonna fry!"

"I know," I drop my arms to my sides. "It's just, this is the only sensible thing I have to wear. None of my summer clothes are classy enough."

Amanda removes the toothbrush from her teeth and spits in the sink. "You can always wear a tank top under a light blazer."

"A blazer? Come on, Amanda, you know me better than that. When have you ever seen me in a *blazer*?"

"All right. Hang on." She gargles a handful of water and replaces her toothbrush on the sink counter. "I have something that might work." She grabs a hand cloth and heads to her bedroom.

"Now, I just bought this last week," she says, ducking into her closet. "But I don't mind you wearing it. Just be careful you don't get any stains." She emerges from the closet and hands me a smooth gray skirt suit. I check the label—DKNY. Then, the size—six.

"You're crazy!" I hand her back the suit. "I'll never fit in that."

"Sure, you will."

"No, I won't."

"I think you're wrong. You've lost a lot of weight recently."

I have?

"I have?"

"Here." She disappears back into her closet and rattles around for a bit. When she climbs back out, she has her most precious possession gripped tightly in her clutches. It's her scale. She places it delicately on floor.

I blink at her, uncomprehending.

"It's okay." She nods at me. "Go ahead. See for yourself."

I suppose sucking in my gut won't help. And keeping my eyes sealed shut only serves to stave off the inevitable. Still, I climb onto the scale gingerly, setting each foot down with trepidation. Then I open my eyes and look.

One hundred and ten pounds.

"Holy shit! I haven't weighed 110 pounds since high school!"

"Not bad, huh?" Amanda grins slyly. "It must be all that great sex you've been having."

I blush. Furiously. But it doesn't matter. I feel fantastic. To be almost too specific, I feel fifteen pounds lighter.

Now, nothing can ruin my day!

I'm waiting on a comfortable couch in the WCA lobby, and I'm trying to act all cool and collected, but it's really hard 'cause I just so happen to be sitting *right next* to that really hot actor whose name totally escapes me. You'd know him if you saw him. He's that gorgeous blond Brit or Aussie (I'm pretty sure it's Brit) who married Jennifer Connelly and, after years of playing to sidekick to Russell Crowe, has finally come into his own as a dashing leading man? Anyway, it's just the two of us sitting here. I mean, there is a receptionist, but she's lost in her own world, living between the twin earpieces of her headset. And there was another girl who walked in earlier, too, but she disappeared into the bathroom about forty-five minutes ago and still hasn't come out. I suspect she's touching up her highlights.

And so. Just me and Mr. Hot Movie Star. He's reading today's issue of *Variety* and I've got the *Hollywood Reporter*. That way, when we're done, we'll have something to talk about. I half expect him to turn to me—any moment now—and say, "You get to the part about the veep who ankled the weblet?"

Any moment now. Any moment—

"Sarah?"

Crap. I look up. A woman with really taut skin and eyes that don't blink approaches me like a crazed mannequin.

"Yes?" I jump to attention. Rather than salute, I thrust out my hand for a stiff handshake.

"Hi, Sarah, I'm Gail." The skin behind her ears twitches. I think she may have smiled at me. "This way, please." She beckons me with a bony finger.

Naturally, she leads me through a series of security doors. This is a talent agency, after all. And talent is a rare and highly valuable commodity in desperate need of good security.

We arrive at a room that appears a little out of the ordinary. For one, it's soundproof. And two, there is a glass partition in the middle of it. Gail takes me past the glass, into the tiny adjoining room and motions for me to sit. She doesn't need to point out which chair—there is only one.

"Why don't you get comfortable? Bob should be here any moment."

I can only nod in response. Because I have no idea what the hell she's talking about. Then, sure enough, the door swings open and a pudgy bald man—presumably Bob—shuffles in.

"Great! He's here!" Gail's ears twitch again when she looks at me. "Why don't we just get started, then? Would you like a glass of water?"

"Uh, no, I'm okay."

She smiles and taps me on the back with her long fingernail. A gesture of affection, I assume.

I watch in dismay as she sails out the room, a heavy door lurching closed behind her. Like a caged animal, I pivot my head back and forth across the glass windowpane between me and my tormentors, trying to get a better fix on the commotion on the other side of the room. Gail stands behind Bob. Bob puts on earphones. He smiles at me and points downward. Gail's hand lowers on a table in front of her and pushes a button I can't see.

"Sarah?" The room rattles with the echo of her voice. "We're going to get some levels. Just talk into the microphone like you would normally."

Now, I have no doubt that Gail is insane. But at least she's not hallucinating. There is, indeed, a microphone protruding from the table in front of me. I blink when I see it. I mean, really, are these people serious? To Laurie's credit, she did warn me that there would be a high volume of phone calls. But this is just ridiculous.

"Um, okay," I say, leaning toward the microphone. Bob flashes me a thumbs-up. I clear my throat. "Marianne Langold's office, please hold."

There is a moment of silence. And then the room shakes with

laughter. Possessed laughter. Demonic laughter. And I grin oafishly like the unwitting comedienne that I am.

"Very funny!" Gail chortles through the speakers. Her cackle is interrupted, however, when the door behind her flies open.

I see only a silhouette at first. Then the figure steps into the light and I recognize the girl I spotted earlier in the lobby. Her highlights look fabulous. The rest of her—well, not so much. Her arms are folded over her chest and her eyes are narrowed. Suffice it to say, she does not look very pleased.

I hear nothing. I see hands flail, and heads shake, and Gail's face pull further and further against her skull until I can almost see through her forehead. Eventually, after a moment of confusion I am not privy to, Bob heaves open the door to my room and hoists me out of the chair by my elbow.

As he leads me graciously out of the recording studio, Bob explains that the pretty girl with the lovely touch-ups is none other than Sarah Wagner, a gifted voice-over recording artist recently signed to WCA.

"You have a nice voice, too," he assures me.

"Oh, why, thank you—"

"But I think you're late for your interview."

See, this is the problem. As it is, I already feel like a dime a dozen. It's bad enough that I fit so nicely into the overwhelming statistic of the unemployed. But why do so many people have to be running around with my name too? It's no wonder none of my prospective employers find me all that distinguishable. When I made the conscious decision to lie on my résumé, I should have just gone the extra mile and called myself Persephone. Do you know anyone named Persephone? No, I didn't think so.

As I scramble through security door after security door on my way to meet Ms. Langold, it occurs to me that instead of letting my mind wander so inanely, I should try to regulate my breathing and focus. If this woman is anything like the monster Laurie made her out to be, I'm going to have a fine time trying to work my way out of this one.

"I am so sorry I'm late," I breathe at her door. "But I can explain—"

"No need." Marianne Langold uncrosses her legs at her desk. "I just heard from Gail. How hilarious!" She lets out a peal of ringing laughter. Not demonic, not possessed. A singing laugh, the way laughs are supposed to be. She wipes a tear from the corner of her eye. "I'm surprised it doesn't happen more often."

"Really? I was hoping you'd tell me it happens all the time."

She laughs again. And I think she's quite beautiful when she does. Not your normal standard for beauty, but the kind that doesn't come with a tuck behind the ears or an injection to the lips. It's the beauty that keeps her eyes bright and lively, that smooths out the hint of wrinkles at the corners of her mouth.

"Here, take a seat," she says. "And let me look for your résumé. I had it right in front of me a second ago."

I settle down in the chair in front of her desk and take a deep breath. It's Showtime.

"Ah, yes." Marianne picks up the sheet of paper. "So you graduated in May?"

Here goes nothing. "That's right."

"And what have you been doing with yourself since?"

"Actually, I went to Europe." There. That was easy enough.

"You did?"

"Oh, yes. I traveled through the south of France with my college roommate for the first month. A friend of ours from Harvard was writing budget hotel reviews for *Let's Go* in Paris, so we met up with him later and helped lighten the load. He compensated us, but only very modestly."

Please, bear in mind. These aren't all just outrageous lies. I did go to France with my roommate right after college. And the hotel review I wrote for my Harvard friend? Let's just say when the book went into publication, my piece failed to make the cut.

"Really?" Marianne's eyes widen. "You know, my father is French. I spent a couple of years of my childhood growing up on the Côte d'Azur. Did you go to Antibes at all?"

"Of course! I love Antibes!" This too is absolutely true. My roommate and I fell so much in the love with the town, we even canceled one leg of our trip to stay there longer.

Marianne cocks her head and smiles at me. *"Donc, tu parles bien le français?"* she asks, mischief dancing in her eyes.

"Pas couramment. Je n'ai pas assez de temps pour pratiquer."

Mischief stops dancing. Mischief grows so fat and unwieldy, her eyebrows make way to let it pass. She's impressed. And so am I. Who knew those four years of college French would actually stick?

"Okay, Sarah, tell me something." Marianne leans forward on her elbows, her palms pressed down on the desk. Is it time for the curve ball already? I must be doing exceedingly well. "You say you're an avid reader on your résumé," she says. "I'd be curious to know what the last good book you read was."

You have got to be *kidding* me! Man, if all my interviews were this easy, I'd—well, I guess I'd be employed.

"Well, you know," I inch forward a little, as if confiding a particularly juicy secret. "When I was in Paris, I picked up a French translation of a German book that was pretty good. Have you heard of *Die Dämmerung*?"

"You read that?" she asks incredulously.

"Yes."

"What did you think?"

"I thought it was fantastic." I shrug. "I enjoy German absurdism. It's a nice change from all the generic, cookie-cutter romances we have here." Suddenly I remember Marianne Langold's client roster includes a fair number of actresses who have eked out a damn good living playing the heroines in screen adaptations of such generic romances. "But, to tell you the truth," I add, anxious not to alienate her just yet. "I really do enjoy a good romantic comedy, too. It's my guilty pleasure."

Phew. Close one.

There is a rap at the door. Marianne and I both pivot in our seats to find a young man with incredibly chiseled features and amazing bone structure open the door and lean his head into the office. He's wearing a tie to put my entire wardrobe to shame.

Marianne stiffens and scowls. "What?" she barks.

"Sorry to interrupt, Ms. Langold. Do you have a second?"

Her scowl deepens. "Absolutely not!" She gestures to me. "Look who I am talking to!"

The man turns to me, stricken, and studies me with a look of terror I know oh-so-well. It's the same look people gave me at the wedding when I told them I was a Rockette. The same look I know I gave Sarah Wagner when she waltzed into the recording studio. He's trying to place me, trying to figure out what in the world could possibly make me so goddamn special.

His uneasy silence is finally broken. The room chimes with the silver bells of Marianne Langold's laugh once again.

"I'm just kidding." She chuckles and points to me. "She's nobody!"

Her laugh is contagious. Soon, the man at her door has caught it. And then I have, too. I laugh because I have to. Because crying in an interview is against the rules. But, inside I can feel myself shrinking. I am no longer Persephone. I am not even Sarah. I am, in fact, that dime a dozen, that one among many of the unemployed.

I am nobody.

The laughing feels good, though. The laughing gives me the strength to wave good-bye to the man when he exits the office, it gives me the strength to smile politely when Marianne describes the position she is looking to fill. It gives me the strength, in the end, to follow her when she stands and leads me out.

Before she opens the door, however, she leans in and whispers to me.

"Now, I'm not really supposed to say this," she begins. "I don't get final approval on new hires. Human Resources likes to recommend the applicants themselves, check references, that sort of thing. Makes them feel necessary, I suppose. But the job is yours, as far as I'm concerned." She extends her hand. "It was a pleasure to meet you, Sarah. You'll be hearing from me soon."

I am so thrilled, I want to kiss her. So, I do. Twice, once on each cheek.

"*Comme on fait en France,*" I explain.

She beams.

And I? Well, I'm overcome with a strange sensation I can't quite place. Could it be victory?

I yank out my cell phone and start dialing Laurie's work number as soon as I step off the elevator on the ground floor.

"You and I met as interns at the New York Film Fest," I tell her.

"I know that."

"But you're a couple of years older than me. I just graduated this May."

"Ooookay."

"Laurie, please! You're my only reference!"

"Relax. You have nothing to worry about."

"**J**ust pick a restaurant," Jake implores. "Any restaurant."

"Do I have to?"

"Somewhere *nice*," he insists.

I groan. "You know I hate picking restaurants." I really, really do. New York City is like a diner with a daunting ten-page menu— one you know you'll never read entirely. The first time the waiter drops by, you panic and stutter and finally ask that he return in another five minutes. But when he comes back, you still can't quite decide between the chef salad, the tuna melt, or the chili with a side of fries. So you make someone else at your table order first and hopefully their selection will be appealing enough for you to just say, "I'll have the same."

"What about Vietnamese?" Jake asks. "You liked Nam Phuong, didn't you?"

"That's all the way downtown."

"How about Pastis?"

"Too expensive."

"I told you. I don't mind. I *want* to take you out."

"But we have to make reservations—"

"I'll call right now."

"No, no, no," I shake my head adamantly. "They'll still make us wait. I hate waiting for food. I'm hungry *now*."

"Wanna go to Serendipity? We can get that frozen hot chocolate you're always talking about."

"Look, Jake. My feet are killing me. I just took off my shoes. Are you really going to make me put them right back on again?"

He burrows his head in his hands. "So that's it? You just want to order in?"

"You mind?"

"What? Chinese again?"

"Mmmm. Perfect." I stretch back on the sofa and prop my sore toes up on the coffee table. Jake sighs and heads into the kitchen to find the menu.

"You sure about this?" he asks when he returns. " 'Cause I'm happy to take you anywhere you want to go."

"I don't get it! Why all the fuss?"

"Because I want to do something *special* for you. I want to celebrate."

"Why? I didn't get the job yet."

"So? She said it's as good as yours."

"Still . . ." I trail off. There really isn't a good reason for me to so stubbornly refuse Jake's sweet offer. But celebrating this early on has a troubling fall of Troy element to it that I just can't shake.

"Chinese is exactly what I want tonight," I say resolutely. "Order the House Special Chow Fun. And we'll use the real plates."

"Fine," he grumbles as he picks up the phone.

The food arrives twenty minutes later and by then I'm ready to tear open the paper bag with my teeth and burrow in for my spring roll. Jake, however, shoos me out of the kitchen and makes me clear off the coffee table. He sets down two bamboo place mats.

"Where'd you get those?"

"They're yours." He eyes me curiously. "You don't recognize them?"

I shrug. "Must be Amanda's."

He ducks back into the kitchen and returns with a saucer for the duck sauce. Then it's two small plates for each individual spring roll, and after that, two larger plates for the noodles.

"Sit down already, will you?" I plead.

"No, this still isn't right," he says, chewing thoughtfully on his thumb knuckle.

"It looks wonderful. Can we eat now?"

"Hang on a sec." Before I know it, he's trotting into my bathroom. I dip my spring roll into the duck sauce and take a bite.

"He we go!" He emerges proudly displaying two of my vanilla-scented votive candles.

"What do you think?" He digs around in his pocket for matches.

"Very nice," I say with my mouth full, patting the sofa cushion beside me. He doesn't sit until the candles are lit and appropriately positioned. I shove the duck sauce toward him. He doesn't touch it.

"You know, I got you something."

I swallow hard. "You did?"

"Yeah."

"Like what?"

"A gift. More like a reward. For a job well done today."

My heart sinks. The whole night he's been nothing but kind and considerate and loving, and here I am with duck sauce on my chin and a stray noodle stuck to my lap.

"Oh, Jake," I say softly. "You didn't have to do that."

"But I wanted to." He grins and hands me a small package wrapped in simple brown packing paper. I take it from him eagerly, then freeze at once.

I don't even have to unwrap the gift to know what it is. It's a book. And the reason I know this is because there is a silver sticker on the crease, just underneath the ribbon. The name on the sticker, in elegant bold font, is "Regal Bookstore."

"Go ahead. Open it."

Wordlessly, I peel back the wrapping and try to keep my trembling fingers from betraying my rage. I flip the book over to the front cover. *A Tree Grows in Brooklyn*.

"I noticed you finished those other two manuscripts," he says. "You left one at my apartment. I figured you probably needed something new to read."

I put the book down on the table and look up at him, feeling my eyes burn. "Where did you get this?" I demand.

"Huh?" My reaction has startled him. "Oh, just this little bookstore in my neighborhood. A couple of blocks away from where I live."

"Why did you go there?"

"I thought it was obvious." He shrugs. "I went there to buy you a book."

Subtle tactics are beyond me at this point. I start spewing the angry words before I have a chance to rethink them. "You sure this has nothing to do with your ex-girlfriend?"

Jake blinks at me. "How did you know—" He stops himself, his eyes narrowing. "Have you been going through my stuff?"

"I don't think it matters right now."

"*I* think it does."

For a moment we say nothing, silently fuming, letting our heated glares do the fighting for us. Finally, Jake looks away, focusing his attention on the dancing flames of the candles. "For your information," he says, "she wasn't working today."

"And how would you have known that?"

"I don't think it matters right now."

I seethe through clenched teeth. "*I* think it does."

"Know what? I've told you a million times before. I'm not going to talk about this." He rises stiffly and grabs his wallet, stuffing it angrily into his pocket.

"Fine." I remain seated. And even though there is a knot gnawing at my stomach, even though my throat feels parched, and my eyes are stinging and a wave of nausea is welling up inside me, I clench my fists and wait for the anguish to subside.

"I'm leaving now," he tells me coldly, probably waiting for me to stop him.

"I think that's a great idea."

chapter nineteen

You could look at my day in one of two ways. You could say I've spent the entire morning waiting for the phone to ring. But that sounds pathetic. True, but pathetic. And so damn obvious. Of course I spend the morning waiting for the phone to ring. I am always waiting for the phone to ring. No matter what I'm doing, or how much I'm enjoying it, believe me—I will stop *cold* if I think I've heard ringing. Because there is always that chance, that thrill—the mystery! Answering that phone could change my life completely. You just never know.

On the other hand, you could also say I've spent my entire morning smoking. Which is also true. And also pathetic. But at least it sounds more productive, as if I've accomplished something. The ashtray holds the proof that I have been hard at work for the last few hours burning the hell out of the last of my nicotine supply.

In times of great desperation, bad habits fit most comfortably. And smoking is no exception. It's a familiar cycle I can easily slip into. Inhale and exhale. My yin and yang. Like entertaining thoughts of calling Jake and then firmly deciding to wait for him to call me. Hating myself for overreacting. Then hating *him* for having the power to cause me so much grief. What is my chief complaint anyway? The only glaring mistake Jake ever committed was the fact that he had the gall to exist before I met him. He's probably had torrid affairs, he's probably fallen in love, and he's probably even had his heart broken—all before I ever came into his life. It kills me! All I ever wanted was to believe that we were meant to be, that I conjured him up out of thin air expressly to be my soul mate. I'd like to think that I wouldn't have handed over my heart to just anyone kind enough to take it. Or would I?

If Jake is going to reduce me to this, if his admittedly minor transgressions can cause me so much distress—even unintentionally—than he damn well better earn the right. He better call me. He better apologize for being the only person in the world who could possibly make me feel this weak and vulnerable.

Or should I just grow up and call him?

By 3:30 p.m., I've run out of cigarettes. Grumpily, I slide on my sneakers, stuff my keys in my pocket, and head to my front door. I skid to a stop before I even reach the hallway.

Could it be? Did I just hear—my phone ring?

I alter my course and make a mad dash for the telephone.

"Hello?"

"Sarah?"

"Yes?"

"This is Catherine at WCA Human Resources. I've got good news. Marianne Langold expects you to report for work starting tomorrow at nine a.m." She lowers her voice. "Just between you and me, we don't usually hire people so quickly. But Marianne gave you a fantastic recommendation. We'll do your background check and call your references while you're at the office. It's just a formality really."

"Catherine, thank you! This makes my day!" I gush.

"It's my pleasure to welcome you onboard. I'll need you to drop by the offices some time today to pick up your orientation manual and security key card. Is there any time you know you'll be free?"

"I can be there in twenty minutes," I say.

I'm actually there in fifteen.

"That was quick," says Catherine, greeting me in the lobby. She is a short, fleshy bohemian wearing a flowing dress. She pumps my hand heartily and the two large fish earrings that dangle below her short, cropped hair swim giddily above her shoulders.

"Come into my office and we'll fix you right up," she says, leading me down the corridor.

I hardly have time to get a good look at Catherine's office. Within only seconds, she's loaded me up to my forehead with a stack of manuals: Orientation kit. Employee manual. Procedural policies. New York staff book. Los Angles staff book. Confidentiality agreement. Operations and Usage manual.

"That comes with instructions and blank forms in the back," she explains. "Messenger forms, fax templates, invoice sheets, time cards. They might seem overwhelming at first, but they'll make sense soon. How are you with computers?"

"I'm very good with computers," I pipe in from behind the volumes of reading material in my arms.

"Great. We might make you sit in during our afternoon training class tomorrow anyway. But definitely take our Computer Operations guide to look over just in case." She tosses the book on top of the pile. "And then . . ." She pauses. "Hmm."

I peer around my cargo and find her frowning at me, holding a security key card attached to the end of a rope.

"Ah! There you are." She hangs the security card around my neck. "Welcome to WCA."

I smile back my gratitude and teeter out of her office.

The manuals, when spread out on my bed, take up every square inch of space available. I myself have been relegated to the floor, a stack of Post-its beside me, a ballpoint pen in my hand, and a yellow highlighter between my teeth.

I've got a long, long night ahead of me.

I sign the confidentiality agreement and cast it aside, making room for the massive Procedural Policies manual. Sighing, I attach a Post-it to the top of page one, and write: *Telephone*. I begin reading the instructions and get my highlighter ready.

The word "agent" does not need to be highlighted. "Agent" always appears on the page in bold capital letters. When answering **THE AGENT's** phone, WCA requires assistants to say, "This is **THE AGENT's** office, who may I say is calling?" It is improper etiquette to immediately put a caller on hold. The assistant must always take the caller's name and phone number before notifying **THE AGENT** of the call. (In case you were wondering, no, the word "assistant" is never capitalized. Why would it be?)

I flip the page and learn that, when entering **THE AGENT's** office, the assistant must always have a pad of paper and pen in hand. No highlighter necessary for that bit of information either. That's just common sense.

In between the chapters titled "Proper Dress Code" and "Vacation Request Policies," my phone rings. This time, it is no longer music to my ears. It is alarm bells, shrieking sirens. I bite down hard on the end of the highlighter and debate whether to answer it. No, rather, I dread answering it. Because I've been burdened with such vast amounts of new information, I've been able to stave off thoughts of Jake for most of the afternoon. The ringing of my telephone is an unexpected jolt of reality that I am not fully prepared to deal with. I chew thoughtfully on the cap of my pen. Reluctantly, I crawl toward the phone.

"Hi, it's me." Not Jake. Laurie. I breathe an enormous sigh of relief.

"Hi, you."

"What happened with the job?"

"I got it."

"Really? Why didn't you tell me!"

"I'm sorry. There's just so much I have to do to get ready."

"That's silly. We should go out and celebrate."

"Laurie, I can't." Call me superstitious.

"Oh, come on. I got you on the list for our movie premiere at the Ziegfeld. I want you to come with me. You know you want to."

"I really, really can't. They gave me homework. Stacks and stacks of it. I'm going to have to spend all night sorting through this stuff."

"You can't be serious."

"I'm afraid I am." I bite my lip. Because I really do want to go to a big-time movie premiere. Maybe I could even snag a seat next to the supporting cast, which, I've heard, includes Andy Richter. And I could wear that Diane von Furstenberg dress I bought for the wedding and might never have the occasion to wear again. And there'd be champagne, and photographers, and goodie bags chock full of airline-sized vodka bottles and stuffed animals.

But what good will any of this do me in the long run? What is one bright, dazzling night when I've got a brilliant new career ahead of me?

"You're definitely not coming?" Laurie taunts me. "You're absolutely sure?"

"Yeah," I mumble. "I'm sure."

When Laurie and I hang up, I stick my pen back into my mouth and think.

I thought I would be relieved that it wasn't Jake on the line. But, goddamnit, why *hasn't* he called?

I pick up the Operations and Usage manual, open it to the first page and try to focus, try again to cast out unwanted thoughts of Jake. For so long, my priorities have been tossed aside, spun in a washer, hung to dry on a clothesline, flapping in heavy gusts of wind. But now I'm reeling them in, ready to fold and sort. I no longer have any time for nonsense. I have a job, a good job, a job I might enjoy. Thoughts of boys—and certainly thoughts of boys with charming, gracious, and beautiful ex-girlfriends—would just be a colossal waste of my time and energy.

In my manual, I highlight a sentence I haven't even bothered to read and have no idea what it says. And by the end of the evening, three of the books on my bed are bleeding highlighter fluid. The yellow lines have leaked onto my hands and thighs, and there is even a streak across my forehead I can't even begin to explain.

At 8 a.m., well before the doors to the WCA building will open, I am seated across the street at a café, smoking my third cigarette of the morning. The WCA New York staff book is splayed open on my lap, stained with yellow ink and fresh spots of coffee. When I'm through memorizing the name, title, and extension of every agent working out of the East Coast office, I order a refill and pull out my LA staff book. I place a hand over the first page and close my eyes, probing my memory for the name of every West Coast agent.

At 8:45, I slide my key card through the security doors and enter the silent offices. After a few minutes spent tiptoeing through the dark, softly humming corridors, I find the pantry. I pull out the can of Colombian roast from top shelf of the cupboard, rinse out the coffeepot in the sink, and start looking for instructions.

Marianne Langold arrives promptly at 9 a.m.

"Good morning, Sarah," she chirps at me.

"Good morning, Ms. Langold." I rise from behind my cubicle.

"Sarah, please. Call me Marianne. Whenever I hear 'Ms. Langold' I feel like a grammar school teacher."

She strides into her office and I hop up after her, holding a pad of paper in one hand, a pen in the other.

"I was wondering how you like your coffee," I say from her doorway.

"Oh," Marianne tosses her *New York Times* on her desk. "You don't have to get me coffee."

"I just made a fresh pot. I was going to get a cup for myself. You sure you don't want any?"

"Hmmm." She sits at her desk and crosses her legs. "Black with Splenda is fine."

I scurry out of her office and jot down on my legal pad, "Black with Splenda."

When I return, I am balancing two generously filled WCA coffee mugs. I carefully hand one over to her.

"Mmm, this is very good," she says, licking her lips.

I realize I am holding my breath. I exhale deeply through my nostrils.

"Here," Marianne nods at a stack of papers on the edge of her desk. "Can you run off two copies of that script for me?"

"Certainly."

The halls of WCA have been filled with new life within the past ten minutes. The ubiquitous hum in the office has now swelled into a great big yawn. It is the sound a car makes in the middle of winter, when you pump the accelerator and wait for the engine to turn over. It is a murmur about to become a roar. The quickening pace of high-heeled shoes clicking against the tile. The trill of a telephone growing more and more insistent.

There is nothing sinister about these cream-colored walls or white laminate desks. If anything, they are warmly inviting and, in their faintly lemon-scented freshness, terribly exciting. Yet, walking down this strange tunnel brings forth a torrent of so many conflicting and overpowering memories. I recall the terror of my first day of preschool, the curiosity of my introduction to high school, the thrill of my first taste of freedom at college. And if I were as young as I was then (as young, even, as I claim to be on my résumé), maybe I'd feel a little more spirited, a little more adventurous. I'd grab the reins, thrust my foot in the stirrup, swing my hat above my head, and yell, "Giddyup!" But I've been bucked off this steed before. And I still have the bruises to prove it. So, this time, I will proceed with caution.

I round the corner of the hallway. A mass of impeccably dressed and neatly coiffed assistants is hovering on the other side of the pantry. They are all waiting in line for the copy machine.

"Oh, no!" I groan.

A young, dark-haired woman in front of me turns and uses her index finger to push her glasses up on the bridge of her nose. "The machine is broken," she informs me. "Sam Larson just called down to Tech Support. They said it would take about thirty minutes to get up here."

"What's wrong with it?"

She shrugs and her glasses slide down her nose again. "Paper jam, I guess."

I heave a sigh and push my way through the line.

"Excuse me," I mutter to the line of pissy assistants.

"It's broken!" shouts an anonymous male voice. I ignore him and put my script down on top of the printer so I can roll up my sleeves. The sleeves, actually, of the Ralph Lauren suit I've borrowed from Amanda. A good reason to be particularly mindful of leaky ink cartridges.

I raise a few flaps of the copy machine, open a few trays, and eventually find the offending sheet of paper coiled around the "Warning: Hot!" cylinder. I use my fingertips to gingerly pry away the page.

I close the lid, and the machine sighs, flashing a ray of yellow light across the glass.

"I am just going to test it," I say over my shoulder at the hoard of wide-eyed, gaping assistants. No one dares challenge me. I slide in my script and hit "Copy." With cheerful compliance, the machine spits out the pristine copies.

"It works!" someone cries.

A chorus of hurrahs, shrieks of delight! I wouldn't be surprised if the assistants hoisted me onto their shoulders and paraded me out to the lobby. I'm an all-around success, an instant victor, lauded by a dozen new friends.

So why do I still feel so sick to my stomach?

I remove my new copies, and the original, from the machine and walk past the sea of outstretched hands. I shake a few, forget every name, and perhaps even fail to give my own. For months, I've grown accustomed to being a nobody. I've learned to live with defeat, grown complacent with failure. It isn't easy to step into this office, to wear these clothes, and pretend to be one of the Happily Employed. Maybe I'm skeptical, perhaps a bit wary, but it just doesn't feel right.

For the rest of the morning, I hide behind my computer screen, tucked into the cavern of my cubicle. I pay no attention to anything that doesn't appear directly on the computer screen in front of me and listen to nothing but the voices that come through the headset of my phone. And in such a deliberate fog of focus, I find myself performing superiorly.

The rapid succession of phone calls doesn't fluster me in the least. I take an hour (two at the most) to create a Filemaker Pro database to serve as a log sheet for both incoming and outgoing calls. Most of the callers I recognize from either my New York or LA staff books. When I hear an unfamiliar name, I am meticulous about taking down the proper spelling and make sure to repeat the phone numbers back my callers.

I hang up line one, answer line two. "Hello, this is Marianne Langold's office, who may I say is calling?"

"This is Peter Owens." Bingo! LA Head of Literary Affairs.

"Hello, Mr. Owens. Please hold for a moment." While speaking to him, I pull up my Instant Messenger window and type to Marianne, "Peter Owens, Line 2." I put him on hold and wait.

A message returns. "Thx." The flashing light on line two clicks open. Line one begins to ring again.

"Marianne Langold's office, who may I say is calling?"

"Yes, hello. This is Gil. Do you know if Marianne has copies of the new Ainsley script?"

I happen to know for a fact she does. I made those very copies myself earlier this morning. But whether Gil—Gil Meadows, in the film production department upstairs, I assume—should be made aware of this fact is unknown to me.

"If you hold on a minute, I'll find out for you," I say sweetly. I type to Marianne, "Gil Meadows, wants Ainsley script."

The message returns, "Come in." I remove my headset and walk into Marianne's office, just as she switches over from line two to line one.

"Gil?" She smiles at me as she barks into her speakerphone. "I've got the script right here on my desk. I'm sending my assistant up with it right now." She hangs up.

"This is for Gil Meadows on the eighth floor," she says, handing me the script. "Room 815. Super nice guy. If he's not too busy, you should take a moment to introduce yourself, let him know who you are. We work together pretty often."

"Of course."

Upstairs, the door to room 815 is closed. So I sidle up to the assistant seated outside his office.

"Excuse me? I'm Sarah, from Marianne Langold's office? I have the Ainsley script for Mr. Meadows?"

She fixes me with a stern look and jabs a finger at the mouthpiece of her headset, indicating she's on a call. She waves me toward the office and mimes a knock. Hesitantly, I tap on the door.

"Come in!"

I nudge the door open just enough to allow a slither of light to fall upon a man behind a large, mahogany executive desk. He raises his pencil-thin, silvered eyebrows.

"Can I help you?"

"I have the Ainsley script you asked for?"

"Ah, yes," he beckons me in. I scurry quickly to his desk. "So you must be Marianne's new assistant."

"Yes. Hi. I'm—"

"Sarah Pelletier!" says a female voice from the couch at the other end of the room. I swivel. Then I leap right out of my skin.

Her little blonde bun is cocked to the side. Her teeth are bared, but where I expect to see blood-tipped fangs instead I see nothing but a pleasant smile. Which is even scarier.

"Sarah, doll, I had no idea you worked here!"

For a split second time stops. Sound all but disappears. I find myself trying to remember where the hell I put my voice.

"Hi, Gracie," I say, although the words sound distant.

"Well, how about that?" Gil snorts, faintly amused. "You two know each other?"

I brace myself for the ax to fall.

Gracie's grin broadens. "We sure do! Small world, isn't it? How've you been, Sarah?"

"I . . . I . . ."

"Been working here long?"

"Uh, no. Today's my first day."

"Really? That's wonderful! Congratulations."

"Um, thanks." I shift uneasily from foot to foot.

"Ah, Sarah?" I wheel around toward Gil. "I'm sorry to do this, but Gracie and I have a lot to cover, and I've got a meeting in half—"

"Right, sorry," I say quickly, hustling out of the door.

"Bye, doll!" Gracie waves jovially to me.

I close the door behind me and wait a while for the throbbing in my chest to ease.

"Sorry about that," Gil's assistant removes her headset and sighs. "Goddamn conference calls go on for hours." She stares at me quizzically. "You feeling all right?"

"Uh-huh."

"You sure? You look a little pale."

I straighten, feeling my heartbeat return to normal and my wheezing subside.

"I'm fine," I say. And the shocking thing is, I really believe it.

Gil's assistant extends her hand.

"I'm Sarah, by the way."

I chuckle. "Me, too."

"Another Sarah? Whaddya know."

I shrug and drop her hand. "It's nice to meet you. But I think Marianne is waiting for me—"

"Go ahead. I'm sure I'll be seeing you around soon."

I wave good-bye and tear down the hall.

Marianne is waiting at my desk when I return.

"Perfect timing!" she says, holding out a sheet of paper. "Can you fax this for me? It needs a cover sheet. It's going to Peter Owens at the LA office."

"You got it."

I take a seat and pull up the Fax Template on my computer to begin composing a cover sheet. Seconds later, a high-pitched trill echoes in my earpiece. I hit line one to answer the call.

"Marianne Langold's office, who may I say is calling?"

"This the Union Square Café. We're calling to confirm Ms. Langold's dinner reservations for tonight?"

"Hold on just one moment." I pull up her calendar. Out of the corner of my eye, I see the other line flashing. "Yes, at eight-thirty."

"We look forward to seeing her."

I hang up and answer the second call.

"Marianne Langold's office?"

"Yes, hi. This is Marianne's husband, Michael. Is Marianne busy right now?"

"Oh, hi, Michael. No, I don't think so. Let me put you right through." I patch him in, the way Marianne specifically asked me to for family members.

I type up the rest of the fax cover sheet and send it off. Then I dial the LA office. "Peter Owens's office, please," I say briskly. The receptionist puts me right through. His assistant Julie answers immediately.

"Peter Owens's office, who may I say is calling?"

"Hi, Julie. It's Sarah from Marianne Langold's office. Just wanted to let you know I sent the fax Peter was waiting for."

"Excellent! I'll get it to him right way." Line two begins flashing. I click over.

"Marianne Langold's office, who may I say is calling?"

"Sarah, this is Catherine in Human Resources. May I see you in my office, please?"

"Sure," I yank off my headset and stand.

My knees feel weak. I have to put my palm down on the desk to steady myself. A sick, overwhelming sense of dread washes over me.

Catherine stands before me, her palm stiff and open. Meekly, I hang my shameful head and remove the security key card from its noose around my neck. I hand it to her without meeting her eye.

"Thank you," she says and sits down at her desk.

"Do I get a chance to explain?" I ask, my voice faltering. I force myself to look up at her.

"Frankly, no. I'm not interested. We both know you lied on your résumé. Here at WCA, we don't tolerate that sort of misrepresentation. It's a firm rule."

I make the effort to raise my chin and act defiant. But my resolve is waning. "I think I have a right to defend myself."

"Well, I'm sorry. You don't."

There is a rap at her door. A man in a uniform leans in. "Catherine, you called for me?"

"Yes, Roger." She fixes me with a pointed stare. "Sarah, please don't make this any harder than it has to be. Roger will escort you out of the building. I will explain the situation to Ms. Langold." With that, she picks up her phone and angles herself away from me. I lower my chin, bite my lip, and try my damnedest not to burst into tears as the security guard leads me out of her office.

Roger follows me onto the elevator and keeps his eyes averted. To avoid looking at him, too, I stare unblinking at the floor numbers above the doors as they light up, silently counting down my descent.

I linger outside the WCA building and cover my face with my hands, my shoulders racked with sobs. Across the street, a group of German tourists snaps photographs of the skyscrapers. A street vendor on the corner loudly hawks his hot dogs, pretzels, and overpriced cans of soda. A homeless man stops in front of me and watches me cry. He soon decides I'm not worth the bother and continues on.

I loiter by the entrance because I'm not ready to go anywhere else. And there I stay until I've smoked every cigarette in my pack except for the last. My fingers tremble when I hold the filter to my lips.

Fired.

I've been fired.

Sentenced to death by a witch trial before I even cast my first spell. Blackballed by HUAC before I even produced a script with Communist undertones. My career is over. And it had never really begun.

Well, stick that on your résumé and smoke it.

I light up the last cigarette, crumble up the pack into a tight wad in my fist, and throw it into the trash can standing beside me. With a sweaty palm, I reach into my bag for my cell phone. I don't really want to talk to anyone. Not Jake, not Laurie, and certainly not Amanda.

I call my mother. She answers immediately.

"Mom?"

"Sarah? What's the matter, sweetie-pie?"

"Mom, I was fired." My voice cracks, suddenly rattled again with heaving sobs.

"There, there," my mother soothes. Already I can imagine myself cradled in her arms, rocked gently back and forth, her face a blur, but her voice—that sweet, supple pacifier—held close to my ear. "Baby," she calls me. "Baby, everything is going to be all right . . ."

chapter twenty

I come home to my apartment and lean my back against the door, letting it sway closed behind me. It feels good to be alone, to let the silence in the room wash over me. I lift my chin and feel the sting where dried tears once streaked my cheeks. It's over now. Forgotten. I make my way toward the bedroom.

I stop when I hear muffled whimpers. Mine? No, they couldn't be. They're coming from behind the closed door to Amanda's bedroom.

Oh, of course! Of all the days to fall victim to a major crisis, natually she would have to pick today. The nerve of her!

You know what? It's not my problem. I don't want to go in. I don't *have* to go in. I'm shouldering enough as it is. I'm at full crisis capacity, I tell you. I'd be no good to anyone in the state I'm in.

Begrudgingly, I shuffle over to her room and knock on her door. "Hey, you okay?"

"No!" she sniffs.

"You want me to come in?"

"No!"

"All right." Don't have to tell me twice.

"Wait!" Damn. I hear her blow her nose. "It's okay. It's open."

Damn, and damn again. I open the door and peer inside. Amanda is propped up on the pillows of her bed, wearing her silk pajamas. Her hair is in a ponytail. Amanda's hair is *never* in a ponytail. She looks like she's four years old.

"Ryan hasn't been returning my phone calls." She reaches for a tissue on the nightstand. "He won't talk to me at the office either. I haven't spoken to him in a week."

"He's probably busy."

Her eyes start to water. "I saw him leave today. He walked out with the new receptionist."

"The receptionist? That was supposed to be my job." Amanda gives me a hard look. I shake my head at my own insensitivity and take a seat on the edge of her bed. "Right. Sorry. This is about you."

A single tear trails down her face. She doesn't use the tissue, though. She balls it up in her tiny little fist. "It's not fair. Why does this have to happen to me?"

"Oh, Amanda. It happens to *everyone*. It sucks, I know, but we all go through it."

"Not you."

"Of course, me! You don't think I understand rejection?"

"No," Amanda shakes her head vehemently. "You don't. You're so happy with Jake."

I suck in my breath. "Who said I was happy with Jake?"

"You don't have to say it. It's obvious." She starts shredding her tissue into thin, even strips. And all the comforting words I can think to say to her get lodged in a lump in my throat.

Amanda looks up at me, blinking away the tears. "What time is it?"

I look at my watch. "Six-ish?"

"Shit." She runs a hand through her hair, her large, glazed eyes staring off into space. She sighs and heaves herself reluctantly off the bed. I watch wordlessly as she slips into the bathroom, the door halfheartedly swinging closed behind her.

Only two hours later, Amanda emerges from her bedroom wearing her best face. And her favorite American Apparel fitted tee and her most flattering pair of Seven jeans. Her hair has been tucked into a buttoned-down golf cap. She takes a seat next me on the living room sofa and fastens a large silver hoop to her ear.

"A couple friends from work are meeting me downtown at the Tribeca Grand if you wanna come," she offers.

"Yeah, I don't know."

"You sure?"

"Yeah," I return my attention to the TV screen. "I'm not in the mood. I don't really feel like getting all dressed up right now."

"Okay," she slides on the other hoop earring. "I got to run. I probably won't be home until late."

"Have a good time," I say as the door slams closed behind her.

How does she do that? It's not fair! I press hard on the volume control of the remote until the sound of the TV drowns out the roar of fury in my ears.

I had the whole night planned out. We'd sit here on the sofa, me in my flannel robe, her in her silk pj's, and we'd pop in her *Centerstage* DVD (which we both agree is, hands down, the best film of 2000) and gorge on her new shipment of Wisconsin danishes and trade swigs of Diet Coke from the two-liter bottle. I'd listen to her sob story all over again—this time in painful detail—and I'd act shocked when she remembered the time Ryan first suggested the firm hire a "hot, new secretary" or when she discovered his office suspiciously locked, with the lights off, even though she was sure she never saw him leave. Then, maybe—just maybe—when she was through, she'd dab her red eyes with the end of her tissue and find it in her heart to maybe—just maybe—listen to *me*. Would that have killed her? Couldn't she have let me have my turn next?

Who I am kidding? I've been so traumatized by the events of my day, I've officially gone delusional. I've painted Amanda in a light so glowingly fierce, it would have seared the pale sheath of skin right off her bones.

Amanda isn't the person I need tonight. She never was.

I reach for the phone on the coffee table and start dialing.

"Hello?"

"Jake, it's me. I want you to come over."

"Oh, yeah?" He hesitates. "Sure, why not? I'll throw my journal into my bag, and maybe my credit card statements. Anything else you'd like to sort through?"

"Please, don't be mean to me." I swallow to keep my throat from constricting. "I've had a rough day."

"Yeah? Having a job wasn't all it was cracked up to be? I could have told you that."

"I got fired."

"Ha-ha. Very funny."

"No. I'm serious."

I can hear the sharp whistle as he sucks in his breath. "Really?"

"Yeah."

He pauses. "I'll be right there."

He shows up at my door an hour later. When I see him standing in my hallway, wearing the same gray, waffled long-sleeved shirt he wore the first day I met him, my heart stops. I have no intention of asking about his day nor do I wish to fill him in on the details of mine. Without a word, with the door still open, I thrust myself against him, grind myself up against his hard ribs, and force my tongue into his mouth. He lifts me off my feet—I kid you not! Me!—and carries me off to the bedroom. Maybe he closes the door behind him, maybe not. Who cares?

My bedroom is a whirlwind of discarded clothes, of sheets and pillows kicked off the bed. And when the angry storm has subsided, I look up to find Jake's smooth, naked body hovering above me. With a gentle smile, he brushes my hair away from my face and kisses me lightly on the lips. I grip his arms tightly, digging my nails into his shoulder blades, as he lowers himself carefully and deliberately.

Jake cups my face with his soft, strong hand and nestles his head against the crook of my neck. I close my eyes and feel his fingertips graze the back of my ear.

"I love you," he whispers.

We stop and pull apart immediately. And we both wait fearfully for my reaction.

I burst into tears.

chapter twenty-one

I wake up the next morning to the pounding of my own heart. For a few moments, I try to string together a hazy recollection of events and vaguely recall having been awakened earlier to Jake's soft lips pressed against my cheek, his whispered promise to call me later. Everything else is a blur.

The mystery of the fog that clouds my memory terrifies me. It's not that I don't know what happened last night—although the specifics remain painfully unclear—but what bothers me most is I still have no idea how I feel about it.

The shrill ring of my phone does nothing to arouse me from my baffled stupor. I pick up the receiver only because that's what my hands have been programmed to do. It is as if I've used an automated finger to click the answer button, a recorded greeting to say hello.

"Sarah, I am soooo sorry," says Laurie.

"About what?"

"I heard about Marianne Langold. I told you she was a bitch!"

"Oh, that. Don't worry about it. It's fine."

"What do you mean, it's fine?"

And then it slams me and knocks me down—each awful, vivid detail of everything that happened the night before. I press a cool palm against my fevered forehead and cringe.

"Oh, no . . ." I groan.

"What?" Laurie demands. "What's the matter?"

I try my best to explain my night with Jake, euphemizing my way through the moments that would normally make me blush.

"And then . . ." I wince at the thought of repeating it. "And then he told me he loved me."

"Shut up!"

"I know, right?"

"When did he say it?"

"Well, you know . . . during."

"During sex?"

"Yeah." Well, wouldn't you know it? I'm blushing.

"Nah-ah!" Laurie lowers her voice. "And what did you do?"

"I cried."

"Oh, *no.*"

"Yeah."

"Was the sex any good?"

My blush deepens, my cheeks fueled with burning blood. "It was . . . well . . ." I sigh. "Yes. It was good. Very, very good." And that's about as detailed as I can handle.

"Oh, Sarah." She clucks her tongue reproachfully. "Don't you know that crying is always a reaction to good sex?" My intercom buzzes. "Was that your doorbell?"

"Umm, yeah, I guess so." I glance suspiciously at my hallway.

"You need to get it?"

"I don't know. Everyone I know is at work. What time is it anyway?"

"Ten."

"Weird. You think if I don't answer it, they'll just go away?" The intercom buzzes again. "Guess not."

"Go ahead and get it. I have to take this call anyway. I'll call you right back."

"If I'm still alive," I mutter. I toss my phone aside and answer my doorbell.

"Delivery!"

I buzz him in.

I open my door and am greeted with an armload of gerbera daisies. The wild array of petals and jutting stems blocks my view, but somehow or another, someone hands me a pen and shoves a clipboard under my bouquet. I hastily sign my name. The clipboard disappears, and so does the pen, and then I hear a merry "bye-bye." I can sense my anonymous messenger scurrying down the hallway. How strange. To have been so close to someone, to have been able, even, to reach out and touch him—and I never saw his face. And how often does this happen? How many times have total strangers brushed against me, grazed my side, only to disappear unnoticed back into the crowd?

I sigh and retreat into my apartment, shutting the door behind me with my foot.

I love you, now flowers too? Forgive me. I know I should be overjoyed. Every girl loves a gerbera daisy. And yet, I'm overcome with the troubling thought that perhaps I've stepped onto a carousel spinning far too fast. Don't get me wrong. I enjoy a carnival ride as much as the next person. But if you stay on too long, the colors become blinding, the music a little disorienting, and the next thing you know, you're puking up funnel cake next to a Porta Potti.

I set the flowers down on the coffee table and pull out the card:

To my darling little girl who is perfect in *every* way. There's always law school! Love, Mom.

The phone rings again.

"Yeah, hi. Everything is okay," I answer.

"Sarah?" Oops. It's not Laurie. It's a voice I recognize but can't immediately place.

"Oh, yes. Speaking," I say, rapidly shifting gears.

"Sarah, this is Kelly Martin from *Aspen Quarterly*. We spoke about a month ago?"

"Of course, I remember."

"Well, I've got good news!"

I got the job.

Making a major decision is like pulling off a Band-Aid. It's best to do it quickly and spare yourself the agony.

Unfortunately, by nature, I'm not very decisive. I envy the sort of people who can walk into a newly renovated apartment, pivot once, and say, "I'll take it." People who can dine at restaurants and, before the waitress has even finished rattling off the dinner specials, can immediately interject, "Oh, that's what I'll have!" Or newlyweds in the throes of passion who can whisper into their lover's ear, "Let's forget the condom this time."

Me, I love to torture myself with second guesses, swilling them like red wine on my palate until I gag and choke. But this time I surprise myself. I accept the job in Aspen without a moment's hesitation. Because, ultimately, saying "yes" is a hell of a lot easier than saying "no." "No" generally requires an explanation. "Yes," on the other hand, is a given, a one-word, irrefutable leap of faith. It's mercifully swift and painless.

It never occurs to me that the possibly life-altering decision I've made so thoughtlessly is one I can change. To be honest, I find the plunge—the leap, if you will—exhilarating. Over the course of the next couple of days, I assign myself the enormously satisfying task of organizing years of clutter into two categories, Toss and Keep. Again, I have no time for long, drawn-out contemplation. I've got only a week to clean up and ship out. Every item in my apartment has become its own Rorschach inkblot, requiring a split-second re-action. And so I hastily decide exactly which memories I wish to keep. And those which I will doom to oblivion.

When I finally stop free-falling, I am appalled to discover I've belly flopped. A hot sting socks me in the stomach. It happens just as I'm sorting and packing my collection of college T-shirts and I find one that doesn't belong to me.

It belongs to Jake.

There are several possible scenarios for my dinner tonight with Jake, none of which are very appealing. For example:

INT. RESTAURANT—NIGHT (SCENE #1)

He's angry, fueled with pent-up, early Marlon Brando–type rage (think *Streetcar Named Desire*). When I tell him I'm leaving for Aspen, he says nothing at first. We sit in stony, menacing silence and for a split second I let myself believe that the moment may pass without incident. But then he tosses his napkin onto the table, choosing instead to graze his mouth with the back of his hand, like he's wiping off blood from his lower lip. In one fell swoop, he flings his arm clear across the table, shattering the plates and glasses. And when he stands, he knocks over the chair. En route to the front entrance, he even shoves the waiter out of his way. The door slams shut behind him, giving all the other restaurant patrons an unexpected jolt. And yet, I'm the one they glare at. Because not only have I just ruined my own life, but I've also just ruined dinner for everyone.

Or . . .

INT. RESTAURANT—NIGHT (SCENE #2)

He's hurt. But in a charming, heartaching Cary Grant kind of way. I break the news to him gently and, for a moment at least, he takes it in stride. He tries to make light of the situation, gesturing comically and cracking a few quips. But amid his nervous fumbling, he accidentally knocks over the salt shaker. We both grow quiet. For although neither of us is particularly superstitious, we know a table full of spilled salt couldn't possibly be a good sign. Now, conceivably, he could just throw a pinch of it over his shoulder and say that's that—but instead he runs his hand slowly over the grains, studying them a little too closely. When he looks back up at me, his eyes are red and shining. In a voice uncharacteristically low and serious, he begs me to change my mind, to stay with him. And I say . . . well, I don't know what I say.

Or . . .

INT. RESTAURANT—NIGHT (SCENE #3)

He's casual. So cool, so nonchalant, so detached, he's practically Bogart. No weepy farewells here. Instead of a kiss, he socks me playfully on the shoulder. Or maybe the jaw. "Chin up," he tells me when he sees I'm on the verge of tears. "There'll be other dames." And when hysterically I insist we can still make it work, we can at least give long-distance love a shot, he'll snort and shake his head. "Not for me, kid."

———

There's also another dinner scenario (SCENE #4), one I'd rather not entertain. But it's an alternative I've been growing fonder and fonder of with each passing butterfly flutter in my stomach. I could simply not tell him at all. Why should I tell him? I haven't told Laurie yet. Or Amanda. I still haven't even called my mother. Telling people about my decision would make it a harsh, cold fact when I've been doing such a good job pretending nothing will change at all. I see no reason to shatter the illusion just yet. Instead, why not just have a lovely dinner and afterward, a night of steamy, passionate lovemaking? And come Saturday, I could disappear without a word, evaporating into thin air like the fragments of a wistful dream.

Wouldn't that be nice?

SCENE #4 IT IS.

It is, perhaps, the longest dinner of my life. The butterflies in my stomach are flapping their wings so hard, I can only assume there has been a tragic series of earthquakes somewhere in Japan. I spend the evening staring at Jake so intently, he keeps patting his face with a dinner napkin.

"What? I have tomato sauce on my nose?"

"No, no, you're fine," I assure him.

And see. That's the problem. He is fine. Perfectly fine. I would love nothing more than to find something wrong with him, something I detest, any little quirk I could force myself to replay over and over again in my head that would make leaving him the easiest thing in the world. Instead, he's been positively wonderful. When he eats, he chews his food thoughtfully, looking up from his dinner plate every now and then to check on me. To make sure my water is always full, to pass me the Parmesan, to grind more pepper for me. He frowns when he notices I've hardly touched my gnocchi at all.

"You don't like it," he says. He sounds dejected. Like he's the one who failed me, not the pasta.

"I'm just not all that hungry."

"Here." He sets down his fork. "Have the rest of my chicken parmigiana. It's really good."

"Really, Jake. I'm okay."

"Just try it," he insists, thrusting the plate at me. I know it's no use arguing with him. I take his plate and hand him mine, knowing full well he can't stand gnocchi. I force myself to swallow a bite.

"Good, right?" he asks, smiling hopefully.

"Yeah, very good." I hand him back the plate. He waves it away.

"Nah, I've had enough. You finish it."

The waiter clears the table fifteen minutes later. And still the topic of Aspen has yet to come up. Not my fault. He just never asked.

"I take it you don't want dessert?"

"No, thanks," I say glumly.

I pick up the check—really, it's the least I can do. And by the time we get outside, I've replayed the line, "Jake, there's something I need to tell you," so many times in my head, it's a wonder I haven't yet said it out loud. Not even by mistake.

Jake hails a taxi. "Your place?" he asks.

"Sure."

As soon as we're in the cab, I lunge at him. I grip him by the arms and draw him toward me. Pull him on top of me, actually. And while we kiss, I wiggle beneath him until all our body parts click and lock into place. And then I hug him to me even tighter, pull him even closer, and the heavier he presses into me, the harder he crushes me, the smaller and safer I feel.

"What's gotten into you?" he pants. His face is so close I can feel the heat of his breath against my neck.

"Shut up," I tell him. Because the cab ride won't last long enough. This evening won't last long enough. This moment couldn't possibly last long enough.

"Jake, there's something I need to tell you."

There. I've finally said it. Only by now the words seem ridiculously inadequate. He's already walked through my living room, somewhat perturbed to spot bare walls and a few empty bookshelves. And he's already wandered into my bedroom, where he stopped cold once he discovered the boxes on the floor, half of them already packed and sealed.

"You're going somewhere?" he asks.

"Aspen."

"Why?"

"I got a job there." I'd tell him more, but I find I respond better to direct questions.

"When do you leave?"

"Saturday."

He winces and shakes his head, the way people do after throwing back shots of Jägermeister.

"When were you going to tell me this?"

"Over dinner."

"The dinner we just had?"

"Yeah."

"Funny, I don't remember you saying anything about Aspen."

"No." I hang my head sheepishly. "But I meant to."

Jake lifts a foot and aims it at one of the sealed boxes. For a moment, I think he's about to kick it and send it flying. The thought of such an unexpected act of rage actually excites me. Instead, he taps it gently with his toe.

"Books?"

"Mostly." I study his face, trying to read his expression. It remains infuriatingly blank. "You're angry?"

"No."

"You're hurt?"

"No." He shrugs. "Okay, maybe a little. But it's not like I'm going to force you to change your mind."

I didn't realize it until he said it—but that's exactly what I want him to do.

I grab his wrist. It stays limp in my hand, but I can feel his racing pulse.

"Jake, I don't *have* to go. I know it sounds crazy, but this whole thing happened so quickly. I can still turn it down. If you want me to stay, you have to tell me."

If his expression has become any more readable, I can't tell. He isn't even looking at me anymore. I can still feel his pulse race, but his hand stays limp. I feel like an idiot clinging to him like this. I give him back his hand, which he promptly shoves in his pocket.

"So, you want me to beg you not to go?"

"You don't have to beg." I look down to study my own hand, which feels empty without his. "Just tell me you want me to stay."

He shakes his head. "I can't do that."

"So that's it? We're just going to end it like this?"

And that's when he looks up. He glares at me in a way I hadn't expected at all. Those hard, unforgiving eyes are the weapon he's been concealing all along.

"*We* didn't end anything," he says coldly. And with that, he turns, carefully sidestepping the boxes so that he doesn't trip on his way out.

When the door slams closed behind him, I deal a swift kick to the box of mostly books.

chapter twenty-two

At 1 p.m., on an unusually balmy August after-noon, I take a seat on the bench outside my apartment building and pull a manuscript out of my bag. I open it on my lap but don't bother reading it just yet. Instead I scan the crowd of pedestrians, searching the frowning masses for any sign of a familiar face. The deli owner next door waves to me through the window. I wave back. He reaches for a Snickers bar and presses it against the glass. I shake my head, no thanks.

A heavy black woman waddles past me and smiles. "Hi, sugar," she says. It takes me a moment, but when I run her though my head several times—in different places, in various roles—I put her in a uniform and place her on duty at her post by the ATMs of my neighborhood bank. So long, Miss Security Guard. Bye, sugar.

The subway station on the corner spits up its most recent wave of exiting commuters. Among them, Laurie, elbowing her way past the horde on the stairwell and jostling an elderly woman with her oversized messenger bag. She marches down the street to the beat of her own New York staccato, pausing for a stroller, veering right for a dog, leaping over a puddle beneath an air-conditioning unit.

A taxi screeches to a halt. The back door flies open, but Amanda waits patiently inside until her driver coughs up the exact change and a receipt. She'll offer him a buck and a smile to make the whole ride worthwhile.

Across the street, Princess shimmies past the storefronts, gazing into the windows to admire her voluptuous reflection. She'll pause to examine the new season fashion displays and spy a scarf she simply must have. She'll check her watch. Yes, she has another fifteen minutes to spare.

And directly below me, in the tunnels that meander underground, my headhunter, Mr. Mark Shapiro, is whizzing by in a number 2 express train, reading the *Wall Street Journal*. The market is still down, the unemployment rate is still high. He's thrilled.

One of the New York City tour buses pulls off to the curb beside me. My mother and father step down, tightly gripping their wallets because they know this town is notorious for pickpockets. With the rest of their tour group, they'll huddle in the middle of the sidewalk, mindlessly blocking pedestrian traffic, subject to rude shoves and evil glares. From what they see on this nondescript strip of Broadway—the Gap, Starbucks, identical apartment buildings—they won't be impressed. They shuffle back onto the bus, wondering why on earth New York is such a big deal.

When the bus pulls away, there he is, across the street. Jake. He looks a little worse for wear, his hair disheveled, his clothes a mess, but there is light in his eyes and an enormous grin on his face, and he's waving his arms in the air and shouting above traffic. And he's saying—

"Hey, 4B!"

I blink. In front of me stands the postman, in his dapper blue shorts and knee-high black socks, digging into his mail cart. I check my watch. It is 1:23. He's early.

"You expecting something good?" he asks.

"Not really." I shrug. "But maybe I'll be surprised."

He chuckles. "One can always hope." He hands me a small stack of envelopes.

"Actually, I was wondering if you had any change of address forms. My roommate told me I might be able to get them from you."

"You're moving? After all this time? That's a damn shame."

I offer him a helpless smile. "I got a job in Aspen."

"Oh, yeah? Colorado, huh? I hear it's nice out there." He pulls a sheet from out of his bag and hands it to me.

"So, I just fill this out and take it to the post office?"

"If you know your new address, you can fill it out right here and I'll take it with me."

"You don't mind?"

"It's not a problem."

"Thanks." I put the form down on the bench. Until I procure a permanent residence in Aspen, I plan on having my mail temporarily forwarded to my parents' home in Denver. As I jot down my childhood address, I feel a stab of nostalgia. How pathetic, how defeatist, to have ended up exactly where I started.

"You take care," says the mailman, taking the form from me.

"You too."

He heaves his mail cart onward and I take a seat back on the bench, wrapping my arms around myself to shield my bare arms from the unexpected chill in the air. Summer in New York is officially coming to a close, and the city no longer feels like an oppressive, sweaty palm crushing me facedown onto the pavement. New Yorkers walk taller when they sense autumn approaching, and I see they've already traded in their sluggish footfalls for a lighter, carefree bounce.

A small gust of wind stirs up the debris on the sidewalk and makes it dance. I lower my head against the breeze and study the small stack of mail in my lap. Only two letters have been addressed to me—and, curiously, they've both been sent from the WCA offices. I select the longer envelope, with my name and address typed and neatly centered on the front, and rip it open.

To: Sarah Pelletier
From: New York Human Resources
Re: NEW YORK TERMINATION POLICY

Dear Employee,

It has come to our attention that your course of employment at WCA has come to an end. Please take the time to carefully review your Health Coverage continuation options attached—

Of course, I don't intend to take the time to review anything. I shove the letter back into the envelope and seal it up. It occurs to me, however, that as much as I find my official termination letter highly depressing, I still feel strangely flattered someone bothered to send me one at all.

The second letter intrigues me far more than the first, anyway. On the envelope, my name has been delicately scrawled in loopy black ink. The return address bears the stamp of Marianne Langold's personal suite number. I cautiously pull out the slender square of pink-stained notepaper inside and try to decipher the elaborate cursive.

Dear Sarah,

I have been informed that Human Resources has taken it upon themselves to relieve you from your position as my assistant. I am truly sorry to see you go. It was a pleasure to have met you and I wish you all the best. Please know that I still think very highly of you and I would be happy to provide you with a recommendation as you continue your job pursuits. I've already mentioned you to several acquaintances at similar companies who are currently looking to hire. Feel free to contact me at my office at any time, and I will gladly discuss the details with you.

Best,
Marianne Langold

Hmpff. Isn't that just a kicker?

I wish there were a scientific approach to judging traffic in New York. I wish it could really be as easy as avoiding the early-morning and late-afternoon rush hour or the big holiday weekends. But traffic in the city is a crapshoot, a guessing game, and today I've drawn the short stick of the lot.

As suggested by the 1010 WINS radio traffic report, I decide to avoid the George Washington Bridge because I'm told congestion is heavy on both the upper and lower levels. But the line for the Lincoln Tunnel seems equally unappealing, so I maneuver my way back onto the West Side Highway, much to the dismay of my fellow drivers. I wave politely to a man in a Porsche who lets me slide back into the steady stream. He doesn't slow down so much as he careens his car to the side on two wheels and flips me the bird as he speeds by.

I miss the turn for the Holland Tunnel too when, after half an hour sitting in standstill traffic, I discover too late I'm in the lane that doesn't even exit the highway. To my left, an entire fleet of Atlantic

City casino buses veers off and ducks into the tunnel. And not even the Mini Cooper driver in front of me can spot a large enough break to try to wiggle into their tight formation.

Then I pull to a stop at the traffic light just as the cabdriver beside me decides he likes my lane better and positions himself diagonally in front of me. When the light turns green, he remains motionless, biding his time before he makes his turn.

"Goddamnit!" I slam my hand against the steering wheel, missing the car horn entirely. Although I haven't caused even a minor stir outside of the car, inside I am wreaking havoc amid the flimsy upholstering, screaming obscenities at my windshield.

Man, I am so not going to miss any of this shit. I am so glad I will never again have to deal with ruthless cabdrivers, Porsche drivers with death wishes, idiots who stop to read street signs when they should already know that Fourteenth Street is below Fifteenth Street.

I follow the flow of traffic. And as soon as I've charted one alternate route after another, I've already missed the turn I was supposed to take. Before I know it, before I can navigate my course elsewhere, I find myself leaving the city through the only porthole left to me—the Battery Tunnel. In the dark, winding cavern, I curse myself the whole way through.

It is downright eerie, lingering in this dark, smoggy canal. And what makes it even worse is listening to the garbled cackle and hiss coming from the car stereo. I flick over to the FM stations, hoping to find a voice that sounds even remotely human. Failing that, I turn off the radio entirely and continue to creep along in dreaded silence.

I finally emerge back into daylight and pull onto the Brooklyn-Queens Expressway. Although the traffic is no less daunting, and I'm still muttering a few choice adjectives under my breath, I can feel the tension lifting from my shoulders and my minor bout of road rage starts to subside. I flip the radio back on. An announcer ticks off a list of bands I really couldn't care less about. But compared to the dismal traffic reports, names like "Bad Company" and "Grateful Dead" sound relatively soothing. I let the station stand.

In the reflection of my rearview mirror, I catch a fleeting glimpse of the New York Harbor. How funny. I keep forgetting that Manhattan is an island. Which, when you think about it, makes perfect sense—the pink-skinned Scandinavian tourists in tank tops and short shorts, the unbearable smell of fish in Chinatown, the sidewalk vendors who don't speak a lick of English. As on any island, an extended stay here means risking a bad case of overexposure. At best, you'll suffer from a minor heat rash. At worst, you'll feel trapped and suffocated, pining for—

Suddenly, I freeze. I realize I'm singing along with the radio. And, as far as I know, I don't know the words to anything. I turn up the volume.

Wait a second. Did he just say . . . *sugar bear?*

After all those years building up a firm resistance to love songs, now I discover, much to my disbelief, I'm completely powerless against it. Two things happen immediately. First, I start to cry. The tears spring up so quickly, I wonder how on earth I could possibly have been caught so off guard. Not just any love song could have done it. It had to be this particular song. It had to be the fuck-you to all love songs. Elton John is a sneaky son-of-a-bitch to creep up on me like this and to break my heart so effortlessly.

And second, my foot eases off the gas pedal and I find myself, rather inexplicably, pulling off the highway at the next exit.

"Ha!" I laugh, overcome with head-spinning, palm-sweating giddiness as I realize I'm driving past a familiar row of brownstones, on a street lined with lampposts and cherry trees.

Now, see these are the decisions I like the best. Not the bold, spontaneous ones. Not the agonizingly slow and dubious ones. I like the decisions that make themselves. Of course the route I've chosen to take out of Manhattan just happens to lead through Brooklyn. Of course there's an exit ramp off the BQE that just happens to lead directly to Jake's apartment. And of course I could only be driving down this final stretch drumming my fingers against the steering wheel and belting out the lyrics to "Someone Saved My Life Tonight."

The safe thing would be to end my story here. Before the car runs out of gas, before I get hit by an oncoming bus, before I spend hours frantically searching for recognizable street signs or an open parking spot while truckers and gypsy cabs honk and scream at me. And all of this is even before I discover Jake isn't home, or he's reunited with Simone, or he wants nothing to do with me. When I look back on today, whether it's from Denver, Aspen, Manhattan, Brooklyn, or wherever, all I want to remember is that I was singing in the car, loudly and off-key, and it was one of those miraculous moments when every traffic light I hit along the way was green.